CUENTOS FILIPINOS

CUENTOS FILIPINOS

JOSÉ MONTERO Y VIDAL

Translated from
the original Spanish by

RENÁN S. PRADO
EVELYN C. SORIANO
HEIDE V. AQUINO
SHIRLEY R. TORRES

Edited by

RENÁN S. PRADO
LOURDES C. BRILLANTES

Department of Modern Languages
School of Humanities
Ateneo de Manila University

Department of Modern Languages
School of Humanities
Ateneo de Manila University
Loyola Heights, Quezon City
P.O. Box 154, 1099 Manila, Philippines
Tel. (632) 426-60-01 Loc. 5350 & 5351
Fax No. (632) 426-60-01 Loc. 5351
E-mail: modlang@admu.edu.ph

Book design by JB de la Peña
Cover design by BJ Patiño and Robert S. Prado
Cover Photo from:
Habitants de Manille, Malais de I'lle Luçon
Publié par Dufour Mulat et Boulanger
Laurent imp., Paris, 1843
Renán S. Prado Collection

The publication of this volume
has been made possible through the support of the
Office of the President, Ateneo de Manila University and the
Program for Cultural Cooperation between the
Ministry of Education, Culture and Sports of Spain
and Universities in the Philippines and the Pacific Islands

The National Library of the Philippines CIP Data

Recommended entry:

Montero, José V.
    Cuentos Filipinos / José Montero y Vidal
; translated from the original Spanish by
Renán S. Prado ... [et al.] ; edited by
Renán S. Prado, Lourdes C. Brillantes. -
Quezon City : ADMU-School of Humanities-
Department of Modern Languages, 2004
    1 v

1. Short stories, Philippine (Spanish).
I. Prado, Renán S. II. Brillantes, Lourdes C.
III. Ateneo de Manila University. School of
Humanities. Department of Modern Languages.
IV. Title.

PL5542 899.21'03 2004 P041000579
        ISBN 971-92296-5-9

CONTENTS

FOREWORD

As envisioned by its translators, the English version of *Cuentos Filipinos* aspires to be counted among similarly rendered works, which have contributed to the expansion of literature, the enrichment of libraries, and the illumination of generations.

From nineteenth-century Filipinas, Montero y Vidal collected cultural, political, economic as well as geographical data, and historical facts and treasures that would provide further information about the islands. Culture and its manifold manifestations— customs, fashions, cuisine, even personal hygiene—occupy much of the setting and texture of his fictional *cuentos*, which are valuable sociological revelations.

In a candid style—too candid, perhaps, for the fiction-writing standards of his time—Montero y Vidal narrates dramatic situations. For instance, he writes of people who, awaiting news brought by mail boat that could define their fate, struggled to grab the letters from the hands of the mail carriers. Two young lovers, believing that God created them for each other, become hunted fugitives after the girl rejects her prearranged marriage in defiance of her parents, to whom she owes absolute obedience and whose word was considered law at that time. Another story relates the misadventures of madness, the tragicomic travails of lunacy, which, the author suggests, was a widespread malady in those days. The assassination of a revered citizen of Pampanga province is well avenged by the *calao,* like the raven croaking in his own way, "Nevermore."

In his depiction of natural calamities, Montero y Vidal never fails to emphasize Madre España's sympathy and support for the victims. Most of all, he emphasizes the warmheartedness of the Filipinos. Describing the aftermath of a storm in his story "The Student from La Laguna," he writes: "Philanthropy being a distinctive characteristic of the inhabitants of the Philippines, Peninsulares and the natives as well, you can be sure that in a short time a large amount was collected . . ." for the relief and rehabilitation of the calamity victims.

Montero y Vidal spent many years in the Philippines and traveled all over this country, which he describes as "awesome and beautiful. It thrills the imagination and lifts the spirit . . . whosoever was born in that land can say with pride: 'I am from the Philippines.'" Clearly, Montero y Vidal was not a polemical pamphleteer but an artist with a great respect for his material.

Despite what present-day critics may dismiss as simple narratives, hackneyed themes, and antiquated techniques, Montero y Vidal's stories have accomplished what the literary artist always aims for, namely, the infusion of fiction with reality, of literature with life.

Cuentos Filipinos is written in an apparently spontaneous style using the typically long and flowing sentences of that era. For the most part, the translation follows the idiom, word order, and syntax of the original. The reader must bear in mind, though, that since the English patterns are more rigid than the Spanish, deviations are necessary. Literal interpretation is not totally avoidable, but a free or reverse translation has been resorted to as needed without prejudice to the substance.

The footnotes in the text are the author's. Our own addenda include a glossary of italicized words and explanatory notes on textual references to which the author alludes.

The translators, as well as the editor, are faculty members of the Department of Modern Languages of the Ateneo de Manila University. We took up the challenge to translate this work by Montero y Vidal, a rare book from the 1870s that has long been inaccessible, with a view to opening windows to the past for those who might find valuable revelations in it, especially students.

We acknowledge with gratitude Dr. Dominador M. Almeda, who very kindly provided the original book and the pictures for its English version. It was his wish to see the book translated by the Department, but before it could be done he passed away. We thank the members of his family who continued to lend their assistance to this project. A short message by Dr. Almeda before his death appears on the next page.

Lourdes C. Brillantes

MESSAGE

When I was practicing medicine in New York, I spent my free time searching for rare books on the Philippines. Once, I was greatly disappointed because I was unable to buy a particular book on Leyte. Someone with an inexhaustible supply of cash simply outbidded me. But on a happier occasion, my attention was caught by Montero y Vidal's *Cuentos Filipinos*. The author's introduction informed the reader that though his characters were fictitious, his real intention was to show the awesome beauty of the Philippines, its rich flora and fauna, and the many different and interesting customs and practices of the people. As he wove the story around a rich Spanish mestiza, for example, he described how the rich entertained in their houses, their clothes, the varied food and drinks served, their music, and their lively conversation. The carriage rides at sunset at the Luneta and the bustling trade in Binondo and Escolta came alive before my eyes.

I bought the book and became even more fascinated as I read on. I was regaled with the stories of a rich pageant of characters: Chinese, Creoles, Moro pirates and sultans, *frailes*, and many native men and women busy at their occupations. There were the *cigarreras* working by the thousands in the tobacco factories in Quiapo, and the *sinamayeras* selling the abaca and pineapple fibers that were delicately woven into fine cloth in the provinces of Pampanga, Bulacan, Camarines, and Iloilo. The men, when not hunting, harvesting, or fishing with great skill, were excellent carvers, silversmiths, and boat makers.

MESSAGE

A pleasant break from their daily occupations were the numerous town fiestas of Obando, Antipolo, and Intramuros, which were celebrated with great pomp, with processions, bands of musicians, thousands of candles, glittering carriages, and fireworks. Occasional typhoons and earthquakes, however, would come to wreak havoc on the people's lives.

After seeing the great value of *Cuentos Filipinos*, I gave a copy to the translators, who are also my friends, to read and, if possible, to translate. I was very pleased to see that they were more than equal to the task. It is my fondest hope that this book will reach a wider range of readers who, like me, will be greatly enriched by the wealth of material in it.

Dominador M. Almeda, M.D.

ACKNOWLEDGMENTS

The Department of Modern Languages of the Ateneo de Manila University takes pride in publishing an English translation of *Cuentos Filipinos*.

I wish especially to thank my creative colleagues, Evelyn C. Soriano, Heide V. Aquino, and Shirley R. Torres who assiduously worked on the translation, and the editor, Lourdes C. Brillantes, who lent her invaluable expertise.

All of us in the team are deeply grateful to the Reverend Father Bienvenido F. Nebres, S.J., for his assistance and encouragement, and to the Program for Cultural Cooperation between the Ministry of Education, Culture and Sports of Spain and Universities in the Philippines and the Pacific Islands, headed by the Reverend Father Jose M. Cruz, S.J., for their approval and support of this project.

There were people who lent a helping hand during the difficult stages of this manuscript's publication, among them, Reverend Father René B. Javellana, S.J., Ángel González Lara, Edgardo Tiamson Mendoza, Iñigo J. Cariño, Kendrick U. Pua, Mike S. Santos, Tony G. Padilla, and Joco I. San Juan, friends who all kindly responded to our quest for details.

Fel S. Ibarrola and Marie Christine P. Samala gave unstinting support: the first encoded the text, and the second put in the last entries.

ACKNOWLEDGMENTS

Special mention should be made of my *hermano*, Robert S. Prado, who provided technological expertise in scanning the pictures, and Angelita S. Prado, who shared valuable data from the past.

Renán S. Prado
Chair, Department of
Modern Languages

A. M. D. G.

AUTHOR'S NOTE

When the first edition of *Cuentos Filipinos* was published in 1876, all media praised this humble work in which we have attempted to faithfully portray the customs of the inhabitants of our oceanic archipelago. We have presented a multitude of historic, geographic, statistical, commercial, and descriptive data, as well as every detail related to the political and administrative organization of their country. The public in Spain hastened to get hold of our modest book, but in the Philippines, the success it received was even greater as all four thousand copies of that edition were sold out.

The opening of the tobacco market led to a change in the constitutions of various corporations that had invested capital there. These corporations decided to take advantage of the new provision. Thus, with the ending of the tobacco monopoly, the Philippine Islands drew the attention of thousands of individuals interested in such a profitable business, so much so that there is now a greater interest in this country about which, in Europe, there is scarce and generally erroneous information.

This concern has impelled us to publish a new edition of our *Cuentos Filipinos*, a title that may not reflect its true nature but which we have retained since we have yet to find another that could express the exact character of this book. We are confident that the text can satisfy the demands of those who long for reliable news from the archipelago. We take pride in our adequate knowledge of the place since we have spent a good part of our life there.

PROLOGUE TO THE FIRST EDITION

There are two main reasons that impelled us to publish this book. The first is to reawaken the zeal of the native Filipinos to read the history of their country so that they may know a little more about it. The second is to provide the Peninsulars with some knowledge of the customs, organization, products, industries, and commerce of the archipelago.

Nowadays, no one denies that the ability to read is one of the most powerful tools of modern civilization. Statistics on literacy confirm that reading produces a cultured people, negating whatever objections might arise.

To awaken the desire to read, it is necessary to provide the readers works that they can enjoy.

There is no doubt—and every literate person knows this—that people have a marked tendency to get involved when reading works about themselves. Readers think of themselves as characters in the fable or novel they are reading.

Sustained by these reflections, we believe we have given the natives of the Philippine Islands something useful by writing this book.

The natives are extremely fond of anecdotes and stories, and if reading is not popular among them, it is because they lack works of interest to them. It is true that not everyone knows Spanish well, but this inconvenience will disappear if we give them books that will acquaint them with their own customs, that will make them conscientiously analyze in-depth their instincts, desires, passions, and idiosyncrasies.

Our *Cuentos Filipinos*, though inadequate, will help overcome this difficulty and fill part of the great void.

The Peninsulars may be interested in knowing that in spite of the lack of organization, the facts and information stated here from historical, geographical, agricultural, industrial, and commercial points of view are valid, owing to the many years we have lived in those Islands.

We do not pretend to have produced a perfect work, but we believe that in spite of its deficiencies, we have accomplished something worthwhile.

ENRIQUETA

I

Enriqueta Amalia de Alba was the toast of Manila's high society, being one of the richest and most beautiful young ladies in the country. An orphan, she lived with her uncle and aunt, her guardians who loved her dearly. The couple belonged to a prominent family, known for their gentility and their immense wealth. Enriqueta was an *española filipina*, as those children were called, who were born of a Peninsular father and a Manila-born mother of Spanish descent.

Race is a relevant issue in the Philippines, and that is why it is given so much importance. From intermarriages come the half-castes, more or less ranked according to whether they are of European, Chinese, native, or mestizo parentage. The Spanish-Filipinos, the most prominent racial group, are looked upon with disdain by the Europeans, who speak contemptuously of the country and its customs, which, in their view, are quite different from theirs. There are Filipinos who are ashamed of identifying themselves as such, and Spanish Peninsulars who regard them as their inferiors for not having been born in Spain.

Neither group is right. Both the Filipinos and the Peninsulars are children of Spain. And if there is any difference between the laws in the provinces of the Peninsula and those overseas, all of which territories constitute Spain, it is to the benefit and honor of its overseas provinces not to damage or discredit them.

Setting aside the legal question and turning to the climate and the land, if the Peninsulars feel proud because Spain is one of the most beautiful regions on the globe and its customs bring such pleasant memories to one far from it, the Filipinos cannot be less proud of the beautiful land where they were born and of the customs and conditions of their peaceful life.

The Philippines is, without exaggeration, a bountiful land. Its climate is healthful and pleasant like the soft, refreshing breeze. The land is extremely fertile. Its forests, rivers, mountains, volcanoes, delightful valleys, smiling meadows, wide fields, the bounty of her soil, the majestic beauty of the changing elements, whether the storm rages or when the *baguio*[1] prevails, whether the rains fall torrentially or the sun shines, vivifying the plants—the land is awesome and beautiful. It thrills the imagination and lifts the spirit.

There are terrifying earthquakes, but which region in the world is not exposed to great dangers?

---

[1] Violent weather that lasts twenty-four hours with gusty winds and rains.

This is the land that grows tobacco as good as that of Cuba's; that produces abacá, a textile plant of indisputable superiority for making rope and mesh, whose fibers are sewn into finest cloths; sugar of unparalleled quality; indigo the equal of Hindustan's; cocoa and coffee of excellent varieties, highly valued in foreign markets; palay,[2] so useful, so abundant, and so varied; cotton, *sibucao*,[3] *carey*,[4] and thousands of other products, the exports of which, despite the natural indolence of the natives and the scarcity of cultivated land, amount to some P17 million annually. This is the land that yields 730 varieties of wood, the majority of which are very good; that has countless minerals and abundant livestock of all kinds; that produces trees like the coconut, which gives wine and oil; that grows the ilang-ilang, a delicate flower whose fragrance delights the aristocratic ladies of the world—this land, I say, is a land blessed by nature. Anyone born in this land can say with pride: *I am from the Philippines.*

And if we leave the splendor and the prodigious fertility of the land and focus on the moral conditions of the inhabitants, we will find that if some of them fall into vices, which entrap even the more civilized, they do possess praiseworthy qualities, which, if weighed against the virtues and vices of the more advanced cultures, will tip the scales in favor of the Far East, where moral degeneracy in all aspects is infinitely less than in many other places in the world.

II

Let us continue our interrupted story.

Enriqueta's uncle and aunt often hosted parties in their house, where the crème de la crème of Manila's society would gather. They

---

[2] Unhusked rice.
[3] Logwood or campeachy wood.
[4] Tortoise shell.

frequently held dances, an entertainment much favored in the country in spite of the warm weather. At these dances would gather young men of all professions, some of whom, captivated by the charm of the beautiful Filipina, hoped for a relationship that would fulfill their amorous dreams.

Enriqueta was seventeen years old. She was svelte and elegant, with thick blond hair that reached the floor. Her eyes were bright, large, incomparably beautiful, with an irresistible brilliance. Her white complexion, slightly pinkish, had the freshness and loveliness of the rose. When she smiled, her small mouth opened to show a fine set of teeth; from her smile sprang such unique enchantment as to bedazzle any mortal. Her brilliant wit, high education, special talents, pleasant conversation, and good manners—all these qualities made her worthy of the esteem, respect, and even the worship of those who had the pleasure of knowing her.

When she sang, her audience was carried away by the pleasant timbre and tenderness of her voice and would interrupt her a thousand times, lavishing their ovations on her. When she played the piano, everyone listened with undivided attention in order not to miss a single note. She possessed the secret that only genius possesses, of playing with both sentiment and delicacy, touching even insensitive hearts.

With these traits, it was easy to understand why many of her suitors would have been happy just to receive a nod or a smile from her, and what noble passions she inspired in those who often beheld her beauty.

Enriqueta had no wish to be separated from her uncle and aunt, who treated her like a daughter. She spent the day doing pleasant chores, in leisurely reading, in sessions of music and painting, for which she felt a genuine passion and to which she devoted much of her free time. At other times, she amused herself by tending the flowers in the garden that she herself watered. How it pleased her to smell their delicate fragrance!

In the afternoons, her uncle and aunt usually went for a ride in their carriage. They would go down the main streets to the Malecón, a seaside promenade where many distinguished families gathered to enjoy the pure sea breeze. At nightfall, the carriages would take the elegant ladies and gentlemen to the wide field of Bagumbayan or to the Luneta, where they would go for a stroll. The Luneta Park used to be the favorite of the city folk. Today, it is almost abandoned.

On Thursdays and Sundays, the Luneta would come alive with music from the military band, while the people enjoyed the view and the fresh sea breeze. The promenade is incomparable for its poetic ambiance. On a clear moonlit night, it is a favorite spot for numerous and select gatherings.

On some afternoons, the uncle and aunt would go around the neighborhoods of Uli-Uli, Santa Ana, or Mariquina, where the countryside is very picturesque. As one moves from the outskirts of the old barrios to the capital, a beautiful panoramic view of enchanting vegetation unfolds—small towns with cheerful homes encircled by bamboos and covered with vines and houses between banana leaves and coconut palms. Finally, we see groups of natives engaged in cockfighting, and women naked from the waist up, shelling palay in a big mortar made from a tree trunk. With mallets, they alternately pound the *lusong*[5] to clean the grain.

This simple pastime of Enriqueta's relatives is common in Manila, where ladies do not like traveling on foot and are rarely found on the streets, except when riding a carriage.

The theaters are not always open, nor do many ladies gather here, except on special occasions. Neither do the ladies go to the cafés. They normally stay at home, where pleasant soirées, or family

---

[5] Name of the mortar from which came the name of the island Luzon.

tertulias, are held. In the Philippines, it is important to have a carriage with swift horses, which are indispensable, because people are eager to overtake one another.

Enriqueta also enjoyed going around the city in her carriage. She also frequently attended exclusive parties, standing out wherever she went because of her charm, her beauty, and her natural elegance.

III

Let us say something about Manila, Enriqueta's hometown.

Manila, the capital of the Philippine archipelago, is located on the west coast of the island of Luzon. In relation to the China Sea, it is at 124 degrees, 37 minutes longitude and 14 degrees, 36 minutes latitude. It has spacious houses and long narrow streets.

The most important of its plazas, called Palacio, forms a quadrilateral of 9,000 square rods. In the center, surrounded by a garden with an iron fence, stands a majestic bronze statue of Charles IV, a true work of art cast in Mexico. It was erected in his honor for ordering the mass vaccination drive. For this sole purpose, he arranged for a steamship to arrive in Manila on 15 April 1805.

Fronting one of the sides of this plaza, which looks out to the sea, was the captain-general's magnificent palace, with an elegant Doric façade, built in 1690.

On the other side was the cathedral, which cost 10 million *reales*. The upper portion of the façade was of the Ionic order, and everything was made of stone. The construction was completed in 1671.

The *Cabildo*, or town hall, occupied the third side. It was a modern structure inaugurated in 1738.

These three magnificent buildings collapsed in the earthquake of 3 June 1863. The palace and the town hall are still in ruins. The cathedral is undergoing a luxurious reconstruction.

The best buildings in Manila are the convents. The community of Franciscan friars and their church occupy 30,000 square yards; the Augustinians 25,000; the Dominicans, 15,000; and the Recollects 12,000. They are magnificent structures.

Other impressive structures are the Santo Domingo Church, in the Gothic style, erected for the fifth time in 1868; the temples of San Agustín and San Francisco; the church and the convent of the Jesuits, which measured 34,000 square yards before the church was destroyed by the 1863 earthquake.[6] There are the Universidad de Santo Tomás and the Colegio de San Juan de Letrán, properties of the Dominicans who are their administrators, and the Escuela Normal for teachers, as well as the Ateneo Municipal of the Jesuits. There are also schools for the ladies: Colegio de Santa Isabel and Santa Rosa; the Beaterio de Santa Catalina; the Escuela Municipal for girls, managed by the Sisters of Charity; the Convent of the Sisters of Santa Clara. There is the college for natives founded by a mestiza under the direction of the Jesuits, as well as the Archbishop's Palace.

The strong government buildings destroyed in 1863 have not been rebuilt. The *Maestranza,* the Parque de Artillería, and some military quarters in Manila are in good condition. The houses in Manila, in general, are spacious, solid, perfectly structured, and built low for fear of earthquakes.

The San Juan de Dios Hospital is an excellent building. It was destroyed in 1863 and reconstructed through public charity and rentals from houses the hospital owns in Manila and from the income of its hacienda in Bulacan. On the average, it has 250 patients under the care of the Sisters of Charity. A board of directors and the administrators run the hospital. The admission of the sick, who are well cared for, is unlimited.

---

[6] The convent is now occupied by the Paulist priests.

Manila is surrounded by massive ramparts, with moats and countermoats, redoubts, bulwarks, and a well-defined fort called Santiago. It was constructed before the arrival of the first governors of the Islands. The walls that enclose the city are 1,080 meters long and 626 meters wide, and with a circumference of 3,510 meters. Eight huge gates with drawbridges manned by the garrison facilitate entrance to and exit from the plaza. On one side, the sea laps the walls, while on the other side the Pasig River bathes them. Beyond the walls lie the suburbs, which, linked to Manila by various bridges, form the capital. The population is no less than 260 thousand.

In the environs of the gate by the Pasig, called Magallanes, stands a graceful monument dedicated to the illustrious discoverer of the Philippines. It is a column crowned with an armillary sphere of copper on a marble base with the name of the ill-fated navigator sculpted in gold letters. At the end of the isthmus, where this obelisk stands, there is a beautiful tree-lined promenade constructed in 1872. At the end of the promenade fronting the Parian Gate is a magnificent iron bridge that links Manila to the suburb of Binondo. Constructed with materials fabricated in Paris, it was inaugurated on 1 January 1876 with the name of Puente de España. It measures 457 feet long by 24 feet wide. In the same place stood a stone bridge built in 1626, made impassable to vehicles after the 1863 earthquake and finally demolished in 1867. Shortly after the opening of the Puente de España, one of the adjacent embarkation points on the river collapsed after many years of service to the populace.

The settlement on the outskirts, Binondo, which is the center of commerce, is very busy and alive. Its streets are wide. The main thoroughfare, Escolta, bustles with activity and has become in Manila, in a modest way, what Canebière is in Marseille and the Rambla in Barcelona.

Navigable canals used for minor embarkation points cut across the suburbs of the city. If more attention is given to these, Manila can be a second Venice. The natives, using light vessels, travel through these canals to all points of the city.

Binondo is where the Europeans have the best commercial houses and the Chinese their numerous bazaars. In this populous suburb extending to the Pasig River are located the *Capitanía del Puerto* and the *Comandancia general de Carabiñeros*. At the end of the wharf is the lighthouse of the bay, inaugurated in 1843. It has a red light, which can be seen even by a light vessel 14 miles away. The Binondo Church, which has a Doric façade, is huge. The earthquake of 1863 destroyed the famous tower, which had as many windows as days in a year. The existing tower is lower. Halfway along Anloague Street is the *Administración central de Rentas estancadas,* the *Hacienda pública,* the *Tercena,* and the *bodegas* for goods monopolized by the government.

The suburb of Tondo still conserves many nipa[7] hut settlements. The most noteworthy are the Divisoria Market and the Tobacco Factory of Meisic, where six thousand women are employed. The Tagalog theater of Tondo has become famous for its *sui generis* productions that are presented by the natives in their own dialect.

The suburb of Santa Cruz enjoys a vantage point. On the wide street of Iris there is the public prison, an attractive structure, and fronting this is the coliseum called Circo de Bilibid, which was built in 1870 and can comfortably accommodate 2,500 persons.

Under the jurisdiction of Santa Cruz are the San Lazaro Hospital and the Chinese Cemetery of La Loma.

The central market is in Quiapo. This suburb is connected to the place called Arroceros by a hanging bridge. Constructed by a private firm in 1852, it measures 110 meters long by 7 meters wide and proudly stands over the river.

---

[7] A palm, the leaves of which the natives use as roofs for their houses. The fruit is fermented to make a drink.

Arroceros, as it is still called today, was originally a rice market. Here, we find buildings like the Teatro Español, of standard capacity and well-decorated, where the Italian Opera companies stage operas when they come to Manila. There is the Jardín Botánico, with an abundance of rare plants though not all of good quality; the Fábrica de Tabacos del Fortín, where 8,000 women work; and the Arroceros Factory, where 1,500 men are employed. There is also the Administración central de Colecciones, various tobacco warehouses, the *Intervención general de aforo,* the printing press, the Military Hospital, the Infantry Barracks, and the Slaughterhouse.

The suburb of San Miguel, located by the banks of the Pasig, has magnificent houses with beautiful gardens. There is a beautiful manor called Malacañang, the residence of the captain governor-general of the Philippines. There is an islet in the middle of the river, which is in a deplorable and unsanitary condition. On this islet stands La Convalecencia, where patients from San Juan de Dios Hospital go to recuperate. There is also a place in San Miguel for the demented and the poor, called Hospicio de San José.

The barrio of Sampaloc, a name that comes from a tree abundant in this place, is well-known for its residents who, almost without exception, serve as typesetters in the first printing press established in the Islands. The women of this barrio are laundrywomen. Europeans occupy many houses in Sampaloc. The high society of Manila has chosen this picturesque area as the place to go for a ride. The houses are almost completely of nipa.

The town of Ermita is well-known for women skilled in embroidering *piña*[8] cloth while the town of Malate is known for its residents who are mostly office clerks and are skillful in embroidering slippers. In Malate there is a mausoleum erected in memory of

---

[8] A plant which produces a fruit also called piña. The cloth is made of woven filaments of its leaves.

the naturalist Pineda, who came to Manila in the beginning of the century. There are two barracks, one for the cavalry and another for the infantry.

In the town of San Fernando de Dilao is the public cemetery of Paco, which is also the other name of the town. The well-constructed cemetery is circular and has sixty-four Doric columns. The wall for the niches is 8 feet thick. Several streets with shady trees surround the cemetery. The oval chapel serves as the pantheon for prelates and for men with the rank of captain-general. It was built by the Ayuntamiento in 1820. It has the disadvantage of being located very near the capital.

In San Pedro, Macati, the Protestant cemetery has some grand and artistic mausoleums.

Since the capital city lacks water, most houses have big tanks to conserve rainwater.[9] Spacious markets provide an abundance of all kinds of food products brought in from the nearby provinces.

The climate is healthful. In spite of the city's large population, there are days when no death is recorded at all, and weeks when no Peninsular dies.

In Manila, there are as many carriages as in any important capital in Europe. The horses are small and strong. They run swiftly and need no horseshoes because their hooves are rough. Many horse owners, however, have them shod anyway. The streets have no stone pavements and are flat and well-cemented. There are many good streets for carriages to drive on. They are wide and are lined with thick trees that lend to the freshness and beauty of the surroundings. On one of the main streets is the Engineers' Barracks, a beautiful one-story building.

---

[9] Currently, there is a project to channel water to Manila. The illustrious General Carriedo left a legacy with that as an objective. In spite of problems, the project now amounts to P250,000.

Manila has one of the most beautiful bays in the world. It measures 30 leagues in circumference and bathes the boundaries of Bulacan, Pampanga, Cavite, Corregidor, and Bataan, the provinces that border Manila. The bay is quite busy with commercial activity and could be busier even without competition from the free ports of Hong Kong, Shanghai, and Singapore, which are colonies of England. Manila is where the prominent members of society live, as well as the consuls, most of the Spanish Peninsulars and foreigners, the provincials and the priors of religious Orders, the artillery regiments, some natives, and some special local military units. The arsenals and the ships of the Armada are located in Cavite, a port near Manila.

Manila has the title of Distinguished and Ever Loyal City. Her armorial bearings consist of a coat of arms. The upper part shows a closed gold castle on a red field with a door and blue windows and crownlike structures on top. In the lower part, on a blue field, one can see the upper portion of a lion tied to the midlower half of a silver dolphin; the right claw carries a sword, its guard and hilt exposed. Surrounding the coat of arms are red heraldic branches. Above the principal merlon of the castle is a royal crown. The Ayuntamiento enjoys the title of Excellence.

IV

We have said that the uncle and aunt of the beautiful Enriqueta often hosted parties in their house. Here the most prominent people, the most beautiful ladies, and the most distinguished young men gathered. One evening, during a lively dance, a friend of the family introduced a young man. He was around twenty-five years old, pleasant looking, well-mannered, and elegantly attired.

Don Gustavo Alarcón, as he was called, was an employee of the Finance Ministry, where he earned a modest salary of P1 thousand a year. A thousand pesos in Manila, where the cost of living is high, is equivalent to less than 6,000 reales in Madrid.

Notwithstanding his limited resources, Alarcón rode out every afternoon in a rented carriage. He had a reserved seat at the theater and often dined in cafés. He dressed in style and attended all socials and dances. There was no family to whom he was a stranger, and no house where he was not warmly welcomed.

Sensible persons did not find his luxurious lifestyle a mystery. Alarcón was a swindler who owed the tailors, the carriage owner, the innkeeper, the Chinese shoemaker, and everyone else who trusted him. He had many debts, continually falling into all kinds of vices, and always devising ways to take advantage of his neighbors. He was, moreover, a cynic and a fraud: A cynic because he flaunted his insulting excesses before the victims of his deceit, and a fraud because everywhere he went he claimed that he was the son of a marquis who had sent him to the Philippines as punishment for his escapades but who provided him with a comfortable income, this being the reason why he was in the country with such a modest job.

The young ladies, who usually do not bother to get to the bottom of such matters, swallowed Alarcón's words, and because he was roguish and foolish, they respected and adored him. Usually, the fair sex is impressed by appearances more than by the real merits of a person.

Enriqueta had heard her friends praise Alarcón. She saw him and found him charming.

Alarcón had the superficial trappings of culture that could make others like him pass themselves off as men of talent. With his good looks and expressive face he won the great admiration of the ladies. The night he was introduced to her uncle and aunt, he danced with Enriqueta and took the opportunity to shower her with praises. The beautiful Filipina, so disdainful of the others, listened with pleasure to the arrogant young man without being aware of her attention to him. Resting after a dance, she felt happy and satisfied. Memories of that pleasant evening deprived her of sleep. These memories, pure as the dew on flowers and innocent as an angel's thoughts, were all related to the name Alarcón. She closed her eyes to sleep, and saw that gentleman's handsome face. She imagined that she heard his pleasant and alluring voice. Finally, while thinking of him, she fell asleep.

When she woke up the following morning, the first thing that entered her mind was the events of the previous night. When she heard a carriage coming, she ran to the balcony, driven by curiosity, and she saw the charming young man. Alarcón greeted her courteously. She moved away from the window, bewildered and wondering how it happened that the first carriage to pass by should bear the man whose memory so haunted her.

From that day on, Alarcón invariably passed her street, followed her when she took a walk, and appeared in the houses she visited. Many times they talked, increasing the affection and delight that the young man had inspired in her, until she fell in love with the passion of a first love. This she confessed to Alarcón, when he swore to her one day that he adored her and begged her to be kind and put an end to his tormenting doubts by telling him that she felt the same about him.

Happy in his love, Enriqueta fostered the most pleasant illusions, thinking incessantly of him, while Gustavo thought of the fortune that could be his if he obtained the rich young lady's hand.

V

As there are no secrets in Manila and word gets around, it soon became public knowledge that the most beautiful of the city's ladies was carrying on a relationship with the most amiable of young men. Everyone talked about it, each one judging it according to his fancy.

Some criticized Enriqueta, contrasting her proverbial disdain for men with her current behavior. Others felt sorry for her. Many of her girl friends envied her, and everyone was surprised at how the fortunate Alarcón had won her affection.

The rumor reached Enriqueta's uncle and aunt, who noticed the man and their niece meeting regularly. It was not difficult to guess the motive of his frequent visits to the house. Since they loved their niece, they tried probing into her heart, finding out to their dismay that she was passionately devoted to Gustavo. They inquired about his conduct and received extremely unfavorable information. All his vices, debts, falsehoods, and cynicism were revealed to them. They found out that he was a heartless young man and that he feigned love for their seduced niece out of self-interest more than the purity of noble sentiments.

One day, concerned about their niece's future, they said, "Enriqueta, do not forget that at your father's death he left you in our care. You know how we have always loved you like a daughter. It is our duty to give you good advice, to let our experience guide you, and to help you avoid committing the mistakes common among the young, which can cause terrible misfortune in the future. Since we are convinced that you love Don Gustavo Alarcón, we have inquired into his family, his life, and his character. Based on what we have learned, we can assure you, since we have enough proof, that this man is unworthy of you and is undeserving of your love. We suppose you are sensible enough to understand that it does you no good to carry on a relationship that is in no way favorable to you. If we talk to you this way, know that it is only because we desire your happiness."

"You know, dear Uncle and Aunt," Enriqueta replied, "that I have always taken your advice with due respect and have tried to follow it. Regarding the present matter, forgive me if I don't act in the same way. I am deeply grateful, however, for your concern for me. Let me explain. In the short time I have known the gentleman you speak of, I have felt such great passion that to lose him would be to lose my life. Forgive me if I do not believe what they have told you about him. Do not forget that he has enemies, and there are people who would like to discredit him before our eyes. I do not know why. I know very well that he does not occupy a high position, but this is because of the special circumstances he finds himself in with regard to his family. And in any case, since I am rich, it does not matter if he has nothing."

"We deeply regret, Enriqueta," her uncle said, "that you are very obstinate and that you still believe in him, while all Manila knows the truth and laughs at his tall tale that he is the son of a marquis. You should know that he is from very humble origins, and that no one is interested in discrediting him. His vices, his fraudulent acts—there is no other way to call them—his own actions discredit him."

"Well, Uncle and Aunt," Enriqueta interrupted, "I will be grateful if we say nothing more of this matter and not mind me if I am wrong. If I am mistaken, then no one but I will suffer the consequences."

"You will be unhappy, my dear daughter," her aunt said, crying disconsolately. "You don't know this man. You are being deceived. Think of your actions. Do not seek your eternal ruin."

The loving uncle and aunt insisted that she reconsider her decision, but Enriqueta did not heed their plea. The unpleasant scene ended in silence.

Alarcón, foreseeing this would happen, had prepared Enriqueta. He had told her that her relatives would resort to slander to discredit him before her eyes. The loving young lady swore that she would not be deceived and that despite everything she would be his wife. Many creditors of Alarcón, tired of waiting for him to settle his bills, had met and decided to take him to court;

but they desisted when Alarcón signed a contract promising to pay his debts, including the accumulated interest, after marrying the Alba lady, whose wealth was well-known.

Oftentimes, the lovestruck young lady's uncle and aunt tried to convince her that they had told her the truth about her lover's licentiousness, but always the effort was in vain. Enriqueta, firm in her resolve and more and more in love each day, was deaf to her relatives' advice, her friends' observations, and the pleas of her other admirers, who were much worthier of her than was Alarcón, who professed intense and selfless love for her.

The day came when, in another distressing scene, she hinted, prompted by her lover's insinuation, that her uncle and aunt were against her love not for the reasons they had given but because they benefited as administrators of her properties. And so, with sorrow and with anguished hearts, they decided to leave her to her fate.

Enriqueta was overwhelmed by Alarcón's show of deep and true love. She honestly believed, as she was incapable of thinking ill of her beloved, that he was honest and noble. She did not doubt that whatever they said of him was slanderous. She thought that his escapades, normal for one of his age and kind, had unduly tarnished his reputation, supplying the excuse for others to think him depraved. She wanted to convince herself that Gustavo's love was as selfless, sincere, and pure as hers. This is why she did not hesitate to finally fulfill her desire to unite herself forever with the fortunate Don Gustavo Alarcón, who, a few days earlier, had resigned from his job.

VI

The wedding of Enriqueta Amalia de Alba took place, much to the disgust of her uncle and aunt. They broke all relations with their niece, who had terribly misjudged them. On the day of the wedding, the newlyweds left for the cheerful town of Mariquina, where she owned a beautiful farm surrounded by green banana trees and filled with the fragrant perfume of thousands of sampaguitas,[10] ilang-ilang, and roses from China. Mariquina is a town situated in an extensive meadow of admirable vegetation; it enjoys a healthful climate and delicious water rich in iron. Mariquina is also the source of a spring called *Chorrillo*, on Mount Turco.

The couple spent three whole weeks in Mariquina. Afterwards, Alarcón, who could not adjust to such a peaceful lifestyle, told his wife of his desire to return to Manila. They then elegantly furnished a house on the property of Enriqueta on the main street of San Miguel, by the Pasig River. Since Alarcón only thought of showing off, they started to host parties twice a week. The guests danced and were served splendid dinners. The parties were most appreciated by many who were anxious to enjoy themselves.

Enriqueta preferred to stay on the farm in Mariquina than to continue the exciting life that her husband liked, but to please him she did not oppose him. Alarcón appeared to be living in a whirl-wind, preoccupied only with having fun, squandering money, and going out with his friends, while his young and loving wife stayed home alone on many evenings.

Such premature abandonment made her doubt her husband's love. Wealth was not as important to her as the affection that her heart longed for.

By that time, the annual horse races attended exclusively by the ladies and gentlemen of high society at the Santa Mesa Hippo-drome had begun. The members of the Jockey Club flaunted their extraordinary luxury, and the crowd was bigger than ever. Alarcón had bought at great expense two horses from Batangas and one from

---

[10] A flower similar to the jasmine.

Albay that he himself rode. He placed a number of huge bets, losing more than six thousand pesos in three afternoons. He did not even have the consolation of seeing any one of his horses win a prize, and one of them almost crashed him against the railing.

When Enriqueta found out what he had lost at the races, she reproved him sweetly, saying, "Gustavo, you did not do well to bet so much. While you squandered a considerable amount of money, you also exposed yourself to danger, as the horse could have killed you. See, aren't my fears real?"

"I know what I am doing," Alarcón responded brusquely, "and I don't need your advice."

He asked for the carriage and went out alone, not returning until the next day. Enriqueta stayed up all night crying, seeing that her husband's conduct had changed so soon after the wedding.

She, who adored him, had authorized him to withdraw from the house of Smith-Bell P30 thousand, which her parents had deposited some time ago. This amount was placed in a current account at the Banco Español-Filipino under her name, to cover the household expenses.

Six months later, Alarcón informed his wife that they had no money left. It was true. For the debts he had incurred when he was single, the expensive parties he often threw, the bets he placed at the races, the expensive treats he allowed himself, and the gambling—a pernicious vice to which he devoted many an hour while his wife languished in sad solitude—had drained them of their money in the bank.

Enriqueta was shocked to see such profligacy, but she said nothing, afraid of starting an argument, for her husband's character was no longer what it had been, and more than once she had to suffer his wrath.

Alarcón knew why she was silent, and to offset the negative effects of the news, he said, "I understand, even if you don't tell me, that you are shocked that we have spent so much. Don't forget, however, all the expenses we have incurred to maintain our reputation in Manila. From now on, we will do away with the parties under the pretext of an expedition to *Quingua*. This way we will cut down on our expenses. In three days, we will move there."

Quingua is a town in Bulacan, a beautiful province near Manila, rich for its fertility and for the efficient cultivation of its sprawling lands. Its inhabitants are hard-working; the climate is healthful, especially in Quingua, whose waters are clear; and the land is most pleasant and picturesque.

In this precious garden, so pleasing to the soul, where Nature seemed to have poured all her enchantment, the beautiful Enriqueta could enjoy brief days of solace. Her heart regained the calm that she had lost in Manila at seeing her husband giving in to a wayward life, confirming what her uncle and aunt had told her about his dissipation.

One moonlit night, a night of the resplendent tropical moon, whose light dims the phosphorescence of the *alitaptap*, luminous insects that transform trees into enormous chandeliers of flickering lights that illuminate the way of the traveler, serving as lamps for long distances—on such a poetic night, when the soft breezes refresh the air—Alarcón invited his wife to take a stroll among the banana trees by the riverbank, an invitation she gladly accepted.

They took a walk in that delightful place, lovingly arm in arm. Enriqueta, happy beside her soul's idol, inhaling the delicate fragrance of the flowers, seeing the wide flowing river that the moon had silvered, and enraptured by the voluptuousness of Nature, forgot her bitter moments and completely surrendered to the delights of love. There, fascinated, she heard her husband's most beautiful plans.

"From now on, my love, we will live only for each other," Alarcón told her tenderly. "We will gradually sever ties with people who rob us of hours of joy, and we will be very happy. Don't you see what beautiful scenery surrounds us?"

"Yes, my husband," answered Enriqueta enthusiastically. "We will live here, far away from the world, minding just ourselves, enslaved no longer to a society that does not love us, and if it flatters us, it is because we satisfy its demands and we sacrifice our fortune and tranquility to get its approval."

"Well said, and the better to realize it, let us buy, if you approve, the pretty estate beside ours, which is being auctioned, and let us live in this delightful place."

Enriqueta, who thought she would be overcome with happiness when she heard her husband, replied, "I do applaud your idea. Tomorrow, the contract my uncle and aunt entered into terminates. They have to decide whether to continue or renew it. I have a share in the capital, which will increase in value. I will withdraw this to acquire the property, so we can carry out our plans soonest."

Alarcon replied, "In that case, first thing tomorrow morning, I will leave for Manila with an authorization from you to collect the money. I will auction off the things in our house that are of no value to us here, and I will have the rest transported. In three days I'll come back. You stay here so you can attend to the furniture as it is delivered."

They did as they planned. The following day, Alarcón took the small boat, *Isabel Primera*, in Bulacan, and two-and-a-half hours later, he arrived in the capital of the Islands with a document that would make him richer by P40 thousand.

VII

Three days passed and then three more, but Alarcón did not go back to Quingua, nor did he send any news. Enriqueta was very worried, not knowing what to do, fearful that her husband had met with an accident. Not daring to look for him without his consent, she wrote a trusted friend and asked about him. The answer was that her husband was in the best of health, according to the valets; and that he was spending the evenings somewhere, returning home at dawn. No one knew where he had been going.

The pain Enriqueta felt upon hearing the news needs no description. That same day, she left the province and went to her house in San Miguel. When she arrived, she found her husband asleep. In the room with him was a friend.

Poor Enriqueta was disconsolate. She was afraid of what had happened to the money she had authorized him to collect and sorry to see the ruin of her hopes of living peacefully in Quingua, a place far away from the seductions of gambling and the vanities that so attracted Alarcón.

Alarcón awoke and was confused and surprised to see Enriqueta. She reprimanded him for his silence, for not returning to her side at the time he said he would, which should have been in time for the auction of the country house they were planning to buy.

Her husband, at that moment, did not know what to answer, but recovering from his shock, he got angry with the poor young woman for having left Quingua without informing him.

Alarcón was a wicked man who shamelessly abused his wife's kindness. He introduced Juan Vélez to her as his best friend. Vélez at that moment was leaving the room. Judging from his appearance, he looked more like a bandit than a decent person.

Enriqueta, grieving at her misfortune, did not bother to ask about the money. Alarcón, indifferent to her broken heart, left her alone and went out with his friend to have fun.

Seeing this behavior, Enriqueta could not contain her indignation and felt severe remorse for having ignored her uncle and aunt's counsel and for having given her hand to that debased man who was incapable of realizing her worth. Overpowered by these impressions, she went to see her uncle and aunt to ask for their forgiveness for her weakness and to find relief in their embrace from the anguish she was feeling in her heart. At seeing her so disgraced, they welcomed her with kindness, lamenting her misfortune at the same time. Enriqueta learned from them that Alarcón had presented them the authorization letter, received the amount of P40 thousand that belonged to her, and instead of going to Bulacan, hurried to the cafés looking for friends to spend the evening with him in a scandalous orgy. Moreover, they told her that Vélez, whom she found in the house, was a comrade of Alarcón recently arrived in the Philippines, who had the reputation of being a persistent gambler. The two had gone to the gambling houses with a lot of money because it was the feast of La Naval in Binondo, an event that gathered together people from as far away as the Visayas and many gamblers all over the country.

Since the young woman was so miserable, her uncle and aunt consoled her as best as they could. They agreed, among other things, to find a way to make her husband change his ways. With this thought, Enriqueta went back home more relaxed and determined to be less submissive to the whims of her husband.

For a week, she hardly saw him. He came home at dawn in the company of his friend. They locked themselves in the room and ate there by themselves. Sometimes, they went out to eat. The young woman decided to put an end to such a dismaying situation. One night she awaited her husband's arrival and, on finding him alone, said, "I've been wanting to have a word with you for days. Let me tell you that I did not marry you only to be treated in the offensive way you have been treating me. I've decided to end this situation. So from this day on, I will not allow my money to be used to sustain the vices of one whom I had the misfortune to marry unaware that he was looking for something other than my love. This has to stop. Either we are a couple or we break the bond that unites us once and for all. Treat me the way I think I deserve. Right now, tell me what happened to the P40 thousand you collected from my uncle and aunt, or else, violent as it may seem to me, I will seek the aid of the law."

Alarcón did not expect to see such forcefulness in his wife. Accustomed as he was to her subservience to his desires, he was taken aback by the sudden resolve with which she now threatened him. Afraid that she would carry out a threat that would have dreadful consequences, he tried to calm her, hypocritically answering her in this manner:

"Forgive me, dear Enriqueta, for the way I have treated you. I know that you have a thousand reasons to be disgusted with me, but before condemning me, listen. Vélez is a childhood friend related to my family. When I arrived in Manila, he was introduced to me with instructions from my family that I look after him. He came to our house, and I could not leave him alone, new as he was to the country, with neither friends nor resources. As he is young and single, he likes to enjoy himself. The feast of Binondo being celebrated, I had to accompany him. That is why I kept away from you. I promise that from now on it will not happen again, and that I will be as loving with you as ever."

Enriqueta understood that her husband was trying to calm her with sweet words. She knew that he was insincere and that he did not want to explain what he had done with the money. But because she loved him so much, and seeing him so affectionate, she was inclined to forget all his offenses even if she knew it was impossible for him to keep his promise.

Nevertheless, concealing her sentiments, she retorted, "To take care of a friend you don't have to spend whole nights away from the house. Your obligation to me that you contracted when we got married demands more of you than this friendship. In your excuses, you still have not told me anything about the money, which, according to my uncle and aunt, you collected. And I am not aware of any investment you have made."

"That money," he answered, disturbed, and clearly showing his dishonesty, "I have deposited in the bank to avoid any setback."

"Well, since it is no longer possible to realize the plan that we made in Quingua, it is appropriate that my uncle and aunt use it for our business. In no one else's hands is the money safer and more productive. This is what I promised. They will come for the money tomorrow."

"In that case, I think you do not intend to count on me for anything. You forget that no one has the right to act as your guardian, unlike before when you were not yet married. I find it strange that because of my bad relations with them, you think of such a thing. Don't I know how to manage the funds and make them as productive as when your uncle and aunt managed them?"

"If you will handle the funds in the same way as the P30 thousand I gave you, it is better that they manage the money themselves."

Alarcón let out an angry scream but calmed down instantly when he realized his difficult situation. To end the disagreeable dialogue, he said, "I had a terrible night and I feel sick. Let's talk about this later. I will go to bed now."

Enriqueta, who was good and gentle at heart, did not wish to torment him any more and let him go to bed. She wrote her uncle and aunt, informing them of her conversation with her husband. They went to the bank to inquire if Alarcón had deposited the funds as he had said. In the evening, the uncle and aunt came to their niece's house to inform her that it was not true that any amount had been deposited in the bank. It was public knowledge that Alarcón had lost a considerable sum in gambling. Enriqueta and her guardians lamented his misconduct and the unscrupulous way he handled her money.

The presence of Alarcón, who had left his bed at that moment, made the uncle and aunt leave without greeting him. It was impossible for them to agree with him on anything.

Alarcón, aware of what was happening, spent a restless evening. His conscience condemned him for his criminal behavior. The next day, he left the house very early and went to tell his comrade, Vélez, who was now staying in an inn, that he feared the worst was yet to come.

Vélez, who saw his friend faltering, understood that if Gustavo renounced the kind of life they were living, he too was lost. Inspired by these reflections, he said,

"I see that you do not know how to deal with women. Your woman is smart and you will end up being her slave. If you knew how to control yourself, you would be the happiest of husbands. Your wife is in love with you. Now is the time to make her adjust to your ways. Make her obey and respect your wishes and resign herself to your whims. The question of money, as it is now, is difficult and can have regrettable consequences for you, not only because of the scandal it can cause but also because in the future they will see to it that you do not get a *céntimo*. Be that as it may, Gustavo, you will be a victim. In your own hands lies the possibility that the contrary can occur. Take advantage of the time you still have. Get whatever money you can, and we will take a trip to China. When your wife finds herself without you, she will be unable to live and she will call you. She will then consider all that you have done and will behave properly. You will not want anything more. Your wife will divine your thoughts and try to please you in every way… Is there much left of the P40 thousand from the other day?"

"Around fifteen thousand."

"Great! Do what I tell you and you will not regret it."

Vélez's devious proposal found easy acceptance in the broken spirit of Alarcón. He bade farewell to Vélez, determined to take up the proposal. Alarcón went to a well-known money-lender. Offering as collateral two good properties that Enriqueta owned in Quiapo, he was able to borrow the sum of P20 thousand.

Then Alarcón, feigning urgency, secured passports for himself and Vélez with a guarantee from another friend. With the guarantee required by the authorities, he could not be prevented from leaving in case Enriqueta saw in the *Gaceta* his application for a passport. With everything thus arranged, he left on a boat that afternoon. Three days later, he and Vélez were in Hong Kong, without his wife suspecting anything in the least.

VIII

When news of her husband's departure got to Enriqueta, she refused to believe those who were certain of having seen him embark. It was necessary for her to see in the papers the name of Alarcón on the list of passengers aboard the ship that had left for Hong Kong the other day. She went to the Secretaría del Gobierno Superior to ask if he had been issued a passport, then later to the Capitanía del Puerto to find out if he had embarked.

Finally, convinced of the flight of her husband, she fell into a state of stupor difficult to describe. Her uncle and aunt immediately went to see her, and they found her greatly distressed and in a state of mortal anguish.

In Manila, Enriqueta's plight and her husband's hasty departure became public knowledge and greatly affected the unhappy young woman. Every gossip and scandalmonger had his own interpretation of what had happened. The cruel criticisms of people who thrive on scandalous news added more fuel to the fire, and it seemed that all of Manila knew that the spouse of the Alba woman had departed. To add to her misfortunes, the person who had advanced Alarcón the P20 thousand informed the unhappy Enriqueta of his villainous behavior. Remembering what had happened to the P40 thousand that she had authorized him to collect from the firm of her uncle and aunt, she was convinced that her husband was a miserable wretch, capable of the worst infamies; a hardened gambler who sacrificed everything to satisfy his foolish passion; a shameless man to whom honor had no meaning; an ingrate who neither loved nor valued the distinction of having been chosen her husband among so many others who were worthy. What pained Enriqueta's heart the most—what she could not bear and what caused her maddening anguish—was the indifference with which he distanced himself from her, his unwarranted departure in a way that showed everyone that he did not love her and that he had married her for self-serving reasons. Yet she belonged completely to him, and it was not possible to rid herself of the intense love burning in her heart.

So great was her emotion and so profound her feelings that she fell ill and for a month she was struggling for life. Finally, nature interceded and she recovered her health, but all attempts to cure the sickness in the soul were in vain.

It is sad to cry over a lost love and the absence of a loved one. The light of day only hurts the feelings of one who loves without hope, and the shadows of the night increase the pain of the memories when the lover is convinced that his lost happiness will no longer return. Each hour that passes increases the impatience of the person who suffers, and loses all tranquility. One feels an infinite sickness and melancholy; life becomes insufferable martyrdom. There is no physical sickness, harsh and bitter as it may be, that compares with the sickness of the spirit. Diseases of the soul are more difficult to cure than the maladies of the body. One who recovers from bodily illness, although he may become physically handicapped, can attain happiness, but one who is sick in the soul will never again be happy on this Earth.

The life, the habits, and even the beautiful face of the enchanting Filipina suffered obvious changes from the day her husband left her bed. Her eyes no longer sparkled with its former brilliance. The glow in her eyes was now dimmed by tears; her cheeks, once rosy, turned pale. She could no longer be heard singing in her lovely voice. The flowers, which she had loved and taken care of every morning, withered as if in sympathy with the young woman. She closed the piano, whose delicate notes had appeased her sorrows, and she no longer wanted to touch it. When thoughts are burdened, music increases the heart's pain, and it is almost impossible to overcome the sorrow. Painting bored her. People tired her. In vain did her uncle and aunt and her loving friends think of a thousand ways to soothe her pains.

For Enriqueta, there was no consolation possible. She was aware that Alarcón was unworthy of her love, and yet she adored him. She was troubled by the thought of the happiness that might have been if he had loved her as much as she loved him. There were moments when she feared she would lose her mind, and she lacked the fortitude to bear her afflictions, asking herself what she had done to deserve this fate. Her loving uncle and aunt, who throughout her sickness did not leave her alone at any time, took her into their home. They spent most of their time with her and strived to enliven her in every possible way.

May is the happiest month of the year in Europe because the trees are clothed in green, the meadows are filled with beautiful flowers, and the birds greet the rebirth of nature and the end of winter with their songs. But in the Philippines, where one enjoys eternal spring, the trees never lose their leaves, nor do flowers cease to bloom. The icy north wind never blows, nor does the vegetation wither, so that the mountains are converted into huge flowerpots, and ranks of wild grass sprout from the rocks. In the Philippines, the month of May surpasses in brilliance any other month of the year, and her forests, meadows, valleys, gardens, mountains, and plains are the most delightful in the world. The numerous inhabitants of Manila and her extensive suburbs, the townsfolk of neighboring provinces, and the residents from adjoining towns and even distant places—all head for Antipolo in happy caravans, in carriages, on foot, or on the Pasig River in small boats decorated with pennants and boughs, for the feast of Antipolo is celebrated in this merry month.

Antipolo is a town in the district of Morong, near Manila. The Virgin, who bears the name of the town, is venerated there. The natives of the archipelago feel a special devotion to her. The month of the fiesta witnesses an unending line of people on the road to the sanctuary, where they bear offerings as a sign of their veneration. Countless pilgrims gather together in joyful spirits. Noisy fireworks, music in the streets, songs, dances in the houses, and visits to the shrine, which is never left deserted, complete the pilgrimage.

Although all homes are open to the pilgrims, the Antipolo folk cannot accommodate the immense multitude, leaving many to rest or sleep under the trees, in improvised tents or behind simple *tapancos* or bamboo sheds.

Those who go to Antipolo return with scapulars of the Virgin, amulets, religious cards, and bottles of holy water, the sale of which amounts to thousands of pesos. The procession is most ostentatious because of the crowd and the bright lights, the deafening skyrockets, the Bengal flares, *loas* or allocutions in verse, arches, music—a universal enthusiasm among a varied multitude in a state of religious fervor tourists find amazing. This very famous festival has the distinction of inspiring even the sons of the Celestial Empire, who come to Antipolo in growing numbers. Most devotees help themselves to mineral water from a well, thought to be miraculous, situated on the outskirts of the town of Tanay. The water, they say, has wrought wondrous cures. Neither do they forget to pull leaves from the so-called tree of blood nearby, which, when pounded, produce a red liquid, a phenomenon that is the source of many absurd tales recounted by the natives.

Enriqueta's uncle and aunt brought her to the sanctuary of Antipolo to give her some relief from her bitter sorrows. Undoubtedly, the prayer of the abandoned wife was pleasing to the Virgin, because she returned, if not happy, at least resigned to her situation. Seeing this, her uncle and aunt were determined to go next to Obando, the feast of which is also celebrated in May.

Obando is in the province of Bulacan, not far from Manila. A belief exists among the natives and the mestizos that dancing before the image of Obando's patron saint cures all kinds of sickness and prevents the occurrence of others. The more one dances the more efficacious the cure will be. Such is the fame of Obando that the road that leads to the town is crowded on the days of the feast, with groups of men, women, and children dressed in fancy costumes, their heads adorned with feathers, shaking tambourines, playing small guitars called *cinco-cinco* and other instruments, all of them dancing to the happy music, allowing themselves not even a moment for rest in spite of the long trek in the dust, the glare and heat of the sun.

As the procession goes down the main streets of Obando, the furor of the dance enraptures the people. Upon seeing the statue of San Pascual Bailón, forty thousand people of all classes, ages, and conditions begin to shake, jump, and dance, imploring the saint to cure them of their pains, showing him the sick parts of their bodies; bustling about praying, singing, and dancing without letup even inside the church where the procession ends. To witness so many people in their clothes of a thousand colors praying, singing, and dancing as though in a fit of madness is an experience that is difficult to describe. One must be actually present to get the exact picture of how strange and surprising this animated spectacle can be.

Enriqueta, who went to Obando with her uncle and aunt, saw the scenes we have so succinctly sketched, and there were moments when she forgot her pains, awed by the enthusiasm of the devotees of San Pascual Bailón. At the fiesta, the loving relatives of the unfortunate young woman sought to provide her grieving soul with some consolation; but even if they achieved their noble intentions momentarily, Enriqueta was again tormented by the memory of her misfortunes, and they saw her sinking once more into her eternal sadness. Thus did they spend several months without receiving any news from her husband.

IX

Let us relate what became of Alarcón after his departure from Manila.

As soon as they arrived in Hong Kong, the two friends checked into the best hotel.

Hong Kong is a small island on Canton Bay on the southern coast of China, approximately 11 leagues, about 62 kms. from Macao. The English, who get a share of everything, have converted an arid rock into a garden and a territory that has become an important place alive with commercial activity. The port of Hong Kong, which today is bustling with people, would not be more than an average anchorage if it were still in the hands of the Chinese, for they reject modern civilization and are against the establishment of Europeans in their county.

In this city, there is an agglomeration of people from different countries. There are many centers of corruption, where people of little prudence are ready to squander large amounts of money within a very short time. Gambling and drinking are indulged in to the point of abuse. Without delay Alarcón and his friend formed a group of the most debased gamblers in the English colony and promptly lost to these men a great deal of the money they carried.

Seeing that business was bad, they moved to Macao. This Chinese city in the province of Kuangtung maintains commerce of great importance, and it is famous for being on a hill close to the cave where the immortal Camoens, it is believed, wrote his *Luisiadas*.

The Portuguese did not treat Alarcón and Vélez any better than the English, so that the two, afraid of losing all their fortune, proceeded to Singapore, abandoning the country of Chinese shoemakers who now reside in Manila, a great majority of whom are from Macao.

In Singapore, they found new opportunities for their adventures. The population of this small island of the East Indies is the most heterogeneous that is known. Its port, visited by ships of all countries, is very much alive. The view of the city reveals the creative genius of the English and their magnificent capacity to convert into commercial centers the most rustic of places and to transform into active businessmen the most indolent of beings.

In this city, European and Malayan establishments stand next to each other. Beside the bazaars of the children of the Hindustans are those of the natives of Indo-China. These front the pagodas, where they pay homage to Brahma and Buddha or worship Vishnu and Shiva. Adjacent to the Arabic mosque is the Christian cathedral; and beside the Protestant church is a temple where Confucius is venerated.

In this same throng of worshippers are individuals of all nationalities in the world, speaking in their distinct languages and dressed in different attires. The mixture of various cultures is surprising, but most remarkable is the commotion, the commercial activity of the inhabitants of Singapore, constantly buying and selling. The pier is full of immense deposits of coal, the streets full of sellers and shops. In the surroundings, amid the beautiful gardens, are some country houses and recreational buildings belonging to the rich.

Naturally, in a place where people from all over the world gather, where much money circulates, where every street has a café and where one is easily introduced to whatever circle one wants to get into—for there are agents for everything here—it was only natural that Alarcón and his friend Vélez found someone to help them empty some bottles and try their luck at a game. At first, everything went well for them, and for a moment, they had the illusion that they would win back what they had lost.

Gamblers never lose hope. Ever looking for recovery no matter how adverse luck may be, they end up ruining themselves. Alarcón and Vélez, instead of stopping when they were winning, played on, until the day came when fortune tired of them. At the end of four months, Alarcón's capital was reduced to P5 thousand.

One night he asked Vélez, "Do you know that another loss like last night's will leave us broke?"

"Well, how much do you have left?"

"P5 thousand."

"That's very little. Do you mean to go and see if you can recover?"

"Without a doubt. I have promised to meet the two Frenchmen who won all the money I had with me. I suppose you will accompany me."

"Not tonight. I feel a bit indisposed. I suggest you be cautious, however."

"That I will be, so I won't lose much. I want to leave P4 thousand with you. I will bring a thousand with me. If I fail to win back my losses, I will not play a cent more than that."

"I applaud your prudent decision."

"Well, keep this money and see you later," he said, handing the money to Vélez.

"Good luck. Goodbye."

Alarcón arrived at the house where his gambling companions had been waiting and went straight to the tables. In a short while, he lost the P1 thousand he had brought in the hope of recovering what he had lost. The other gamblers saw that he was not playing anymore. They asked him why, to which he replied that he had no more cash with him. They offered him a P1 thousand, which Alarcón did not want to accept. But his new friends insisted. In the end, he agreed and continued playing, using the thousand they had lent him. He lost, and again they advanced him the same amount. He was afraid to go on, but agitated by passion, he played on, until he came to lose the P4 thousand they had lent him. That was the same amount that he had left in the house.

Now desperate and wanting to try his luck for the last time, he put on the table his watch and his rings, worth a total of P300, begging them to accept this wager for the same amount. They agreed, in consideration of what he had lost. He was so unlucky that he lost again.

He signed a receipt for the P4 thousand that they had advanced him and even if they did not want to accept it, he put it on the table and left very much disturbed. What he suffered on the way to the inn where he was staying is impossible to describe. His forehead was burning; a thousand absurd ideas stirred his imagination and he thought he had lost his reason. In this state of mind, he entered his room.

He looked for Vélez to tell him of his misfortune, but his friend was not in the room nor on his bed. He was about to ring the bell to ask the servants of the inn if Vélez had left when he saw a letter addressed to him on the night table. From the handwriting on the envelope, he knew it was from his companion.

X

Vélez's letter, which Alarcón hurriedly read, went thus:
Dear Gustavo:

There are times when a man, less inclined to excitement, meditates.

And I, my friend, who you know have very little interest in philosophizing, have meditated this evening. The result of my meditations may not please you nor merit your approval. I will be very sorry, because the solution will come late.

I have reflected, dear Gustavo, that you are more of a gambler than I, and that is all that there is to say. And do you know the consequences of being enslaved to a vice that the moralists call the worst? Well, it is very simple. You will lose even the last céntimo that you have and when you run out of money, you will even gamble away your jewels.

On the day that this happens, which will be soon, what will our situation be in a strange country? Without ability or vocation, can we earn a living and not be exposed to the horrors of hunger and misery? Have you thought of this?

I think not, because you have not yet thought of what I know. But I, who have already meditated, as I have told you, see this as clear, palpable, imminent.

And seeing thus, my friend, it would be the height of madness not to avoid so unpleasant a crisis. I have decided, then, to embark on an American boat, which leaves in half an hour for Punta de Gales, and from there take another boat of the Mensajerías Francesas.

Since I am not aware that a way of traveling without money has been discovered, in spite of having the honor of being born in the century of the most pleasant discoveries, I take with me the P4 thousand you left with me. I do this on condition that I return the money when I have more than enough and when you need it, which I think will never happen. In gratitude, I give you a good advice.

With your gains this evening, pay the inn and our other debts. After doing this, do not stay a day longer in Singapore. Return to Manila and throw yourself at your wife's feet, begging her forgiveness. She is an angel. She loves you and will pardon your ingratitude. Beside her you can be happy; but if you do not overcome your passion for gambling, you could end up in a garrison. I, in Europe, will remember you and hope you will not forget me.

Your best friend who likes you,
Eugenio Vélez

While Alarcón was reading his friend's letter, his heart beat so strongly that it seemed it would burst. After reading the letter, blood rushed to his head, and he collapsed.

He recovered a little, and his mind wandered in a sea of ideas. He reflected on the action of Vélez, whom he had considered his friend, on the sarcasm of his letter when it was he who had induced him to abandon his wife, and on the indifference with which he had fled, leaving him without a céntimo in such a critical situation. Later, he remembered that the P4 thousand that Vélez took was for the debts he had to pay, and he thought of the consequences of his failure to settle these debts.

He was penniless, he owed the inn, and the most frightful misery loomed before him.

Finally, the image of Enriqueta crossed his imagination. On remembering how good she had been to him, the vileness of his behavior towards her, the fortune he had squandered, the state of neglect that he had left her in, and the happiness he had lost, he exclaimed, "Vélez is right; I have been a scoundrel."

Incapable of resolving anything worthwhile that would save him from his terrible situation, he got a revolver and left the house in despair. The morning light was beginning to shine. Not a soul could be seen on the street. Battling a thousand sinister thoughts, he arrived at the cemetery.

The cemetery in Singapore is worth the traveler's attention. It is surrounded by an elevated grating and is accessible through a wide iron gate. On either side of the entrance are sturdy trees. The interior is concealed behind the foliage of willows and covered by a variety of flowers. More than a cemetery, it looks like a garden. The artistic monuments are not many, but there are a great number of tombs of different shapes. In the same way that the living are mixed together in the city, the dead are mixed together in the cemetery.

The Catholic sepulchres are distinguished by the crosses raised above them and those of Protestants by their simplicity. On many of these sepulchres are inscriptions in the language of the country to which the deceased belonged.

The Chinese characters, in varied colors, stand out because of their shapes in that vast array of names of those who have ceased to exist. There are some marble mausoleums encircled by iron fences and shaded by tall cypresses, with tombstones that bear the names of important people of the colony. There are also several tombs that contain remains of Spaniards whose misfortune it was to die in distant lands, or on their way back to their country after many years of absence.

It was very silent in the cemetery. The guard who opened the gate for Alarcón asked for the number of the tomb he wanted to visit in order to guide him there, but Alarcón replied that he did not need his help because he knew where to go. He walked on and soon lost his way in the thick foliage that adorned the mansions of eternal repose.

The sun began to color the clouds; the birds were greeting the new day. Alarcón looked sadly around him. Coming upon a small garden where there were many crosses, a sign that those buried there belonged to the Catholic Church, he went in and leaned against the trunk of a cypress tree that stood at the center. There, he stayed pensive for some moments, his face a portrait of deep melancholy. He was, no doubt, retracing in his mind all the events of his life, and he thought of his wife whom he had so cruelly abandoned. He removed his hat, looked up at the morning sky, and prayed. Then, getting hold of the revolver he carried and moving rapidly, he aimed the gun at his temple and fired. He let out a muffled cry and fell at the foot of the tree. Startled by the sound of the gunshot, the guard came running, and upon seeing a man bathed in blood, he blew his whistle. His companions came and while some of them pondered what had happened, others tried to stop the bleeding in Alarcón's head. He was still breathing.

The authorities arranged for him to be transferred to the room reserved for foreigners in the general hospital, where the physicians administered initial treatment.

In his hurry to fire the gun, he had raised his arm too high so that the bullet did nothing more than open a wide wound, which was quite serious but which could be treated.

Alarcón remained unconscious for twelve hours. When he gained consciousness, he noted that the medical practitioner who was attending to him spoke Spanish. He asked the *practicante* where he was from and found out that he was born in the Philippines.

At that, Alarcón revealed his identity, keeping quiet, however, about why he was there. The practicante thought Alarcón was delirious and did not believe him. It would seem unbelievable that the husband of the richest lady of the country should find himself in Singapore without any friends to take him home. Adding to the man's doubts was the attempted suicide.

Alarcón understood that the practicante did not believe him. He told parts of his story, and at last, he got the practicante to believe him. From that moment on, the solicitous practicante did not leave his bed, offering him every kind of care.

The fever allowed the wounded a few moments of serenity, but he used the time to talk about his wife, to recall the happiness he had felt beside her, and to regret the good that he had lost. He knew that his treatment was difficult, and he did not want to die without seeing Enriqueta, without obtaining her pardon, without saying goodbye.

The practicante offered to inform the family, and Alarcón dictated this letter:

My Revered Enriqueta:

At the moment when a man is about to leave this world, he realizes and laments his errors, enduring as punishment the bitter pain of not being able to make amends for them. I, who had the undeserved luck of being your husband, ignored your worth, and instead of living happily by your side, I allowed myself to be driven by my passions and by the criminal advice of a traitor who I thought was a friend. I have now come to end my days far away from you and from my country, in a hospital in a foreign land.

I had the mission to watch over you and I abandoned you. I should have worshipped you like the angels do the Creator because you are good and adorable, but I did not love you. Instead of being a faithful administrator of the wealth that you generously entrusted to me, I squandered it. I have been a criminal, a scoundrel towards you. Now that reason has illuminated my spirit, I deplore my error and apologize for my unjustifiable behavior. Close to dying, my sole grief is not to see you for the last time and to ask you a thousand pardons. Should you pardon me and should I have the joy of seeing you, I would die peacefully. Great is my fault but your kindness is greater.

Goodbye, dear Enriqueta. Don't speak ill of me. . . your wretched husband who dies loving you.

With agonizing effort, he signed the letter. The practicante immediately brought it to the *Irurac-bac*, a Spanish ship that was bound for Manila.

The doctors recommended that Alarcón be kept calm. The fever, however, returned with great intensity. His caring practicante, who never left him, understood the delirium brought by the fever, the cruel remorse the patient was suffering from, and the impatience with which he waited for his wife.

When the fever receded, he and Alarcón talked of Manila. He thought constantly of his wife and his country. The wound, meanwhile, was not healing. Alarcón reached the point of losing hope of seeing the one he now loved very much because he appreciated her kindness. Despair aggravated his condition. The doctors lost hope of saving him.

XI

As she read her husband's letter, Enriqueta forgot all the wrong he had done to her, realizing only that he was dying in a foreign country, that he was disgraced and that he wanted to be with her again.

Immediately, she obtained the necessary papers for travel to Singapore. In the afternoon of the following day the mail boat *Mariveles* would sail and she did not want to lose so good an opportunity.

Her uncle and aunt tried to dissuade her from making the trip, afraid that some danger might overtake her, but she said, "My husband is sick, and my duty is to be by his side to attend to him. He abandoned me and was ungrateful, but he is repentant and he loves me. What I will regret will be to arrive too late. He may die without my being able to see him; without his knowing that I forgive him with all my heart."

Knowing her resolve, instead of trying to stop her, her uncle said that he would accompany her. Enriqueta embraced him warmly, thanking him for the eloquent expression of his love.

The trip was pleasant and rapid.

Five and a half days after their departure from Manila, Enriqueta and her uncle were in Singapore. From the pier, they went directly to the general hospital. The sight that met the eyes of the unfortunate young woman could not be any sadder.

Alarcón was at the point of death; beside him a priest was exhorting him to have faith in the infinite mercy of God while the doctor supported his head in his arms.

On seeing him, the young woman uttered a heart-rending cry and ran towards him.

As it is impossible to give a detailed and faithful account of the tender reconciliation scene between Enriqueta and Gustavo, a situation that made everyone who witnessed it shed tears, we forego describing it. After the first moments of seeing each other, Alarcón made an effort to talk and said:

"Thank you, my dearest wife; you have been very kind. I finally see you again, I know that you forgive me . . . I die happy. If you only knew how I repent for my behavior toward you . . . ; how good you are!"

"Forget that as I have forgotten it. Why didn't you come to me, knowing that I love you? Why did you prefer to leave me when I cannot live without you?"

"If you understood how much I loved you, Enriqueta! Come nearer, I can't see you."

Enriqueta was kissing her husband madly, as though the outpouring of her love would save him from a terrible drought, but his days, nay hours, were numbered, and the coldness of death confronted her. After a few moments, she was kissing a cadaver.

She was beside herself with grief. No human power could remove her from his arms. She did not hear the pleas of her uncle, nor was she aware of what was going on around her. After a few hours of mental disarray, she regained her senses. Her eyes filled with tears, and this expression of sorrow restored her senses.

She comforted her heart, and rising above the circumstances with a spirit that no one thought she had, she gave orders and asked that she be brought to the hospital director. She asked him for permission to have her husband's body embalmed so that she could transport it to Manila.

This done, she had the creditors of Alarcón located so that they could be paid what he had owed them, amounts they thought they had lost when the cause of his attempted suicide was known.

Alarcón's body was embalmed and put in a double lead casket. Then without delay, Enriqueta, together with the remains of her husband, took the first boat bound for Manila.

Enriqueta was the object of her uncle's devoted attention during the trip and she was greatly consoled by the practicante who attended to her husband in the hospital. The young woman, out of gratitude to him and aware of his desire to return to his country, made him board with them and guaranteed a lifetime income for him as manager of one of her haciendas.

All the churches of the capital offered magnificent ceremonies to help the soul of her unforgettable husband. She obtained a special license to inter him in an elegant mausoleum that she had constructed at the far end of her property in the picturesque town of Mariquina. To the mausoleum, she added a chapel. Every Friday, the day of Alarcón's death, a priest came to offer supplications to the Supreme Maker for his eternal repose.

Enriqueta established her residence in Mariquina, where, newly married, she had spent the only days of happiness with her husband. Every morning, she would pray by his tomb, laying on it a crown of flowers that she gathered from her garden and which she herself arranged.

There she spent life with less grief because every place, every tree, every flower filled her with memories. Remembering the hours of pleasure that now seemed so distant, she was distracted from her sorrows and the days that went by very slowly.

THE SULTANA OF JOLO

I

One day in the month of January 1848, the city of Cebu was in a very festive mood. The balconies of the houses were decorated with elegant tapestries; on the streets were arches that had been skillfully built. There were streamers and flags over pathways, greased poles in the plazas, and rich velvet curtains, bouquets of flowers, and a profusion of lights in the churches.

In the port, the ships came into view bedecked with flags and bunting. Bells pealed, cannons boomed, and music wafted harmoniously all throughout the town.

People virtually overflowed from the balconies, dressed in their Sunday best, talking and laughing merrily. They moved around the plazas, on the streets and promenades.

It was the feast of the Santo Niño. Magellan had brought the image to Cebu and since the time of Legaspi the Cebuanos have revered and worshipped the Christ child.

There was only one house, it seemed, where no one was participating in that immense and widespread rejoicing. It was a residence with a beautiful façade, so different from the houses nearby that it easily stood out.

Some thought its inhabitants' disinterest in the celebration was due to lack of religious faith; others attributed it to different reasons that were far from the truth, while many who knew the real reason respected it.

Hypochondria, a terrible sickness of intense melancholy, was slowly consuming the lives of the persons in that house so devoid of exterior adornments while other houses were lavishly decorated.

The profound sadness that embittered the days of Don Vicente Tupal and his wife, owners of the house, could not be more justified.

They had a sixteen-year-old daughter named Lólen, short for Dolores, beautiful as the light and pure as the angels. She was their happiness in old age, the pride of their race, heiress to immense wealth her parents had acquired through a laborious life of self-abnegation and industry. Unfortunately, this beloved daughter, for whom they had endured many hardships and who was now the object of their purest affection, had been abducted treacherously and at that moment was suffering like a martyr.

The unhappy Tupal had a sister in Barili, a port in the province of Cebu. She had written Tupal, inviting Lólen to spend some time with her and to be godmother to her first son. Tupal agreed happily to his sister's request and sent Lólen to Barili.

The more distinguished young ladies of the town were pleased to entertain her and keep her company on her walks. One afternoon, they were running along the beach, happy to see the waves breaking on the rocky shore and spreading on the sand the whitest foam that washed their feet.

Engrossed in their games, they did not notice a vinta[1] quietly scraping the sand. When they saw it, the boat's crew had already come ashore.

Frightened by the fierce-looking men approaching them, they tried to run away. The men caught four of them and forced them on board the vinta. Lólen, the daughter of Don Vicente Tupal, was one of the captives.

On the vinta were some natives, their hands and feet bound, also captured, from the towns of Cebu and Negros, islands separated by a channel.

The abductors rowed vigorously and in a few moments they were far from the coast.

Lólen and her friends, paralyzed with fear, pleaded with their abductors to set them free, but the rowers did not mind them. These were Moros from Jolo, daring pirates who continually scoured the islands of Mindanao and the Visayas in search of captives. They ruined the fields, burned the houses of fishermen who fled upon seeing them, and constantly alarmed the inhabitants of the coastal towns, punishing them with their vandalism and barbarity.

After Don Vicente Tupal and his wife learned what had happened to Lólen, their sorrow was so bitter that life for the couple became mortal agony. This explains why their house remained closed and sad. Their hearts were grieving on the feast day of the Santo Niño of Cebu.

---

[1] Swift sailboat like the pirogues of the indios.

The parents of the young lady captive cried and suffered constantly; the happiness of others and the memory of better times only increased their torment.

II

Cebu, capital of the province with the same name in the Visayan Islands, is an ancient city and the second most prominent in the archipelago. One cannot mention this city without recalling its history, so closely linked to the first stages of the conquest.

It is known that King Charles I of Spain acceded to the request of Ferdinand Magellan, the renowned Portuguese navigator in the service of Castille, to organize an expedition to the Far East. The expedition was composed of 234 men on five ships called *Trinidad, Victoria, Santiago, Concepción*, and *San Antonio*. The largest of these vessels weighed at least 130 tons.

Magellan left with his small squadron from Seville on 19 August 1519, on board the ship *Trinidad*.

On 1 November 1520, after many hardships and setbacks during such a long voyage, Magellan discovered the strait that now bears his name, a stretch of sea 104 leagues of longitude and 8 of maximum latitude that separates the southern American continent from the Tierra del Fuego.

On 16 March 1521, when the expedition was at a critical juncture, they discovered the Marianas Islands and named it San Lazaro, in honor of the saint whose feast day it was. They loaded their boat with provisions from these islands.

Sailing along the coast of Mindanao, they reached Butuan, where they celebrated the first Mass in the islands. It was attended by Magellan and his men. They planted a cross on a nearby hill.

On 7 April, they cast anchor in Cebu. The beach was full of men armed with lances, but there was no combat because Magellan accepted the friendship proposed to him by Hamabar, the rajah of Cebu. Magellan and Hamabar cut and drew blood from their chests. They drank the blood to seal a pact of alliance.

Not far from the beach, they made a cross of stone and erected it under a cupola supported by four columns, of which one remains to this day. Here, a Mass was celebrated, a ceremony that impressed the Cebuanos.

Informed of its significance, they asked to be baptized, and the mass baptism was celebrated with great festivities.

The natives of Mactan, a small island very near Cebu, were at war with the subjects of Hamabar. Magellan thought it proper to intervene in favor of his new allies and set out to fight the warriors of Mactan.

Magellan and his men were repelled and put to rout. The heroic ship captain was struck and killed by a poisonous arrow on 26 April 1521. His death was mourned by the surviving crewmen, a costly tragedy that dissipated the joy of a discovery.

Today, there stands on Mactan a simple tomb where his precious remains repose.

Other adversities following the tragic loss of Ferdinand Magellan compelled his companions to abandon Cebu and go to the Moluccas, notable for beautiful parrots called *catalas*, a species of *papagayo*, and birds of paradise that abound there. The Moluccas are also famous for the battles that the Portuguese fought against the first Spanish expeditions.

Almanzor, rajah of Tidor; Corrale, a gentleman from Ternate; and Yusuf, sovereign of Gilolo, looked after Magellan and his men in the Moluccas.

Unfortunately, the *Trinidad* leaked and had to be abandoned. They set sail on the *Victoria* in 1522, under the command of the eminent Basque, Juan Sebastian Elcano. They passed the strait of Sonda, sailing across the Indian Ocean. They rounded the Cape of Good Hope at 42 degrees latitude south, and after touching the islands of Cape Green, they arrived in Sanlucar de Barrameda on 6 September 1522, three whole years after their departure from Spain. Of the more than two hundred men in the expedition, only eighteen returned to their country.

Sebastian Elcano and his fearless navigators were the first to circumnavigate the globe—a cause for universal astonishment and acclaim.

Three more expeditions under the commands of Loaisa, Saavedra, and Villalobos, dispatched successively, did not yield positive results. Villalobos gave the name Filipinas to these islands in honor of Philip II, at that time Prince of Asturias.

This strong-willed monarch decided to occupy the islands. To realize this objective, he commissioned the distinguished patrician, Miguel López de Legaspi, and gave him the title of Adelantado. With five ships and 400 men, Legaspi set sail from the port of Natividad on 21 November 1564, arriving in Cebu on 27 April 1565.

The illustrious Andres de Urdaneta, a mariner first and then an Augustinian religious, commanded the squadron.

Legaspi established residence in Cebu, whose inhabitants were governed at that time by Rajah Tupas, who welcomed him warmly. Cebu was then established as the capital of the archipelago until 1571. In 1598, it was elevated to the status of Episcopal See.

Legaspi made it a town and created the first city hall that the islands ever had, and whose certification, a curious document, is still conserved in Cebu. Guido de Lavezares was appointed governor.

Later, Cebu was elevated to a city. It occupies a picturesque position by the sea and has a fort to defend it.

Because Cebu lacks rivers, the inhabitants need to store rainwater in large earthen jars. The convents store water in cisterns.

There are well-built buildings of stone masonry, spacious plazas, some beautiful walks, an elegant *pantalán*[2] to attract boats to dock there, and small towns nearby, like San Nicolas, which boasts of lush vegetation.

Cebu is a commercial center and the residence of the superior authority of the Visayas. It is a station for an armada and its port is equipped to serve foreign traffic.

The Visayas consist of six islands situated south of Luzon and north of Mindanao. These islands are rich due to their natural resources and products, abaca being the most expensive. The provinces of Cebu, Iloilo, Capiz, Antique, Negros, Samar, Leyte, and Bohol belong to the Visayas.

The Cebuanos are hardworking and skillful businessmen. They make precious woven fabrics. They have lime, sugar, and oil factories. They deal in pearls, *balete*, tobacco, abaca, delicious cocoa, and cotton. Fragrant tablets used to perfume clothes and rooms, joss sticks to light cigars, cheeses, and exquisite puffed bread exported to Manila and foreign countries are among the famous products of Cebu.

Fruits last all year round in Cebu and their quality is unsurpassed. There are also coal mines that promise a great future for this island of the Visayas. From Mount Buisan enough gold is extracted.

Surprisingly beautiful and unique are the pigeons, which are carefully bred and whose feathers have seven lively colors.

Foreign trade in Cebu counts with representatives from the best establishments in Manila. Their business is worth many millions of pesos. The Spaniards and the mestizos also engage in profitable business. The Chinese occupy a whole district with many bazaars filled with assorted goods. Mestizos form another important group.

---

[2] Wooden port.

There are no tobacco warehouses in the Visayas, unlike in Luzon. Expert appraisers inspect the harvest. The tobacco is received in loads and the planter is paid outright. When production is low, 12,454 quintals are harvested per year; during a good year, the yield is 24,733. Each bundle costs P6.

Many boats commute frequently between Cebu and Manila, a distance of 130 leagues, about 728 kms.

The inhabitants of the Visayas are fairer in complexion than those of Luzon and differ somewhat in customs. The women wear their skirts loose; this makes them look more graceful than the Tagalog women, who wrap around their waists a cloth called *tapis*.

The climate is healthy but warm.

The principal dialect is Visayan.

III

The chapter that we have devoted to a description of Cebu, based on the importance and significance of this city, has prevented us from informing our readers sooner about the fate of our young captive.

The chief of the pirates manning the vinta where we left her was a datu, a relative of the sultan of Jolo.

Having arrived in Balanguingui, the residence of the sultan, the pirate chief went to his master to inform him of the happy outcome of his journey and to beg him to accept some captives. The sultan, awed by the beauty of Lólen, chose her from all the others and made her go to his bedroom. The rest of the captives were either sold or assigned to different kinds of work.

The sultan bade farewell to his kinsman, congratulating him for the beautiful captive he had brought to Balanguingui. Filled with admiration for Lólen, the sultan said in the Visayan dialect, "Calm yourself, beautiful lady; forget the grief that overwhelms you. May you discover from the tears in your eyes that such beautiful eyes shine better when lit by love rather than when moistened by tears! In your land you have no power, here you will be sultana."

Lólen answered: "Sire, I prefer to be the humblest in my country than to be queen here. I pray that you permit me to return to the place where I was cruelly seized. At this very moment my poor parents are dying of sorrow because of my misfortune."

"Should I allow your return to your country? I would be a crazy fool, indeed."

"Why, sire? Is your conduct just? What right do you have to make me a slave when I was born free? Why do you bring me here against my will?"

"I should not discuss this with you. I can only tell you that you are a beautiful enchantress and that you will be mine."

"I will die first."

"How is that? You refuse to be my wife?"

"I prefer not."

"Why?"

"Because it cannot be. If you allow me to stay in Jolo, I will detest you. I do not give my heart to one I do not love."

"And if you were not my captive, would you love me?"

"No, because I love someone else."

"You have a husband," exclaimed the sultan in an angry tone that instilled fear.

"I have a fiancé who will be my husband."

"He will not be while I live."

"Well, I will not have another."

"Yes, you will have me."

The sultan approached Lólen to embrace her. Lólen stepped back and taking a dagger that was on top of the night table, she said with energetic resolve, "If you come near, I will stab your chest or pierce my heart with this dagger."

The sultan became still, restrained by the young lady's determined manner. Presuming that affectionate gestures and flattery instead of violence would produce more favorable results, he said, "You are mad. Drop the dagger and let us talk."

"Talk all you want!" she answered without letting go of the dagger.

"I have fallen in love with you. It is necessary then that you be prudent, for if you irritate me, I will take by force what you do not grant me willingly. Here, there is no power other than mine. I long for your love and I will have it. Contrary to my practice, I will desist from using violent means. You are now irritable because they have seized you from your country. I want to give you enough time to reflect calmly. In the next house, you will have women to serve you. Tomorrow I will visit you."

He then blew a whistle and an elderly woman appeared. He gave her some orders in a language unknown to Lólen. The woman took the young lady to the dwelling the sultan had designated.

Lólen took care to hide the dagger in her clothes. She had resolved to commit suicide rather than suffer the dishonor of uniting herself with the sultan. She did not love him; moreover, they differed in religion and race.

The sovereign of Jolo went to see her the following day. "Are you calmer now, beautiful Cebuana?" he asked.

"I will not be while I continue to be a captive," replied the young lady with bitterness.

"You are not a captive here. You see what captives do and how they are treated. You are the queen of my heart."

"Well, send me to work like the rest and give your heart to another."

"That is impossible. My heart is yours. Since we parted yesterday, I have not stopped thinking of you. I need your love."

"Sire, I cannot love you. If you don't intend to kill me, I beg you to take me back to Cebu."

"To see your fiancé?"

"To return to my parents."

"I will arrange for them to be brought here."

"They will not come."

"I will make them very rich."

"They already are."

"They will have power."

"They don't need it."

"Then, I will lose my kingdom before allowing you to go."

"Sire, stop this persistence and be generous. In Cebu, I will remember your clemency and I will be forever grateful. If you want ransom, my parents will pay whatever you demand."

"It is not possible for me to please you. Your absence would kill me. I love you and I cannot forsake the sweet hope of winning your love."

The sultan spoke the truth. Lólen's beauty, her character, and her wit had impressed him so much that beside her he trembled like a leaf blown by the breeze. Her beauty, superior to the many he had known, put him in a strange situation, his mind agitated by his passion.

The sultan for the first time felt dominated by love. The ease with which he could possess any woman he fancied was why his heart had never had a role in his relationships with the fairer sex.

He left Lólen's room, less deluded by what he desired than when he had entered, but without daring to use any violence on her. His restraint was unusual, given his ferocious temper.

One day he was overwhelmed by passion. His supplications and praises were useless, and after offering expensive presents just to convince her to be his wife, he tried to take her by force. But the impetuous young lady pulled out the dagger that she always carried with her. As she defended herself, she inflicted a slight wound on the sultan, after which she also wounded her own breast. The wound could have caused her death but luckily the dagger grazed a medallion that she was wearing.

The sultan, afraid that she would commit suicide and thus cause him to lose the one he loves dearly, swore never to use violence ever again. He consoled himself with the hope that his love would finally be reciprocated.

Lólen, taking advantage of the sultan's high spirits, obliged him to solemnly swear that he would respect her for a period of six months, offering to unite with him after this period. By that time, she would have the opportunity, she told him, to erase the memories that were making her suffer. The waiting period would enable her to adjust to the life and customs in Jolo.

The sultan happily pledged to abide by her wishes. That was a day for immense rejoicing for his subjects, who acknowledged the beautiful Lólen as sultana.

The sultan said to her, "Do not wonder at what I do for you; I want everyone to respect you and for them to know that your person is sacred, since you are their queen. You will be mine at the end of the agreed period of six months."

Lólen was confident that during this period the chance to escape would present itself. With the hope she had given the sultan, she felt that she could be more at peace and easily succeed in gaining her freedom.

The datus paid their respects to her, and the townsfolk acclaimed her as their queen. To celebrate this happy event, there were three days of rejoicing, music, theatrical presentations, music, merriment, Moorish dances, lavish drinking and dining, and widespread celebration in Balanguingui.

The Cebuana captive, as they called her, was from this day on regarded as the sultana of Jolo.

IV

Jolo is an extensive archipelago with more than 200 thousand souls, situated between Mindanao and Borneo. The Mohammedans, who settled here under the orders of the sultan and various datus, are fierce and brave.

The land is covered with coconut trees. There are thick forests where *balete* and *calambibit* trees abound. There are good quality pearls in Jolo that the Moros sell in Zamboanga, the capital of Mindanao.

Since the arrival of the first Spanish expeditionary forces, the Joloanos have been hostile to them. In 1577, when the Islands were under the authority of Don Francisco Sande, there was already a need to match our weapons with theirs.

In 1602, Juan Juarez Gallinato fought against the pirates but he found it very difficult to win. The same thing occurred in 1609 and 1633, when Silva and Salamanca, respectively, were governing.

In 1638, the captain-general of the Philippines, Don Sebastián Hurtado de Corcuera, led an expedition against Mindanao and Jolo. After a bitter combat, he gained complete control of the Islands. The sultan could not be captured but the sultana and her nephew, Tacun, became prisoners.

In 1731 and 1734, expeditionary forces attacked Jolo. Many pirates were killed, their forts were destroyed, and their ships were either burned or sunk.

In 1836, General Salazar, after punishing the Moros, signed treaties with the sultan. In 1843, General Alcalá, captured the island of Basilan. In other partial combats our navy routed them.

The Joloanos, however, never surrendered. They continued their pillaging and marauding along the coasts of Mindanao and the Visayas. Sometimes, they even ventured up to the north of Luzon, where Pangasinenses and Ilocanos had built fortresses to defend themselves from the Moro invasions. These fortresses still exist. On the mountains of those provinces, there are watchtowers erected to guard the seas. To prepare the towns to resist the invaders, the people use certain signals to announce the whereabouts of pirate ships. From 1843–1848, the Joloanos frequently undertook daring raids all over the archipelago. They captured a considerable number of people, destroyed the fields, burned houses, and robbed the merchant vessels with impunity. Everywhere they committed countless acts of vandalism, decimating the provinces south of Luzon and keeping the inhabitants in perpetual misery.

So much aggression could no longer be tolerated. The Spanish flag had been waving victoriously in the far corners of the world; the glory of Spain had won the admiration of the current generation and was sure to amaze even future generations. The moment had come for Spain to put an end to the reckless arrogance and fierce savagery of the followers of Mohammed.

The illustrious general, Don Narciso Clavería, one of the most eminent governors the Philippines has ever had, decided to personally put a stop to the impudence of the Joloano pirates and deliver the Visayas Islands from their suffering.

The news ran through the archipelago like electricity. There was a shout of gratitude and enthusiasm from the depths of everyone's heart because Clavería's intended war was justified and conformed to the wishes of the people. The opinion was unanimous that it was convenient and useful to subdue by force those who did not recognize any other law, scoffed at the rights of others, and violated the most sacred pacts.

Preparations for the expedition started in Manila. The women made lint, the town gave donations in the name of patriotism, and prayers were offered in the churches for the triumph of our weapons and the destruction of the believers in the Koran.

Some brave natives, lovers of their country, enlisted as volunteers, anxious to share with the army the victory to be gained in rescuing their suffering brothers. The first volunteer to show up was the son of a wealthy businessman from Iloilo, a young man with a military mien, named Ricardo Tagle. This man wanted to satisfy, with the blood of the Moros, the hatred that had grown within him since the abduction of his fiancée Lólen on the beach of Barili.

The wedding of the young couple had been arranged beforehand by their respective families and was to take place shortly after the day Lólen was abducted. For this reason Tagle felt in his soul as much pain as Lólen's parents.

Days before his fiancée left for Barili, Ricardo and Lólen bade each other farewell, their hearts full of love, illusions, sweet longings, and bright hopes. The two were rich and blessed. They loved each other passionately and were full of faith in the future. After staying some time in Cebu with the one who, by marrying him, would soon fulfill his greatest dream, Tagle left for Iloilo to attend to the wedding preparations together with his parents, who wanted to see him united in matrimony as soon as possible to the daughter of their most loyal friends.

When Ricardo learned of the villainy of the Joloanos, his wrath verged on madness. He thought of a daring plan to save the unfortunate young woman by organizing a band of valiant men who offered to follow him even if it should mean certain death. But then he found out that the army had been dispatched to do battle in Jolo.

Ricardo immediately went to Manila without informing his parents so as not to worry them. As we said earlier, he was the first to receive the honor of being accepted as a volunteer. His countrymen in Iloilo applauded his heroic determination.

The province where Ricardo was born is the second most important province in the Visayas. The port of Iloilo with its flourishing trade is even more important than that of Cebu. It has a population of 600 thousand.

There are around 40 thousand looms in the province. Their delicate fabrics of *piña, jusi, sinamay*, silk, and cotton are highly valued, especially those manufactured in the towns of Jaro and Molo. They are unrivalled in the country.

The natives of Iloilo are industrious laborers and active businessmen. Their lands are well-cultivated and sugar is produced in increasing quantities. They also harvest coffee, cocoa, abaca, tobacco, and wheat. The land is fertile. Foreigners, such as Europeans and Chinese, exploit the wealth of this province, where extensive commercial activities are carried on.

As governor of Iloilo, Don Diego Quiñones, and the inhabitants led by their worthy leader, were overjoyed when they repelled a Dutch invasion force of 500 men on 29 September 1716. Don Diego Quiñones was seriously wounded, and subsequently had to be carried about on a sedan chair. The Dutch were completely routed, with eighty dead and a hundred wounded.

Iloilo has been an Episcopal See since 1865, with the bishop residing in Jaro.

The province is located 105 leagues from Manila. Like Cebu, Iloilo is destined to become immensely prosperous.

V

The expedition sent to fight against Jolo under the command of General Clavería left Manila on 5 February 1848. It was composed of 600 infantrymen, fifty artillery pieces with two drummers, three warships, two schooners, six barges, and eight cannon launchers.

Upon anchoring off the shore of Balanguingui, the ships that transported the army started firing their cannons at the Moros. The Moros defended themselves like wild animals.

The expeditionary army displayed heroic valor. The assault began on the *cottas*, which are fortified forts with defensive walls packed with mud and stones. Bullets, upon impact, reinforce such a wall as they become embedded in it.

The Joloanos are strong and daring. Among them are fanatics called *juramentados*, so called because they swear to give up their lives attacking the enemy without ever backing out. They fulfill their oath with blind valor, hoping to be brought to the paradise of the houris. This is based on the law of Mohammed, who promises this grace to those who die fighting the Christians.

The army, in spite of the valor of the Moros, had the upper hand. The cottas of Sungap and Bocotingol stopped firing. The cannonade was horrifying.

The Cotta de Sipac was about to be taken by the troops. The Moros went on the attack and, moved by their barbarous instincts, began killing their women and their daughters to prevent their being taken prisoner.

When he saw the carnage, the heroic Clavería doubled his efforts. After a few moments, the Spanish flag flew over the Cotta de Sipac. The brave general was able to save more than three hundred women and children from death.

Then the attack against all the forces of the cotta of the sultan began. The sultan was not seen leading his forces. We shall say something about him later.

The sovereign of Jolo was loyal to the oath he had made to the captive Cebuana. Even if he repeatedly tried to persuade her to advance the date agreed upon, he never forced himself on her, and instead awaited with resignation the completion of the agreed six months.

Important affairs of another nature detained him in Selangan. When he found out that the expedition against Jolo was led by the governor-general of the Philippines, preparations for war occupied all his time and that of the datus. He had faith in his subjects and never for a single instant did he think that they would be vanquished.

On the day of the attack, and thinking that the expeditionary troops were victorious, the sultan thought that he would lose Lólen forever. With a broken heart, he imagined his beautiful captive regaining her freedom and finding happiness with her loved one in Cebu. Disturbed by this thought, he left the defense of the town to the datus and hurriedly went to the house where Lólen lived.

The women, to whose guardianship the sultan had entrusted her, knelt before him, weeping and wailing sorrowfully.

"What is wrong?" he asked them.

"We beg your pardon, sire. The sultana is not here," they said.

"Where has she gone?"

"We do not know."

"This is how you carry out my commands? Fear for your lives."

"Sire, have mercy on us. The continuous sounds of battle terrified us and we did not see her leave. Perhaps she is not far away."

"Woe unto you if I do not find her!" he exclaimed angrily and left at once in search of Lólen.

He looked everywhere but his adored captive was nowhere to be found. He was desperate when he arrived at his cotta without finding her.

He saw that the besiegers had the advantage, attacking unrelentingly and already securing the ladders to assault the fort. At that moment, other enemies inside the fort attacked the Moros from behind. They were the captives who had been imprisoned in the concealed dungeons at the beginning of the battle.

Surprised to see them free, the sultan ran to the dungeons and furiously asked the guards, "Who ordered the release of the captives?"

"Sire. . . the sultana," they answered, fearing for their lives.

"And where is she?"

"She left with them to defend the cotta as soon as she provided them with arms, assuring us that she was working under your orders."

The sultan left the guards in a fury. Realizing the treason of the one he believed had resigned herself to becoming his wife, he ran to the scene of battle, ready to plunge his sword into the breast of the ingrate.

Lólen was among the captives who had jumped from the parapet, encouraging them to fight while sustaining a Spanish flag upright on her lance.

The Moros defending the cotta, seeing that the besiegers were attacking them on one side and the captives on the other, began to disband. Those who were farthest, upon seeing the enemy's flag inside the fort, thought that the Christians had taken over, and they fled in terror.

Taking advantage of the situation, the army attacked. The cotta was breached by a platoon of soldiers. Some Moro chiefs continued to defend themselves. Others tried to escape, but the sultan stopped them. He rallied a big group, and with him as their head they approached the captives, shouting to his men, "Shoot the dogs!"

The Moros began to aim their guns, but in apparent amazement they brought them down without firing.

"What's happening?" he asked.

"Sire, the sultana!" those close around him answered.

"Allah confound you! Shoot, I said!" he shouted furiously.

But there was no more time. The soldiers advanced rapidly almost without encountering any opposition.

The Joloanos around the sultan advised him to save himself. He was about to retreat but a scene detained him, tearing his soul to pieces: The Cebuana captive was embracing an army officer.

Frantic and raging with fury, the sultan ran towards them, waving his sword.

Upon seeing him, Lólen shouted, "Defend me from the sultan!"

The officer, followed by some soldiers, advanced to meet him.

"Leave the sultan for me," the officer told his men.

A battle to the death commenced right before them. The sovereign of Jolo fought like a lion. The officer was none other than Tagle, whose life was now in imminent danger. The memory that the sultan had separated him from his loved one filled him with great courage to fight against all odds. Taking an unexpected leap, he struck the sultan in the head, wounding him.

The sultan's men, seeing him fall from the blow dealt him by his opponent, rushed furiously at Tagle. The latter, battling like a hero, made the Moros flee in shame.

The sultan, meanwhile, had been rescued by some Moros who carried him in their arms, while others, to facilitate the rescue of their master, fought to the death.

Tagle scoured Jolo everywhere but he could not find the sultan, who had been transported by his subjects to another island nearby.

Balanguingui fell into the hands of the army.

Some 500 Moros died; 124 cannons were taken, the majority of which were those they called *lantacas;* the Joloano towns were demolished; 160 *vintas, pancos,* and *calisipans* were destroyed and 10 thousand trees were felled.

On the side of the army, twenty-one troops were killed. The wounded among the chieftains, officials, and soldiers numbered 160. Among the 200 captives were Dutch subjects who had regained their freedom.

General Clavería warmly congratulated the Cebuana heroine and decorated her with the Cross of San Fernando. Informed that she was the fiancée of Ricardo Tagle, the brave volunteer from Iloilo who deserved to be commended for his bravery on the battlefield,

General Clavería promoted him to captain. This was a reward for the courageous couple.

Lólen's heroism was admired by the army. Wherever the soldiers saw her, they applauded her with enthusiastic affection.

The story of her captivity in Jolo spread; people exalted her virtue and her constancy, and they congratulated her because she loved her country more than the power with which the sultan had tried to entice her if she agreed to be his wife.

Ricardo Tagle was drunk with joy at being able to embrace the one he loved dearly and for whom he had suffered so much. He felt proud to love one who was so worthy of being loved.

Happiness filled their hearts anew. They were so happy that they forgot their past sorrows.

Love gladdens the soul, brightens dark places, and brings happiness to the unfortunate.

He who has never loved or been loved does not know happiness.

VI

The captain-general of the Philippines, Don Narciso Clavería, was triumphantly received by the inhabitants of the capital when he returned from Jolo. The Spanish government rewarded him with the title of Conde de Manila.

The natives of the islands were grateful that national honor had been redeemed.

Ricardo Tagle was assigned to the distinguished regiment in Cebu, where he married Lólen, with the governor-general as sponsor at the wedding.

Don Vicente Tupal and his wife were overjoyed to embrace their daughter once more. They had never expected to feel such joy again. Their happiness almost cost them their lives since an excess of pleasure is just as bad as profound pain.

Ricardo's parents, in order not to be separated from him, moved to Cebu, where they stayed until their affairs obliged them to return to Iloilo.

The natives of both provinces were proud to have these young people belong to them because they had earned public esteem by fighting heroically against the enemies of their country, under the immaculate flag of Spain.

Three years later, the husband of the beautiful Cebuana returned to battle against the Joloanos. The Moro rebels, having recovered from their debacle, resumed their campaign of looting, conflagrations, and abduction of captives all over the Visayas.

In 1851, the estimable General Urbiztondo, Marquis of Solana, left for Jolo in command of the army, and captured the capital, an important event that resulted in the absolute conquest of the sultanate.

Tagle distinguished himself in the campaign, and was awarded prestigious decorations. After returning from Jolo, he learned of his father's death. This led him to retire from military service so that he could handle his late father's affairs. In his grief, he found comfort in his wife, whose love for him grew deeper each day.

They decided to live from time to time in both Cebu and Iloilo. They lived a tranquil life, undisturbed by misfortunes of any kind.

The title of Sultana of Jolo was bestowed on Lólen in memory of the time when the Joloanos recognized her as their sovereign. The people of Cebu still take pleasure in recounting this story after all these years.

The glorious campaigns of the illustrious Generals Clavería and Urbiztondo kept the Moros subservient from then on. Their vandalism along the southern coasts of the archipelago did not happen again.

Minor isolated engagements involving some ships of the Armada, provoked by the piracy of some datus or perhaps the abuses of the Joloanos, may have convinced the current governor of the Philip-pines, General Malcampo, that it was the right time to undertake a new conquest of that territory. In the campaign against the Moros, he led the biggest expedition ever organized, with no fewer than twelve thousand men, and he seized Jolo on 29 February 1876.

The war frigate *Carmen*, the corvettes *Santa Lucía, Vencedora,* and *Vad-Ras*, the schooners *Filomena* and *Constancia*, the cannon ships *Araya, Samar, Joló, Paragua, Mindoro, Prueb, Albay, Filipinas, Mindanao,* and *Calamianes*, and the brigantine *Subic*, also a war-ship, formed a powerful squadron in the bay of Jolo. Their cannon power aided the infantry. Merchant ships, among them the *León*, a big freighter with sailboats in tow, brought the troops and war provisions.

Victory was not won without considerable losses, many caused by the shortage of water. The dauntlessness, however, of the army and the peninsular volunteers and Filipinos from Zamboanga and Misamis stood out. They proved themselves brave and enduring.

May God grant that the precious blood poured on the sands of Jolo during the 1876 campaign be the last to be shed, and from the very costly expedition of General Malcampo, may the Philip-pines obtain the benefits he promised. Well, it is high time that humanity preferred the triumphs of peace to the turbulence of war. War should never be waged except when it is unavoidable and ut-terly necessary, for war consumes in one day the wealth of a country. War is against the best interests of a nation, holds back its material progress, and destroys the worthiest of its sons.

THE NEWCOMER
AND THE OLDTIMER

I

One morning, a coach stopped at the door of a respectable house in the city of Manila. As soon as the passenger got out, he asked: "Is this it?"

"Yes sir," the driver replied.

"Well, wait for me here," he said and entered the house.

In the garage was a coach locally known as *sipan*. Beside it was a coachman wearing a light shirt and knee-length pants, worn by the *indios* for domestic chores. He was busy removing mud from the wheels, throwing buckets of water at them, while the *sota* cleaned the chains of the nozzle.

"Is your master here?"

"Upstairs, sir," they answered.

He went up a spacious stairway made of wide slabs of narra.[1] In the *caída*[2] he found two houseboys, or servants, wearing the same outfit as the coachman. They were cleaning the floor with banana leaves, which give the wooden floor more luster than wax. The terrace was adorned with flowerpots set on pedestals made of Chinese porcelain.

"Tell them that there's a visitor," he said to them.

The youngest of the servants passed the bend formed by the caída and was heard saying, "Sir, there's a *castila*."[3]

"Let him in," a voice replied.

When the visitor saw the owner of the house dressed in strange clothes, he made an effort to suppress his laughter.

He was an old, short, and fat man, clad in Chinese clothes, with a large loose shirt as transparent as crystal. He was seated on a big rattan chair with his head laid back. His feet, resting on the arms of a big chair, were in straw slippers. In his mouth was a long black cigar, his right hand holding a bamboo scratcher and the left holding the *Diario de Manila*.

On a small table nearby a *pebete*, or joss stick, was emitting smoke from a *pebetera*, or metal dish. He fanned himself with a big *paipai*.[4]

When the gentleman entered, the old man sat up with much effort. After the usual introduction, the gentleman presented a letter to the old man.

He read it, and said, "Perfect, my friend. You come with a recommendation from someone I esteem very much. From this moment on, you can enjoy my full trust."

"Thank you very much."

---

[1] A species of red mahogany.
[2] Wide and ventilated part of the house that serves as waiting room.
[3] A Spaniard. This is the way the natives call the white men.
[4] Palm leaf called buri, which serves as a fan.

"No, don't go yet. That's not all. This house is at your disposal. You can come here to eat and rest whenever you please. If you need money or anything, just tell me and I will give it to you. Have you been here long?"

"Thirty hours."

"Same with me," he exclaimed laughing.

"What!"

"Yes, the only difference is that instead of hours, years."

"Thirty years in the country!"

"Short of a few hours more. Tomorrow it will be thirty."

"How awful!" said the interrogator in surprise.

"Do you find it surprising? Soon you will see how other things that take place in this country will make you like them. Here time passes without your noticing it. The less you think about it, the more you will realize that you have arrived in Manila shortly after Legaspi did."

"With me, I assure you that it will be the contrary."

"You say that because you are *vago.*"

"Sir!"

"Don't be alarmed. Here the word vago means someone who has just arrived in the country."

"But this country is infernal!"

"That's what everybody says at first, but opinions change later and many who went back to Europe return whenever they could."

"Well, I don't understand it."

"Later you will. And how was the trip?"

"Very long: We were delayed for forty days."

"And you call that long! What then do you think of my journey, which lasted for six months?"

"Didn't you come through the Suez?"

"I came on a boat through the Cape of Good Hope. That's how travel was undertaken in those days, unlike now. Imagine seeing the same faces for six months, eating salty food, biscuits instead of bread for many days, canned goods aplenty and water without ice. And the sea! There were times when it was dead calm. We didn't move an inch for fifteen days. That was unbearable. The sea was like a silver lake, not a single breeze, and in places like the Equator where it's really calm, the heat enveloped us. When we passed the Cape, the opposite happened. Tempestuous winds rumbled. Waves as high as mountains threatened to swallow us while the ship rocked and moved everything around. It was not possible to cook. The sails were torn to pieces and giant waves destroyed the deck, converting it into a river. The crew could not attend to everything. We had passengers who pumped out the water, helping in the maneuvers while shivering from the cold in the winter temperature of 38 degrees. When we passed the Cape, we feared we would freeze after spending several weeks without seeing the sun. One hundred eighty-four days on board! After several months without seeing land, we were overjoyed whenever we saw a boat from a distance or when it passed us by. The *telégrafo de banderas* gave information about where the vessel was heading, its sailing time, the health of the passengers, and the relation to the latitude it was located in. Whenever it disappeared from view, we felt very sad. Even the sight of fish flying, the catching of a shark or tuna, the sight of some whales, the infinite variety of *petrelos*, aquatic birds that abound in certain places filled us with feverish joy. These were the only interesting sights that interrupted the monotony of our existence. Add to the dangers of so long a voyage the difficulties of some passengers who had to be reassured that bickering and challenges occur in any expedition, that differences should be settled upon arrival. Perhaps as soon as the boat anchors, everything would be forgotten. And you complain about your boat trip of only forty days and with a thousand comforts, which in my time we did not have."

"You are right, but allow me to make an observation. In the past, the employees used to collect their salaries during the trip. Now we only receive a meager salary from Spain."

"That's right. That was our only advantage, and not a small one, in fact. However small the salary that an employee brought, upon liquidating the costs of navigation, there remained about P800 to P1 thousand for clothing adequate for this climate, to build a house or buy a car and possibly, take the family on a trip. It makes sense that at present, government employees who come to this distant country do not enjoy the same benefits, mainly because the voyage has been shortened."

A servant appeared carrying two wine glasses, beer, and cigars on a lacquer tray.

"Try one of these cigars from Isabela, and join me in a glass of beer," the owner of the house said.

"As you wish."

"Are you here as an employee?"

"Yes, sir, with a salary of only seven thousand pesetas."

"It is not much, but you can live on that."

"The salary, as you well know, is little. Most important, I've been told, are the benefits of the job."

"The benefits! Well, if you didn't have any other means of getting food to eat, you could ask for a slot in the hospice."

"What! If not for the benefits, I would not have come on such a low salary."

"But what are those benefits?"

"I don't know. In Madrid, I learned that here one's salary is spent on toothpicks. What is important is what the job brings."

"Well, it's a mistake. You have been deceived. Here you have nothing except what is stated in your credentials: only your salary, and with it you have to meet all your needs. In the offices, instead of benefits, there are other duties to discharge, which you will soon find out for yourself."

"But in Spain, they told me that. . ."

"I believe you. They told me the same things. I never had any benefits, however, other than my salary. Believe me, there is no such thing. Not long ago, a customs employee claimed that he was entitled to a share in the duties collected by the state, and he almost filed a lawsuit against the administration because instead of reimbursing him, they just laughed at him. And like you, he was relying on what he was told in Spain. *Jauja*, my friend, is an ideal city. He who believes that the ideal city is in the Philippines is mistaken."

"What else can I do? There is no other way now but to accept it."

"That's better."

"With your permission, I have to leave you now."

"So soon!"

"Yes, I have some things to do."

"Well, as you wish, Joaquín Alvaredo. I am at your disposal."

"Thank you, Genaro Fonseca, at your service."

"I'll wait for you tomorrow so I can introduce you to my family, since they aren't home today. Come early because we are going on an excursion, and we would be pleased if you could join us."

"I will come."

"Until tomorrow then."

"Goodbye."

II

At seven o'clock the following morning, Don Genaro Fonseca entered the house of Don Joaquín Alvaredo. He did not notice the latter, who said, "We have been waiting for you. Breakfast is ready."

They entered the dining room, where the family and other persons were introduced to him.

"This is my wife, that is my daughter, Nena, and another daughter over there is Chata," Alvaredo said, pointing to them.

Nena and Chata, which names in Manila are used to designate the eldest and the most beautiful of daughters, were very pretty young girls. The first was eighteen and the second was fifteen years old.

"We are frank here, my friend. Sit down and have breakfast," Alvaredo added.

The chocolate was served. On the table were plates filled with *ensaimadas, bizcochos,* red and white *poto, zuman-latic,* and *bibimca,* rice cakes that Filipinos eat with chocolate.

"Did you try the poto?" Nena asked Fonseca.

"You will like the zuman better," Chata said.

"Let him try everything!" Alvaredo said in a loud voice. "You should get used to the food in this country."

Fonseca tasted the zuman, bibimca, and poto, but did not like them. He chose the ensaimadas instead.

"I am not surprised. He will like them later. Since I am a *matanda* in the Philippines, I am used to everything."

"What does 'matanda' mean?"

"Matanda, my friend, means old or an oldtimer in the country."

After breakfast, they got into the carriages that had been prepared for them. Then they proceeded to Pandacan, a happy town about two kilometers from Manila.

"First, we take a bath," Alvaredo told Fonseca. "Next we eat mangoes, which are fun to eat while bathing, and then let's dance and have fun. That is exactly the way to celebrate the thirtieth year of my stay in these islands."

The schedule was followed as planned. They arrived at a beautiful concrete house with a galvanized iron roof located near an estero, or canal. The ladies did not forget the *gogo,* a plant that froths like soap and which, surprisingly enough, cleanses the hair. The gentlemen refreshed themselves by using *tabo,* or small buckets more commonly used than the bathtub. Later, the dancing began.

The men, employees, soldiers, and parents of the excursionists were all young and jolly. There were a dozen enchanting young girls, Spanish Manilans, who were very charming and who, following their whims and caprices, wore resplendent mestiza gowns. They dried their hair by letting it hang loose, showing off the luster of their beautiful black tresses.

The gentlemen had put on their brightly colored *camisas de piña,* untucked, as was the fashion then. They made Fonseca don the same attire. They danced nonstop the whole morning to the music of the orchestra composed of native musicians who played Philippine music masterfully.

At noon, they took a break from their favorite pastime to recover their spent energy. The table, set for thirty guests, was made of beautiful solid narra, a kind of wood that abounds in the archipelago. Of the dishes served, the *morisqueta,* or very white rice boiled in water, was the favorite. Even Spanish children prefer it to bread.

In the Philippines, it is customary to place on the table all the dishes that make up the meal from the first to the last. Fonseca found this strange.

"Will you eat morisqueta?" several young people asked him.

"I will try it, but I don't think I will like it. It must be tasteless."

"Mix it with food and put sauce on it."

"No, I don't like it. I prefer bread," he said after tasting it.

"You will get used to it, my friend," said Alvaredo. You are still vago."

"I don't think so."

"That was what I said then. And for a long time now, I have preferred this to bread. If you only knew how convenient it is for those who lack teeth. When you become bored, you will learn how to chew *buyo.*"[5]

"For God's sakes, please stop! The buyo is the most repugnant thing that exists," Fonseca exclaimed, almost throwing up.

---

[5] A species of climbing plant with big leaves. Lime is spread on a leaf, a piece of betel nut is placed in the middle and then rolled. The natives chew *buyo* at any time of the day.

"It is disgusting to the eyes, I agree, but it fortifies the stomach and strengthens the gums. The tidy *indias* clean their teeth with the bark of the *bonga*, that's why they have very white teeth."

"Yes, but I bet my neck I will never chew the buyo."

"That's exactly what I used to say, and I have chewed it. Dear friend, much later you will chew it, even the *sapa*.[6]

"You must be joking, Don Joaquín."

"You will tell me about that when you start falling in love with indias. It is an amazing phenomenon worthy of deeper scrutiny. They're not really pretty nor are they flirts, but they have driven more than one Spaniard crazy."

"They couldn't be from my own land."

"You still have the blood of Spain; let it turn to *horchata*, and tell me later."

"Do you want me to serve you this, *niña* Chata?" an elderly woman asked Alvaredo's daughter.

"*Usted cuidado*," she replied.

"There are two things that annoy me," Fonseca exclaimed.

"I hear a man who is seventy years old being called Niño Quicoy, an old woman Niña Carmen, and usted cuidado at all times. Would you be kind enough to explain to me what it means?"

"Of course. We say 'Niño' as an affectionate familiar address, as is customary in the country. 'Usted cuidado' is an admirable phrase. It expresses consent but is also a threat or an indifference to the fulfillment of a duty. It has other meanings as well."

"It is truly eloquent."

"You will get to know other expressions that will catch your attention. And do you like the country?"

---

[6] Residue of the masticated betel nut which the indias offer to their lovers to chew to prove their affection.

"I have to be honest. At this very moment, I enjoy your pleasant company, your admirable frankness, and the kindness of these beautiful girls. But judging from the inconveniences in the country, I find life here detestable."

"Let's see, tell us about it," said Alvaredo, who as a matanda delighted in reminiscing about his impressions when he was vago. At the same time, he wanted to explain to his visitor certain strange things, which all the new arrivals in the country wonder so much about.

"In the first place," Fonseca answered, "they talk of the danger of dysentery."

"That's not exactly true. During my long stay in the country I had the chance to experience what I am now going to tell you. Dysentery usually attacks only those who do not practice good hygiene, those who commit great excesses, and a few who have the propensity to contract the illness. Even so, it does not occur frequently. There is a remedy that can cure it. Go back to Europe on time because only a few recover from it."

"They also say that every year, the country suffers from horrible gales called *baguio*."

"That is correct. They often cause great damage on sea and land, but they also clean the atmosphere, thus preventing many illnesses. Because of them the climate of the Philippines is very healthy, so the destruction is compensated for by the benefits they bring."

"And what about the fires that make whole towns disappear in an instant?" Fonseca asked.

Alvaredo replied, "They usually occur where the *bahai*[7] is made of nipa. The natives rebuild them in two weeks at little cost; the streets improve as a result of the new dwellings. Consequently, the fires are to a certain extent beneficial because they improve the view."

---

[7] House, hut in Tagalog, pronounced as *bajai*.

"And what about those *collas* when torrential rains last for months, do you find them amusing?"

"Not really; but they are a blessing to the fields and they cool the temperature, a pleasant thing here, where summer is perpetual. Besides, one can use a coach. Who in the Philippines does not always have a peso in the pocket for these setbacks?"

"The mosquitoes irritate me."

"Put a mosquito net over the bed and they won't bother you."

"The heat suffocates me."

"That's because you are not yet adjusted to life in the country. In the Philippines, one does not go out during the hot hours unless he rides a coach. It costs very little to maintain one. Stay at home clad in Chinese attire, which is the most comfortable wear; take a bath every day; always have a paipai handy, and recline comfortably in the *butaca*. Since fresh breezes blow continually and the houses are big and well ventilated, one does not feel the heat much."

"And the skin rash?"

"To avoid it, do not overeat the rich fruit called *manga*. The rash disappears when you bathe in rainwater and the last recourse is the cane scraper that you will see in my house."

"And what about the servants who do the opposite of everything you say?"

"Learn to talk to them in the *sui generis* language, which we call here *español de cocina,* or broken Spanish, repeating what you want to say three times. You will see how well they understand you.

"But one needs the patience of Job."

"Once you get adjusted, you will have it. Here it is indispensable to take things very calmly and not argue anymore. Imitate the indio who is the most patient person I have ever known."

The young people enjoyed listening to the vago's complaints and the matanda's explanations. Some time after they had finished drinking coffee, Niña Chata said to Fonseca, "Come on, stop asking questions and let us dance. Remember that I promised to dance the *habanera* with you."

"Let's dance! Let's dance!" shouted everybody as they stood up.

Suddenly the house began to shake; shouts of joy turned to sounds of terror, and faces turned pale. They hastily went down to the basement, sheltered under the door arches, mumbling prayers continuously, afraid the house would collapse on their heads at any moment. The musicians and the native servants, with their faces on the floor, could not utter any word except, "Earthquake! Earthquake!" It was the matanda who was the most scared. Only Fonseca, who went down the stairs slowly, remained calm. He was laughing at Alvaredo, as if indifferent to the danger that caused everyone so much fear.

Fonseca shouted at Alvaredo, "Didn't you say that all phenomena in this country were blessings? What about earthquakes?"

III

The earthquake lasted some forty seconds and stopped without causing any damage because, though strong, it had made the house swing like a pendulum.

After everybody had calmed down, Alvaredo, who saw Fonseca laughing, said, "You, young man, have no idea what earthquakes are like, nor do you know their dreadful consequences. Earthquakes are the worst calamity that the country suffers from. At first, I, too, wasn't afraid of them. Many times, whenever an earthquake woke me up, I would just turn on my side half-asleep. I would not bother to run, unlike now. I hardly saw a lamp move. Nowadays, whenever there is an earthquake, my hair stands on end, I tremble like quicksilver, I gasp for breath, I lose my speech and I experience great agony while it lasts. This has been happening to me since the disastrous earthquake of 3 June 1863. That frightful catastrophe will never be erased from the memory of the survivors in Manila. The collapsed buildings are proof of the monstrosity of that earthquake, which filled Manila with grief, leaving it in ruins for many years. Remembering that disaster makes my whole body shake. That explains why I was terribly scared a moment ago."

"Actually, I have seen ruins in various places in the capital," observed Fonseca. "But I did not know what caused them. I would like very much to know the details of the 1863 earthquake."

"Well, I will satisfy your curiosity because I was a witness to the disaster," replied Alvaredo. "I remember all the circumstances as if they happened only yesterday. Listen. It was 7:25 in the evening of that fateful day. A loud underground noise was heard, and immediately the earth trembled, causing many buildings to fall down with a frightening, deafening sound.

"That strong quake was followed by another shock and some circular movements, causing the houses, which had been weakened from the first shock, to fall to the ground. The rest lay in ruins. A kind of blaze mixed with a column of dust rose from the city. The agitated waters of the Pasig River turned a leaden color. The ground opened up in various places. The bells from all the churches kept ringing lugubriously by themselves until the towers that held them collapsed. A loud scream from the city dwellers, shouts of agony from the victims, cries of anguish from their relatives, of panic and terror from the rest filled the air. There was tremendous confusion. It was not possible to be calm during the first moments of the dreadful cataclysm.

"The aftermath was overwhelming. No words could describe it. The cathedral was leveled, burying in the rubble priests, chaplains, singers, and the people who were celebrating the eve of Corpus Christi there. A few survived because by a stroke of luck, they were pulled out from hollow spaces formed by the beams of the roof. The best buildings of Manila were destroyed, among them the palace of the *capitán-general*; the Casas Consistoriales, or town halls; Intendencia; Aduana; Audiencia; the tobacco factories; the Consejo de Administración; the churches of Sto. Domingo, San Francisco, San Juan de Dios, Quiapo, Santa Cruz, and the Recollects; the Carenero; Meisic & Fortin quarters; the Military Hospital; the Divisoria Market; the city jail; and many others. The Tribunal de Comercio, the Dominican Convent, and the Colleges of San José, Santa Catalina, and Sta. Rosa were uninhabitable. Only the San Agustín Convent, constructed by a nephew of Herrera, the architect of El Escorial, remained standing.

"The stone bridge was very much weakened. The dead numbered more than three hundred; the injured were approximately of the same number. The garrison had fifteen dead, eighty-eight injured, and forty-one with contusions. Forty-six buildings of the state collapsed, leaving twenty-five more greatly damaged.

"The number of ruined private and public buildings rose to 570 and 530 respectively.

"Public as well as private losses in Manila were incalculable. Almost all public buildings were destroyed completely. The terrified residents of Manila abandoned the city and transferred to houses made of wood and nipa in the neighboring small towns. We went to live in Malate. Rent, which is normally very cheap, rose because many people came to rent houses. Five days later, there was another earthquake. It destroyed the buildings greatly damaged by the unforgettable and unfortunate earthquake of 3 June. For a long time, life was a continuous torment for the residents of Manila. Every night, they dreamt about earthquakes. Since then, many who escaped from sure death on that day have feared earthquakes more than all calamities put together."

"And did the earthquake last long?"

"Half a minute; if it had lasted longer, the city would have disappeared completely. What a terrible scene, Fonseca, my friend!

I still seem to hear the agonized voices of the wretched souls trapped in the rubble, begging for water, for the love of God, and imploring that they be extracted from the tomb. Nothing could be done for them because a slight movement of the rubble would hasten their death."

"And are earthquakes frequent?"

"The famous ones recorded in the history of this country are those that occurred in 1600, 1645, 1658, 1754, 1824, and 1852. Tremors, like what you have just witnessed, cause only a good scare. When Mother Spain learned of the enormous damage caused by the earthquake of 1863, a fund-raising campaign was launched in the Peninsula and in the Antilles to help the victims. The public treasury raised P2 million. The longest known earthquake occurred on 1 October 1869. It lasted for two minutes, and its movement was oscillatory; it did not produce any damage. I assure you that such tremors leave me sleepless. I detest them with all my heart."

"Alvaredo, you have to return to Manila, in case something happened to your house," said a woman who was listening to his story.

"As you wish," he answered.

Everybody got ready. The happy caravan that had spent a very pleasant time in Pandacan returned sadly to Manila, bringing with them the horrors of 3 June 1863. They feared another misfortune. When they arrived, they learned that the earthquake had not caused any harm to anybody.

"Mr. Fonseca," Alvaredo said, "we trust that you will come to see us often."

"I will be most glad to do so."

"If you wish to stay for dinner, don't leave; but I warn you that I eat a moderate dinner. At night, food should be easily digested. I do not take anything except *tinola* with fried rice and poached eggs.

Usually I alternate it with *puspas* and *basa-basa*, which are all excellent stews to maintain a light stomach. Are you interested?"

"No sir; I am extremely grateful but I am going home. I feel I should rest."

"Be very careful with the native lasses," Chata advised.

"After having met you, the prettiest natives look ugly to me."

"What a flatterer you are!"

"I am just being fair."

The excursionists bade goodbye to one another. Out in the street, he heard Alvaredo shouting after him:

"Always sleep dressed and with the light on in the dormitory. If there's an earthquake, go down to the mezzanine. You are new here, so it is important for you to know what to do."

"Thanks, I'll do that."

"Come on," Fonseca said to himself while walking toward the inn. "This matanda is something and he has two daughters who are well worth the pain of enduring his idle talk. He was not a bad recommendation. I will visit him frequently. I like Niña Chata very much. She was so pretty in her mestiza dress, with her hair unbraided! I have never seen anything like her before. And how well she dances! Come now, I should think about other things, I should not go crazy over her."

The beautiful image of Chata continued to haunt Fonseca.

Perhaps he had fallen in love with the beautiful Filipina.

IV

In the same inn where Fonseca stayed was a soldier, surnamed Gómez, whom he befriended. Together they often went around the city and its suburbs, his friend serving as his tour guide.

One afternoon, as they were taking a stroll, Gómez said to this companion:

"Tonight, pleasure awaits us."

"Why?"

"Because it is the celebration of the feast of Santa Cruz."

"And what kind of a celebration is it?"

"Very exciting, delightful like all fiestas in the Philippines. Here, where political feuds are unheard of, one does not think of anything but fun. The indios spend much of their earnings in church activities, in fiestas, and in gambling.

"One is born, christened with bells ringing, and music and a banquet in the house. A wedding takes place, more bells, the church is lighted and covered with bunting, while the table overflows with food at all times. Someone dies, a first-class burial; three priests accompany the corpse from the mortuary to the church, to the cemetery, and then to the grave. There are responses from the bereaved, and nine days of prayers, and later the *pamisan*, a day where after mass there is drinking, eating, dancing, and games, all done in honor of the deceased. When the feast of the patron saint of the town is celebrated, as you will see in Santa Cruz, there is no house, no matter how small, that does not prepare a grand dinner, drinks, sweets, music, and a dance for those who wish to come. The *principales* shoulder the cost of a castle of fireworks, without which no fiesta will be considered happy. Millions of skyrockets and a multitude of enormous paper balloons rise up to the sky to the delight of a huge crowd that comes to enjoy the spectacle. Now you will see how we dance and enjoy ourselves greatly."

"But do you have to know the people who give those dance parties?"

"It is not necessary. In town fiestas, the generous community gladly receives as many people as there are who want to honor them by going to their houses. The amiability of the Filipinos is proverbial. They are happy when their guests leave their dance parties contented. It means a lot to them when their guests accept what is offered; a refusal could make them feel slighted. They put on their admirable best, and they are refined, courteous, obliging, and generous with the Peninsulares who visit them on the day of the town fiesta. It doesn't matter whether they are known to them or not, nor do they expect to meet them again in the future."

"It is a quality that makes them look charming to my eyes."

"What's more, they carry those qualities very well."

They were talking this way when they arrived in Santa Cruz.

At every street intersection, there was an elevated monumental arch lavishly adorned. All the houses had bunting and banners. The balconies were filled with people. An immense crowd walked the streets, and bands roamed the streets playing lively marches. The metallic sound of the bells could be heard.

The carriages could hardly move. They were not allowed to take many streets.

Gómez and Fonseca got off the sipan.

"Let's enter this house where I hear some music," the former said.

"I don't think that is proper," his companion objected.

"Have no fear. You will see people with patriarchal customs."

The owners of the house saw them and hurried to invite them to the receiving room where they could sit. The room was full of elegant *dalagas* and *bagong taos*[8] in their colorful attire.

Some of these young men were accompanying on the guitar several women who were playing the harp. The harp is an instrument popular among the native Filipinos, who play it admirably.

Some of the dalagas with very good voices were singing lively songs in Tagalog. When they finished, a native started to sing the *kundiman*, combining popular *coplas,* or verses, in broken Spanish with Tagalog lyrics.

---

[8] Young single ladies and gentlemen.

Some of the coplas ran this way:

Cundiman, cundiman	Kundiman, Kundiman
Cundiman si jele,	Kundiman, lulls you to sleep
Mas que está dormido	But when you are asleep
Ta soña con ele.	You will dream of him.
Desde que vos cara,	I can see it,
Yo ta mirá	In your face
Aquel morisqueta	That fried rice
No puede tragá.	I cannot swallow.
Cundiman, cundiman,	Kundiman, Kundiman,
Cundiman, cundiman,	Kundiman, Kundiman,
Mamatay, me muero,	I die, I die
Sacamay mo lamang.	Only in your arms.

The music of the kundiman is melancholy.

After the song, some servants placed a small table before Gómez and Fonseca on which were two cups of chocolate and different kinds of pastry.

"It is not wise for us to drink chocolate because we have just eaten," they said.

"It doesn't matter, gentlemen," replied the owner of the house. "You can take it even if you are full."

"No, no, we can't. Please forgive us, but at this moment it would cause indigestion."

"Then eat some ice cream. I cannot allow you to leave my house without eating anything."

"Very well, we will have ice cream to please you."

They served themselves and left the house shortly.

"Ten more steps up," said Gómez:

"Let's go up the house and you will see the *balitao*."

"What is it?"

"A dance from Mindanao and the Visayas."

The balitao is graceful. The natives dance it while singing coplas to the rhythm of the music. Fonseca enjoyed it very much. There they were made to drink cold beer, the only thing they found acceptable. The table was full of cold cuts, desserts, and wine.

At night, all the houses, arches, the church tower, and even the trees were illuminated with many colored lights, paper balloons, and Chinese lanterns. Everybody was happy. The excitement and the sounds of merriment were indescribable.

After the procession, which amused the indios very much, dancing in many houses began. Gómez and Fonseca entered several houses and witnessed great excitement. They danced nonstop. Ice cream, desserts, and hot soup were passed around in big quantities for the ladies. For the gentlemen, there were rich, pure cigars, punch, and beer. The tables were filled with turkey, ham, and different kinds of roasts, fruits, and sweets. Each got whatever he wanted without anybody objecting in the least, unlike before, when a hundred people were required to serve the guests. During the buffet, the table was replenished six times. The menu was exquisite, abundant, and varied. The wines were the best.

The dances ended at dawn. The evening party was delightful. Fonseca left, enchanted by the praiseworthy customs. He was beginning to realize that life in the Philippines could be wonderful.

This kind of celebration takes place there almost daily, since each of the many small towns on the outskirts of the city celebrates its own feast on a different day. In that way, a good part of the year is spent on pilgrimages and dances.

The most popular celebrations in the city are the Naval de Binondo, the fiesta of Santa Cruz, and those of Quiapo and San Sebastián. In the last two places, the fairs last several days. All of them end ostentatiously like the one we have just witnessed.

The native Filipinos worry little about the future. After meeting the basic necessities of the day, which are not costly since their meals are modest, they do not think much about other needs. As a result they spend on the feast of the patron saint everything they have earned in a year's time. If they do not have money, they mortgage their lands or pawn their jewelry, everything, so long as they appear generous to their guests on the day of the big celebration, when the rest of the neighborhood literally throw the house out of the window, to put it vulgarly.

V

After a few days, Fonseca went to visit Alvaredo, to whom a young woman was making *mata-mata*.[9]

"Lucky are the eyes that see you," exclaimed the former affectionately, extending his hand.

"It is good to know that you are beginning to like the country even if you are busy," Nena joined in.

"Keep quiet, for God's sake. I think they are driving me crazy."

"Why, what happened?"

"I left the inn and now I have become the master of the keys," said Fonseca.

"Who accompanied you when you brought your *casancapan*?"

"What is casancapan?"

"The furniture, my good man. Haven't you transferred yet?"

"Yes, sir, since the inns are expensive and it's not good to stay there, they advised me to rent a house. I took the advice for two reasons. The captain who used to live with me left with his men for Mindanao. Of course, I enjoy more freedom and comfort, but I am not one who can put up with the local servants."

"Come, come, and tell me, it must be interesting."

"I rented a mezzanine with two pieces of furniture for P12 a

_____

[9] The action of pressing the roots of the hair with the nail of the thumb.

month, which I think is expensive because it has neither a kitchen, a bathroom, nor any other amenity."

"Here houses cost much and the rent goes up each time," exclaimed Alvaredo's wife.

"I bought the furniture I needed from a Chinese cabinet maker," Fonseca continued. "And the truth is, I find it strange that in this country where people have a penchant for luxurious living, the beds do not have mattresses."

"And who can stand them in this heat! A good bed made of narra, its center made of reed, wide enough, together with a mosquito net, mat and pillows made of cotton, and at most a light mattress, is enough. When you get accustomed to sleeping on it, you will find it indispensable for this type of weather. Because here one spends half of the day in bed!"

"What I think is a happy invention is the *abrazador*."

"The abrazador! Well, I think so. Placed between the knees, this pillow allows the circulation of air, giving the body a good rest. But what about the houseboys?"

"Their passive resistance to my orders is very annoying. They say yes to everything, they never deny anything, they do not move, not even beating their bodies with a bejuco. They always do what they want. The cook filches from the market money . . ."

"That happens in other countries, too."

"Some days, he serves a lot of food . . ."

"When he wins in the *tiangui*."

"On other days, he either serves very little or nothing at all, on the pretext that he lost the money. He tells me that whenever I am already at the table."

"That day he lost in the *palenque*."

"What are tiangui and palenque?"

"The market. The cooks, before buying food, gamble among themselves with the money they bring. The employers of the winners are happy that day because they have delicious food; the others fast. It is already a custom."

"Well, there's no doubt that the custom is good, as good as serving morning and evening chicken cooked in different ways."

"An indication that there's abundance."

"That's why they are tiring. I will tell you what happened with a *bata*. He came to me looking very sorry and asked me to pay him a month's salary in advance because his mother had died. I obliged, sympathizing with him in his misfortune. That night, his mother came to see him and when I told her what had happened, she answered that since it was a Sunday, he wanted the money to place a bet in the cockfight. Later, when I confronted him for telling me that his mother had died, he answered with impudence: 'Ah sir, I could have been wrong because she was revived.' The laundryman asks for money for soap in advance; the cook, because his wife is sick; the coachman, to pay taxes; the grass cutter, for the boat; everybody asks but nobody complies with my orders. If the cook is absent, the bata does not want to cook because he says it is not his obligation; if the bata is absent, the cook does not clean. I tell you, I am fed up with them."

"The servants here are bad, my friend Fonseca, but you don't have to do anything rash. Be calm and take things in stride. Don't give salaries in advance even if they assure you with tears in their eyes that the whole family has died. All the relatives of the domestic helpers die several times whenever they need money. You should know better in the future. On the other hand, you benefit from their sewing your buttons, mending your clothes and the other womanly tasks they do. They are so skillful. They know something about all kinds of housework. They sew clothes, wash and cut each other's hair."

"Well, mine, if they are not sleeping, which is a daily habit, they amuse themselves by pulling the few hairs of their moustache one by one with two small sticks like pincers. Or they get my combs from my dresser and use them to fix their hair; they use up my pomade, perfume, soap, and rob me of my cigars and still have the nerve to deny it even if they are caught red-handed."

"That is nothing. You should know that they wear the clothes of the master, and amuse themselves by imitating his posture, voice, and actions! You ought to go and live with a republic of friends."

"A republic! And with what job?"

"You don't understand me. In Manila *república* refers to a group of friends who share a house and contribute equally to the total expenses. Every month someone takes charge of running the house. It turns out cheaper and better whenever the persons in charge are of sound judgment. For you who still do not know the country, it would be more convenient because you avoid much frustration. When your turn comes, it would be four months since your arrival and by then you would know the customs already."

"And where can you find these friends?"

"You can always find them among your office mates or you can meet them through referrals."

"Too bad I did not know that before."

"It is your fault for not approaching me. You vagos shun our advice saying that we matandas are crazy. I will not deny that some are crazy, but thinking that we all are is a notorious exaggeration and is obviously unfair."

"There's one custom I find nice."

"Which one?"

"That one practiced in the groceries, the cafés, and all kinds of establishments. They make it easy for you to buy something on credit by giving you a *vale* even if they hardly know you.

"I think that is disadvantageous. Making a vale is easy, but the problem is that at the end of the month the debts add up. Then there is one who has carelessly spent more than necessary and ends up penniless only one day after receiving his paycheck."

"What about the guarantee of payment?"

"It can be explained. Manila is a capital city where many receive their salaries from the state. Since the vale means I will pay, it will surely be honored."

"Were you at the Santa Cruz fiesta?" asked Chata.

"Yes, ma'am; I was certainly amused. I admired the generosity of the natives and the amiability they showed to those who went to the houses, even though they were strangers."

"That very admirable custom," answered Alvaredo, "is already disappearing, because unfortunately, there are always foolish people who abuse it. Before, sincerity used to prevail in the fiestas. The residents of the towns, especially the *hermano mayor*, considered it a great honor when their houses were full of people."

"Apparently not everything looks bad to you in this country," Nena said.

"There are some things I find so strange, but I cannot figure out why."

"Let's see, Mr. Fonseca, what are they?" asked Alvaredo, smiling.

"I noticed that women never walk in the streets."

"Don't consider that strange. Laziness is prevalent. They prefer to ride a coach."

"And what about those who cannot afford such luxury?"

"They stay home, knowing that in Manila the coach is not a luxury but a necessity."

"Neither are they seen in the orchestra seats of the theaters."

"It is a useless preoccupation."

"Nor do they go for a walk."

"Yes, they gather in Magallanes for evenings of music. Before, they used to go to the Luneta."

"When there's no music, the place is deserted. But even when there is music, many do not get out of their carriages. This is hard to explain because evenings are the right time to enjoy the fresh breeze that reduces the heat at those hours."

"They are lazy."

"Well, the people in this country are very lazy."

"The same thing will happen to you *cuando se aplatane*."

"Do you mind explaining to me what *aplatanarse* is?"

"Getting acclimated, acquiring the customs of the land."

"As soon as you learn how to eat bananas, you will slow down. An easy life will diminish your strength."

"If that is the case, I won't eat them anymore."

"Only if you have eaten too much. You will also lose the colors of your face as it will turn greenish like mine. Even the heat of the sun is of no use."

"What about those indios I have seen carrying a cane for fishing in the middle of the fields? They must be crazy."

"No, they are fishing."

"Fishing on land? You are joking."

"Fishing, yes sir. When water from the sown fields floods the canals, mud puddles that stay for several days are formed. The fish bred there are eaten by the indios. They catch them in the middle of the field, as they would do in the sea. Fishing brings them a big profit. In the rivers and by the bay, they build bamboo fences where they catch abundant fish that they sell afterwards. Fish, especially *dalag*, *hito*, and *halobaybay*, is their main course."

"I heard that the country does not celebrate the carnival."

"That's right. They don't like masks here."

"And there are no donkeys or mules either."

"What would we need them for? The carabaos are enough."

"I have also observed that the women and children smoke enormous cigars."

"The same thing occurs in all coastal countries. The weather dictates it."

"I think the water coming from the water tank is bad for the health."

"No, it is not, but it is necessary to mix it with red wine, cognac, or some sugar, especially when going on a trip. Keep this advice in mind. All underwear should be made of cotton. Linen is harmful because it stops circulation. Avoid getting hungry or not eating at the usual time. Doing the opposite would give you a bad stomach, which is fatal in the Philippines. Be very careful of the smell of the earth. Never go out right after the rains. Wait after some time has passed. Fear the sun and the showers. Try not to feel bored, because the moment loneliness steps in and you start thinking about the country, you are bound to go crazy."

"I will follow your advice to the letter."

Alvaredo was right. Madness is a real disease in the Philippines. It comes in different forms to everyone. Seldom can one find one who doesn't have it but nobody wants to admit that he is crazy, and gets mad if people tell him so.

There are different kinds of madness: sentimentality, muttering, flippancy, lovesickness, indifference, offensiveness, the tendency to harm others. Monomaniacs are the real mad ones.

Fonseca and Alvaredo's family continued conversing for a long while about the country until the semaphore interrupted them, signaling that the mail boat was in sight.

Fonseca excused himself, went home, and ate. He later proceeded to the Central Post Office to wait for the distribution of letters from Europe.

The day the mail boat arrives, there is unusual excitement in Manila. The entrance to the administration hall is filled with employees with their hearts in their mouths, anxious to know if they will get a notice of dismissal. When their fears are confirmed, they leave the hall downcast. If not, they breathe freely for another fifteen days. Some come hoping to receive a much-desired promotion. Still others fabricate news that circulates with the speed of light around the whole town, affecting the people depending on what the lies are all about. The most stupendous news tells of new ministries established, the killing of half of the world's famous personalities, and declarations of war, if there is really a war. Battles are invented or peace pacts announced. For a while, it is impossible to know what is certain, as everyone feels excited. Carriages fill the grounds of the Administration Building. The postmen jostle each other to get to the post office boxes fast. Those present snatch the letters away from their hands, devouring their contents, sighing impatiently for the distribution of flyers or supplements that the newspapers give, together with the important news and telegrams.

Since there are neither political issues nor news of recent events published, the rumors circulated upon the arrival of the ship are generally believed. People comment, belie, confirm, and discuss them until the next fifteen days, when the next mail boat arrives and new lies replace the old ones. It is so hard to learn the truth about happenings in the Motherland because of its great distance from here.

VI

Fonseca was beginning to fall in love with the country as time went by.

Life is made pleasant by all the comforts that everybody enjoys. In Europe, only certain classes have the privilege to enjoy themselves. Life in the Philippines is peaceful. So as not to degenerate in monotony and boredom, however, one should befriend families who receive guests every day or on certain days of the week.

Coffee shops are hardly crowded. The theaters are seldom open. Some matandas usually gather at the door of Chinese bazaars on Escolta Street.

There, they reminisce about their happy arrival in the country, when they wore only the white drill, a hat made of *nito* or *jipijapa*, and a Chinese parasol—a fortunate time when the dictates of fashion did not impose imperial tyranny in the Philippines.

Clothes worn nowadays, made of flannel or wool, with the annoying *frac,* gloves, and top hats, were unknown then. The streets swarmed with young soldiers who offered to light one's cigars in exchange for a stick of cigarette. There was no need, unlike now, to carry matches, which were being imported in big quantities, putting an end to the practice of lighting someone else's cigar. Unemployment was yet unknown. Employees served meritoriously in their offices. After thirty-five years of serving in the same office where they eventually became officers or chiefs, they retired with the maximum pension.

Soldiers who died after fifty years of service were honored for not having used the swords they carried. They departed with a note on their clean record of service stating "valor se le supone"—which means they could have shown valor, but for lack of wars they were not able to prove themselves. For example, there's a part of Malaya where the natives search for locusts to eat, which the army lacked the resources to catch.

Only one letter a year was received. The arrival of the *Nao de Acapulco,* which brought the awaited coins, provisions, and passengers from Mexico, was met with church bells and music. Today people meet the mail boat with a somber countenance, afraid of the news it carries which, in general, is sad.

Money did not grow on trees during those times, as some old people say, but at least people were free to spend. The community, however, did not contribute even a little for the maintenance of the public lighting system that uses coconut oil. Thus, the streets were as dark as they had always been.

Fonseca, well advised, preferred the gatherings in the houses of many friendly families. There one could spend pleasant times singing, dancing, and playing the piano, or sitting on a bench with the admirers of Confucius and some matandas who extolled the good things of their time, but kept to themselves the terrible ills of the present.

His favorite place was the house of Alvaredo. It was not clear whether it was due to his desire to know more about the customs of the country, which Alvaredo, like all matandas liked to relate, or to the joy of conversing with Niña Chata. Fonseca could not tell what he admired most in Chata. Was it her small mouth and very white teeth, or her beautiful black eyes which, when she looked at him, were as ardent as the sun in the tropics? Was it her thick ebony hair, which shone when left loosely to dry after a bath; was it his own physical sensitivity to the climate, or the tiny feet he could see in the small pearl-beaded slippers she wore at home?

Fonseca's life was as follows: he would get up at seven, drink a cup of chocolate, and at eight, go to the office. There he worked a little, read the newspapers and got to know about the scandals they reported. At twelve, his bata brought him lunch on a lacquered Japanese dinner tray. At two in the afternoon, he left the office and took a nap until 4:30. At five, he went to the Malecón in his sipan, traversing the streets toward the barrio of Sampaloc. Along the way, he greeted the many ladies who were either going out for a drive or who were on the balconies of their homes. He ate supper at seven. The evenings he devoted to visiting friends. His last stop was Alvaredo's house, where he stayed until midnight. It was like that for three months.

One day, the supplement distributed by the newspapers that arrived from Europe did not contain any interesting news. Instead, it listed three columns of names of public officials who were declared fired. The first name in the list of casualties was that of Don Genaro Fonseca.

Dismissal is the sword of Damocles hanging over the heads of government employees. When it falls on someone, he dies for the sake of the all-important budget.

Upon reading the obituary notice, Fonseca felt colder than the inhabitants of the Pole, despite the 40 degrees the thermometer registered in the shade. Being fired thousands of miles away from his country, hardly recovered from the nausea of the trip, not having even saved five *céntimos* to buy a *mecate*, or rope, with which to hang himself and having to borrow money at usurious rates, proved too much for a Christian to endure.

Fonseca, despite being a Christian, thought of suicide. Struggling with that idea, he realized that he could not end his life so easily because he did not have any money to do so. Jumping into the river or from a balcony seemed too vulgar for him.

Fonseca's thoughts were interrupted when his servant came in to hand him a letter from Alvaredo inviting him to dinner.

I will see Chata before ending my life, he told himself. He ordered his servant to prepare his clothes right away.

The servant went to the bedroom and, returning shortly after, said, "You do not have any more clothes, sir."

"What do you mean there are no more clothes?"

"That's right, sir."

"It can't be. The laundrywoman came two days ago."

"Worse than that, sir. Everything is gone."

"But how is that possible? What do you mean?"

"The *anay* ate them all, sir."

"What is anay?"

"The anay, sir."

Fonseca could not understand his servant. He rushed into the bedroom.

The houseboy had left the closet open for Fonseca to see right away the extent of his tragedy. All the clothes in the closet had been reduced to dust.

Fonseca's expression was indescribable.

The night before, his clothes were intact. Twelve hours later, he did not have anything, not even a miserable handkerchief to dry the tears in his eyes caused by so much misfortune. To someone more ignorant, it would have seemed like something the elves had done.

Impatient to know what anay was, he went straight to Alvaredo's house. He wore the same clothes he had worn the day before, the only clothes spared because they were in another place.

He narrated to Alvaredo what happened. The latter explained, "The anay, my friend, is a species of very tiny white ants, armed with two sharp teeth with which they bore through wood, pulverize cloth fabric, and destroy in seconds the wooden framework of a building as well as the biggest file of papers, as you have seen. This little insect multiplies rapidly. The house you live in must have been built of badly cured wood or it is not made of molave, the durability and bitterness of which the anay respects. Provide yourself with drawers or chests made of *alcanfor* imported from China, since the anay or any other kind of insect does not attack such material. I am very sorry about what happened, especially your dismissal."

"Will you go back to Spain?" asked Chata in a soul-piercing voice.

"What else can I do?" Fonseca answered sadly.

"Do you feel like leaving the country already?" asked Alvaredo.

"Yes, sir. I'm very sorry," he replied, giving Chata a meaningful look. "I was beginning to fall in love with this beautiful land and it saddens me to separate so soon from the people with whom I have forged a sincere friendship, above of all you. If I knew a way of earning a living respectably, I would stay."

"If that is the case, then you can stay. My family and I appreciate your goodness. That's why as soon as I heard of your termination, we were really sorry. I thought of a way of trading profitably. If you agree, we will start right away."

"I'm listening."

"When I myself was fired, I was able to survive, even without work. But I did not want to be idle and I devoted myself to doing business. I don't regret it because I made in a few years what I would never have earned if I had been employed. My project is what I am going to explain to you. In the provinces of Cagayan and Isabela, rice is very scarce because all the lands are planted with tobacco. Neither do they have textiles. You will go to these provinces with a good quantity of rice, fabrics for *sayas*, shirts, *tapis*, scarves, and other articles for daily use. Not having received payment for their tobacco, they will be in need of money, but you can give them the articles they need in exchange for promissory notes or tobacco receipts, with proportionate interest. It is a sure business and very profitable, the details of which I will tell you. The net profit you make, we will split in half, as I provide the capital and you go through all the trouble. What do you think?"

"I accept gratefully."

"Well, you will leave eight days from now on a boat scheduled for Aparri, the port of Cagayan. From now on, we will arrange everything. You will bring letters for people who will attend to you in those provinces. The trip will familiarize you with the country because it is only in going to the provinces that you will get to know it. He who does not leave Manila does not know what the Philippines is like."

"It is done."

Chata expressed her joy with a gracious smile.

Fonseca spoke to her in a low voice, "Had I not seen you, I would have felt less sorry to leave for Spain, but after having met you, it would be a tremendous sacrifice to do so."

"You are always very kind!"

"It is nothing compared to your beauty."

"Thank you for the flattery."

"Will you remember me sometimes when I am away?"

"Why not? You heard Father say that we hold you in high esteem."

"What I need more is your respect."

"Don't doubt it."

"Thank you, Chata. Your beautiful image is engraved in my soul. There and here, your memory will stay with me."

A servant, announcing that dinner was served, interrupted the conversation.

"Let's eat," Alvaredo said. "I have already ordered champagne. We will toast to the success of our enterprise."

"And for my dismissal, the cause of our newly forged partnership."

"That's right. Now instead of offering condolences, we must congratulate him," Nena and Chata said.

"I accept."

VII

Cagayan and Isabela, provinces situated in the north of Luzon, have the most important tobacco plantations in the Philippines. The tobacco they produce when well-cultivated could compete with that from the Vuelta Abajo of Cuba. All the inhabitants of the two provinces are dedicated to tobacco plantations.

The Ministry of Finance oversees the harvesters through the inspectors and appraisers who make sure that the established guidelines in producing the best harvest are observed for the benefit of the tobacco industry.[10]

This plant reaches the maximum height of 2 yards. Its leaves, generally green in color, measure about half a meter long and 5 to 7 inches wide. To grow them, seedlings are first produced. During the first days they are covered with cogon awnings to protect them from the sun and the strong rains. After forty to sixty days, the shrubs are transplanted to the appointed land, which has been plowed and

---

[10] General José Basco y Vargas established the policy on income for tobacco in 1781.

cleaned beforehand. Weeds that grow with the tobacco are pulled out every day and the earthworms that damage them are exterminated. After a month, they are trimmed and the shoots are removed. When the leaves are mature, marked by a yellowish color, and the veins rustle when separated, they are cut, hooked on sticks and are hung for airing in chambers made of bamboo with a nipa or cogon roof. As soon as they are dry and have turned dark in color, they are placed in big pyres and covered with *alupasi*, the bark of the banana plant, on top of which a weight is placed. They have to be turned around every twenty days to avoid fermentation or the parching of the leaves. When they are cured, they are arranged in bundles of a hundred leaves of the same size and are taken to the bodegas of the state for appraisal.

The people, with the approval of the chief collector of the province, and under the inspection and supervision of the intervening appraiser, appoint six sorters who separate the leaves into four classes according to the size and quality of the tobacco. After an estimate of the merchandise is made, a card justifying the delivery of one's tobacco is issued to the harvester, who can collect its value on payday. There are collections where no receipts are issued. In this case, the harvester is paid according to the Manual of Appraisal where his name is listed, together with the tobacco he brought in. The harvester himself bundles or wraps up the tobacco with alupasi, putting forty clusters in each bale.[11]

In the towns of Ilagan and Maquila in Isabela, there are tobacco presses that divide the harvest into three parts of 400 pounds each. These substitute for the usual bundles. The tobacco is thus prepared for shipment to Manila.

Unbundled tobacco leaves, as well as those bound in the two systems of collections, are then auctioned or sold at reduced prices

---

[11] The Ministry of Finance pays for each bale of tobacco from Cagayan and Isabela P9.50 for first class tobacco; P6 for second class; P2.75 for third class and P1 for fourth class.

for export abroad. Tobacco from the Mountain Province and from the Visayas is sent mostly to Spain, while that from Nueva Écija is mixed with the inferior classes from Cagayan and sold in the country. There are three factories in Manila, one in Malabon and another in Cavite. There are 26 thousand female machine operators and about 1,500 males. These five factories can manually process 360 million pure cigars annually.[12] The revenue from tobacco is the biggest remittance to the Philippine Treasury.[13]

Whenever conditions in the Treasury allow, payment for the collections of tobacco is organized by the *cabecería*. On the very same day, the harvesters spend almost everything they receive, settling debts, buying necessities, paying taxes, and making other contributions. Around the Tribunal, the Chinese set-up numerous stores selling all kinds of articles.

There are fifty-five rivers crossing the province of Cagayan. There is a small lake called Carue, measuring 11,800 meters in circumference, where crocodiles abound. It is a province rich in cattle. Isabela produces excellent tobacco. If gathered on time, tobacco becomes a gold mine for it.

In the interior part of these provinces, there are settlements of wild people who plant tobacco. Famous for its good quality is the tobacco from Calauas.

---

[12] In a 5-year period, the factories have processed 507,383 ½ *arrobas* (1 arroba or 25 lbs.) of superior sized tobaccos, and 552,183 arrobas of inferior sized tobaccos.
[13] According to the 1868-69 Budget in force in the Philippines, the annual estimated income is as follows:

sale of processed tobacco for local consumption	$ 4,550,000
sale of processed tobacco for export	$ 1,000,000
sale of tobacco in loose leaves for export	$ 1,162,500
scrap from damaged tobacco	$ 2,000
Total	$ 6,714,500
After expenses, the income is around	$ 3,000,000

This revenue, if well managed, can be doubled.

After giving this brief report on the tobacco trade, we resume our narrative of what happened to Fonseca.

The boat he took anchored in Aparri. Then he boarded a *barangayan* that embarked in the town of Lal-lo. From there he went to Tuguegarao, the capital of Cagayan. In these places he did good business, disposing of the merchandise he brought for tobacco receipts. He did the same thing in Tumauini, the capital of Isabela.

After having disposed of the goods, he wanted to return to Manila as soon as possible, spurred by the desire to see Chata. Since there was no boat, he traveled in a *pontín* towards various ports in Ilocos and continued his trip by land back to Manila. Although he could have taken the Cagayan route, he feared the difficult passage from Mount Caraballo.

He was delayed at the bay of Aparri for two days because the boat was unable to pass through the mouth of the river, which at times makes the port unnavigable. Once in the wide sea, the waves seemed to swallow the fragile vessel. At nightfall, a very strong wind blew. The *arráez* of the pontin gathered all the crew and sang the Ave María in a monotone. Afterwards, he entered his small cabin, telling the crew to keep close watch. Some seamen slept on the prow of the ship. Fonseca was uneasy. On seeing that the wind was getting stronger and the seamen were not doing anything, he spoke to the steersman. Ropes held the rudder and the steersman was sleeping. He woke him up right away, but the indio, without getting up, asked him:

"Do you want anything, sir?"

"You are sleeping peacefully and you left the rudder in this kind of weather?"

"There's no danger, sir, I am tied to it."

He thought the indio was drunk so he looked for the arráez. "We are going to sink," he said. "The wind is blowing terribly and you have not taken any precautions at all."

"There's no need to worry, sir. This always happens."

"What will happen is we will be thrown out. They have the rudder tied."

"It is the practice, sir."

"What practice? These people are crazy!"

"Go to sleep now, sir."

Fonseca left for the deck. The indios' calm behavior before the threatening danger scared him. He thought his end had come. He wanted to surprise death by sleeping like the crew of the coastal vessel, but it was impossible to sleep. The night wore away. Nothing unusual happened. At dawn, the wind stopped. Not faraway was land.

"Where does that coast belong?" he asked.

"To Ilocos Norte. The town of Bangui is there," they answered pointing to it.

"Let's dock there. I want to get off."

"It is better in Dirique, sir," the arráez said from his cabin.

"Why?"

"It will be less troublesome for you, sir."

"In Dirique then, if we can dock soon."

Dirique is a dangerous port of Ilocos Norte. There is a cottage that belongs to the hacienda where tobacco is deposited before a contractor transports it to Manila. The one in charge of the cottage is a robust Catalán surnamed Martínez. He was kind enough to provide Fonseca with a guide to accompany him to the town of Pasuquin. They made the trip on horseback. The trees standing on both sides of the road were full of *chongos*.[14] They jumped and made gestures to Fonseca whenever he looked at them. Most of them were brown in color; a few were white, black, or red.

From Pasuquin he went to Bacarra, a big town, arriving at night. He saw numerous bats called *paniques* on some kapok trees. He amused

---

[14] Monkeys.

himself by catching them while the horses were being prepared. He arrived in Laoag, the capital of Ilocos Norte, an hour after leaving Bacarra.

After the town of Taal was divided, Laoag became the biggest town in the Philippines.

In Ilocos Norte, there is a collection of good quality tobacco harvested on the Eastern side.

From 1864 to 1871 the province was under an illustrious and dignified chief who left a lasting memory for his honesty and wonderful character. Ilocos Norte prospered from trading. The tobacco the province produced was superior to other brands, except those from Isabela and Cagayan, which are still the best in quality.

In Nagpartian, a small town near Dirique, there is a big lake called Banban where crocodiles abound. In Paoay, a town where the best blankets called Ilocos are woven, there is another lake.

The province is famous for its woven articles of *guingon*, cotton and silk, tablecloths, abundant cattle, horses, and forests. Different Igorot tribes live in the mountains. There are also many wild boar and deer. The inhabitants are docile, honorable, and hardworking. The land is fertile and the climate healthy. When the north wind prevails, it is cold in the Ilocos region. The province has a population of 160 thousand and is 88 leagues, about 493 kms. away from Manila.

Fonseca stayed for six days in Laoag because of a slight fever. A countryman treated him. A native of Medina-Sidonia, the man was named Don Manuel Ortega and he was the official vaccinator of the province.

Since there were no inns in the Ilocos, Fonseca stayed at the Tribunal, or the town hall. From there, he was brought to the home of a clerk, also a countryman, being a native of Antequera, who, according to Fonseca, was famous for his generosity and excellent character.

From Laoag, Fonseca went to Vigan, in Ilocos Sur, where he made arrangements with the driver of the mail coach for his trip to avoid the inconvenience of arguing with the authorities. He liked the province of La Union for its good roads and its fine location.

The tobacco collection in Ilocos Sur is very important.[15] The Igorots who reside in the mountains harvest it on a large scale and when they bring the tobacco down for appraisal, they also bring gold in bullion or in powder form gathered from the rivers. The precious metal is sold at a low price if it is of inferior quality.

Fonseca was sorry for leaving Cagayan in a hurry without waiting for a boat. Land trips during the rainy season are very dangerous, costly, and exceedingly troublesome. The mail coach, which does not have provisions for passengers, is the only means of transportation and should be taken only in extreme emergencies. Passing through the Amburayan, a rich river that separates the provinces of Ilocos Sur and La Union, and flows between Tagudin and Bangar, the coach almost sank because of the strong current. It had to cross on bamboo rafts towed by *polistas* immersed in water. Travelers and carts are transported this way from one shore to the other. The rivers in the provinces do not have bridges. During the dry season, wooden planks are constructed and are removed during the rainy days so that the floods do not destroy them.

Every time the coach crossed a river, Fonseca trembled all the more. At times the rowers could not counter the current, and the rafts were either pulled very far or sunk. Encountering setbacks and obstacles in fear, they passed through a slope between Binaca and Tarlac. The route through Pangasinan was considered dangerous because of the terrible bandits who had already killed many travelers there. The mail coach had to be pulled by carabaos because of the bad state of the roads. This, together with the proverbial calm of the driver named Lladoc, caused them to arrive very late in Guagua, a place in Pampanga, where boats from the

---

[15] The price satisfactory to the Ministry of Finance of tobacco from La Union, Masbate and Ticao, Ilocos Norte, Ilocos Sur, Abra and Nueva Ecija is at P8.00 per bale of the first class, P5.00 for the second, P2.50 for the third and P0.75 for the fourth.

capital dock. Fonseca boarded one of these boats and after four hours reached Manila.

He told Alvaredo, "We did good business because I was able to dispose of all the goods I brought. After deducting all the expenses, we made a profit of from 50 to 100 percent. But if I were to travel again on a pontín or by land, I would rather be poor. What natives, what rafts, what rivers, what downpours, what heat, what courts, what roads, what dangers, what coach, what nuisance, what driver, what hunger! I have never suffered so much. There were moments when I feared that we would never see each other again."

"Of course, you have suffered a little, but in turn you have made a fortune. Even here in the Philippines, money is not earned without working and suffering," said Alvaredo.

Chata welcomed Fonseca with a gracious smile, and instantly he forgot all his sufferings. For two hours they talked about what lovers normally tell each other after a long absence. They realized they loved each other; they believed they were born for each other, and they promised to be faithful to one another forever.

The matanda, whose consent they sought, gave his favored vago a good mark. They asked the government in Spain to send them some documents, and as soon as everything was ready, Julia Alvaredo, or Niña Chata, as she was called at home, was united in indissoluble matrimony with D. Genaro Fonseca. Happy and growing more contented each day, Fonseca decided to spend the rest of his life in the Philippines with his adorable wife.

May God grant them long life and a lot of money. For although married couples swear to be happy with only rice and salt if they are Filipinos, or with bread and onions if they are Spaniards, they get to know each other's faults after a few months. And if there is no flour, as the saying goes, everything turns sour.

For love to grow, it has to be well-nurtured. At least in this case, both the vago and the matanda are in complete agreement.

Rosa Yacson:
The Mestiza Ilocana

I

Europeans unfamiliar with the character and nature of the Filipinos presume that great passions born of love, which in other places cause some dramatic events, do not exist in this country. They base this misconception on the indolence of the *indio* and his calm attitude toward anything except his favorite pastimes—cockfighting and gambling.

Such an impression is not accurate because when inspired by love, the Filipino overcomes his passivity, which is attributed to the tropical climate, and can become capable of heroic deeds.

ROSA YACSON: THE MESTIZA ILOCANA

Let us tell the story of some loves, which in constancy, sincerity, and unselfishness can compare with great and immortal love stories. The heroine in this story is modest and unknown. But that does not matter, since sacrificing one's life for the sake of love is appreciated as much as adorning with a royal crown the most humble daughter of the town.

In the year 1865, a young mestiza was the toast of Vigan, the capital of the province of Ilocos Sur. She was called Rosa and was as beautiful as her name. She was the only daughter of the richest man in Vigan, the former capitán, Don Mariano Yacson.

The *capitanes* and *gobernadorcillos* belong to the aristocracy of the towns. They enjoy certain privileges, like a special pew in the church, the right to be called "Don," and to be eventually considered for the highest post in the municipality. They are the most respected among the *principalía*.

All this, and the fact that Capitán Mariano was the owner of several houses, two of which were of stone, a schooner, two coastal vessels, agricultural lands, and various animals, made his family the richest in Vigan, and Rosa an enviable catch for anyone.

Rosa had many suitors, but still innocent about love; she paid no attention to them. She listened to the songs dedicated to her from below her window, and the continuous serenades called *emprentadas*, with the same indifference with which she listened to the sound of the rain.

Moreover, when she was still a child her parents had betrothed her to Ramón, the son of Juan Álvarez, a rich *cabeza de barangay*.

For reasons of convenience or to put an end to old rivalries or to bolster kinship, it is customary for the families in the Ilocos to arrange the marriages of their children even when they are still being breastfed. Once agreed upon, their settlement is to be carried out regardless of whether the young couple is of age, whether they love each other or not or whether they will be happy or miserable.

Because of this deeply rooted practice, the submissive Rosa calmly accepted the husband chosen for her. She hardly knew him. His parents had sent him to Manila at an early age to study at the San Juan de Letrán College hoping he would be a lawyer some day.

II

Rosa was a very beautiful young woman. Her well-shaped eyes were very expressive, tender, and sweet. It was impossible to look into them without getting fascinated by her magical charm.

She had very beautiful black hair, so thick and so long that when unbraided, it reached the floor. Her feet were small, her hands dainty, her body poised and shapely. She was fair, almost white but slightly rosy. Her mouth was small, with white perfectly formed teeth; her neck was pretty, and her nose, although small, did not diminish her beauty. She was very charming, remarkably simple in her ways, and distinctly graceful. She had a sweet melodious voice and played the piano well. She was well-educated.

Rosa's parents had given her all the comforts of life. This she repaid with tenderness, graciousness, and excellent manners, and she was loved more for these traits than for her physical beauty. With such attractive qualities, she obtained from relatives and strangers alike whatever she fancied.

She had a pretty carriage, a complement to her elegance, and on many afternoons she would go for a stroll at the Mira, a picturesque place where people viewed magnificent scenery.

Often, in the evenings, some of her friends, together with their brothers and relatives would gather in her house. They sang and danced sometimes. At other times, they played selected pieces on the piano, a very popular instrument in Vigan.

She offered them cigars from Cagayan that by chance had found their way to Vigan. Her guests liked this tobacco as much as the popular *buyo*; they also enjoyed her homemade sweets. All were so gratified by her kindness and cordial ways that no one could ever dislike her.

III

Every 25 July, many people from Ilocos Sur went to celebrate the fiesta in Bangued, the capital of Abra.

"Are you going to the fiesta in Bangued, Rosa?" her friends Juanita and Társila asked her several nights before the forthcoming fiesta.

"I don't know if my parents will allow me to go," she answered.

"They don't deny you anything. Tell them to take you along and we will go together."

"And what are we going to do there? I don't know anybody in that province."

"It doesn't matter. We have relatives there. Make up your mind to go and you will see how much fun we'll have. There will be a play, horse racing, and a ball at the Tribunal. Last year we were there and we enjoyed ourselves very much. It is a very beautiful province and to go by raft on the river of Santa is a pleasurable and very poetic experience."

"All right, as you wish," Rosa told them.

She spoke to her parents about going to Bangued.

The trip was pleasant, as her friends had said.

Several families from Vigan went to the fiesta and stayed in the house of a capitán in Bangued, who welcomed them with a big banquet.

The first thing they did on the day of the fiesta was to hear the High Mass, which was celebrated with great pomp. After the Mass, they visited the principalías of Abra and paid their respects to the gobernadorcillo of the province, accompanied by musicians, as was the custom. Then they went to kiss the hand of the parish priest and later spent the rest of the morning watching the *comedia* in Ilocano.

The spectacle charmed the Ilocanos so much that they even forgot to eat. They liked the show very much and were delighted by the *bolbollagao*, or jester. In the afternoon, there were *carreras de caballo* and *juego de sortijas*, which everybody enjoyed.

Rosa was happy and her friends who noticed it said, "Don't you think that we did right in urging you to come? See how much fun this is!"

"Yes," Rosa said, "and I thank you for it. The play was very good. The juego de sortijas is very exciting and I am impressed by the skill of the rider who caught three rings."

"Which one?" they asked her.

"That young man wearing a cap with feathers and a blue band."

"Oh yes, he's so handsome. And what a fine figure he cuts on horseback," Társila said admiringly.

"He's probably the son of a principalía," remarked Juanita.

"No, he isn't," interrupted one of the daughters of the capitán in whose house they were staying. "His origins are somewhat unknown. It is said that his parents were rebels in the hinterlands and he was captured when he was only six years old. Since then he has been living in Abra under the care of the chief of the military detachment that arrested him. The officer taught the boy very well and loved him so much that when he went to Spain, he left all his property for him to administer until his return. He is honorable, hardworking, and of good character. He showers his old mother and little sister with all the comforts since they came in search of him many years ago. They were converted to his religion. He awaits his master and we believe he will be well repaid for his loyalty."

"What an interesting story," Rosa said.

"I am not surprised. There is no person here who doesn't notice him. He is handsome, generous, and talented. He is so pleasant that people around can't help but like him."

"Does he have a sweetheart?" Rosa asked.

"There's no one we know of. He treats everyone with the same gallantry. He is always friendly but he does not pay special attention to anyone."

"That's strange. And what's his name?"

"Luís Domínguez."

"Look! There!" People were shouting. "He got another one!"

"Bravo!" everyone exclaimed. "Bravo!"

IV

The young man looked towards the group from Vigan and when he saw that they were clapping, he stood in front of them, bowed and thanked them.

When he saw Rosa, he paused in midstride and then went on with the race, looking back several times to get a better look at her.

Rosa, who kept watching him, felt embarrassed when their eyes met. She looked down as if she had done something wrong.

Luís had already hooked four rings, winning the admiration of the spectators for his bravery and skill. He carried the rings on the tip of a cane without offering them to any young lady. Other gallants would have quickly offered the rings to their favorite ladies.

Now the most important ring was the only one left. It was the most expensive, and had been bought and decorated by the daughters of the principales. He who ensnared it would win a prize and receive the honor of being crowned by the daughter of the gobernadorcillo.

All the riders did their best to win it but their efforts were all in vain. Luís Domínguez, who until then had not joined in the game, hooked the last ring on the point of his cane with admirable dexterity and galloped on at full speed. This triumph gained him spontaneous and frenetic applause.

The gobernadorcillo's daughter put the attractive crown on the head of the winner. Luís then ran towards Rosa and very tenderly said:

"Lady, if you would be so kind as to accept this crown and the rings I won, I would consider myself most fortunate and deeply grateful."

Seeing that all eyes were fixed on her, Rosa blushed. She was speechless and did not know what to do.

Her friends signaled for her to accept it. She did so and thanked the gallant youth with a meaningful look no words could describe.

She felt the objects burn in her hands. She did not know why, nor was she aware of what was happening to her, but she felt something strange in her heart. It was something she had never experienced before and she could not understand why.

The memory of the gallant young man haunted her without her wanting it. Instinctively, her eyes started to look for him in the crowd that was leaving and she did not try to move.

"Aren't we going?" her friends asked.

"Let's go," exclaimed Rosa, absentmindedly.

While they were taking their *merienda* in the house where they were staying, the conversation turned to the events of the day.

Rosa was oblivious to what was going on. She neither said nor heard a thing because she kept thinking about the winner in the *juego de sortija*, whom everyone praised. Without wasting much time, the girls started to dress up for the dance.

V

Rosa dressed and adorned herself with much care. Over a beautiful blue skirt she placed a silk *tapis*, which she flirtatiously tied around the waist. Her blouse, made from very fine *piña*, did not fall below the waist, in keeping with the fashion in the country. A shawl, also of piña, was fastened by a precious diamond pin. Earrings, a comb, pins, several rings of the same shape, a beautiful pearl necklace with a small diamond cross, and a filigreed silver fan completed her costume.

Her small bare feet were partly hidden in a very pretty pair of gold-embroidered slippers abundantly adorned with pearls.

Some very fragrant sampaguitas artfully placed on her head interplayed with her diamonds, making her look more radiantly lovely than ever.

All who beheld her couldn't help but admire her beauty. She was the envy of the women and the delight of the men. She was the belle of the ball and everybody hastened to compliment her.

Rosa seemed distracted. Her eyes were fixed on the entrance of the Tribunal, as if expecting the arrival of someone special.

The hall was luxuriously adorned; numerous lights illuminated it. Various dance tunes, such as the waltz, the *habanera,* and the polka, were played alternately. The governor was there, together with public officials and visitors from Spain. Well-dressed bachelors from Abra and Vigan, native and mestizos alike, moved about courting the ladies. There was excitement, noise, and joy everywhere.

But Rosa was distracted. She seemed isolated from everything around her. Her friends, thinking she was ill, asked what was the matter. But she replied that it was nothing. They went on dancing and they did not bother to ask her anymore.

Suddenly, Rosa's face lit up. Spontaneous joy brightened her eyes. She liked the change she felt, which without doubt was caused by the arrival of Luís Domínguez, the handsome horse rider who had charmed everybody that afternoon.

He was elegantly dressed according to the fashion in the country—a shirt made of first-class colored piña, pants of white wool, shiny boots, and a set of inexpensive but elegant buttons on the chest. His black shiny hair was carefully combed.

His large dark eyes were beautiful and bright. His skin was dark but lighter than that of most natives. His nose, although a bit flat, was shapely enough, his body well-proportioned and poised, his walk elegant without any affectation.

He greeted familiar faces with ease and spontaneity. The young men in turn welcomed him with fond smiles, which he did not reciprocate because he seemed to be looking for something that he finally found.

Rosa and Luís exchanged a deep and passionate look revealing the sympathy they had for each other.

VI

Sympathy is the precursor of love, but for them love came ahead of sympathy.

Luís approached Rosa. She was trembling like a leaf in a tree when the wind blows.

They shook hands anxiously and the touch made more intense the fire in their hearts, like air that ignites a flame when it blows on a smoldering fire.

"Thank you very much, señorita," were the first words of Luís, "for accepting my insignificant gift. You are as kind as you are beautiful."

"I should be the one to thank you for your attention," a blushing Rosa answered in the dialect of the province.

"People living in Vigan are happy. There are young people there, like you, who touch the soul, making life desirable."

"It must be because you want it. In this hall I see a few who are much more beautiful than all those in Vigan."

"That is simply gallantry towards my town mates."

"There must be pretty girls here as there are in Vigan, but there is something superior to beauty, and this I have not seen among those from Abra, nor do I see it among those from Vigan, except in you. It is something divine I have never seen before and which I cannot explain. It is an irresistible attraction that subjugates and enslaves the will. I, who up to now was not interested in getting close to anybody, feel myself being dragged towards you by a superior force. What it is, I wouldn't know."

"Thank you for your flattering words, but I know very well that they are either meant to deceive or are praises said out of sheer courtesy."

Luís invited her to dance. They continued talking. The conversation heightened the pleasure of knowing each other. Soon that sweet trust, which sympathy, if not love, had planted, grew between them.

He regaled her with ardent words: how sweet life would be to be near her and enjoy her pleasing ways, how painful to separate from her so soon after knowing each other. Her memory would then cause sorrow, no matter how pleasing it was to meet her.

"I would be very happy to see you often!"

"Why don't you come to Vigan where it is more fun?" Rosa said, trying to hide her excitement.

"I would really love to, but right now it is impossible. It would, however, be a great pleasure to see you again. Perhaps it won't be long."

They talked for a long time, revealing their affectionate feelings, their mutual inspiration. When they parted, affection had blossomed into love.

VII

Rosa became melancholy. She who was so happy before was now sad and perturbed. She couldn't keep her mind off the first man she had ever taken any interest in.

Her parents could not ascertain the cause of her sadness. They thought she was sick. A doctor was called but to no avail since her illness was one for which no cure could be found in the pharmacies.

Twenty days after their meeting in Abra, Luís, who could not forgive himself for not seeing her sooner, arrived in Vigan bringing commercial goods. He knew how to transact business with Capitán Mariano, who welcomed him to his house.

Rosa's happiness on seeing Luís was indescribable. Soon, her cheeks regained the color they had lost. She became lively and the seductive smile that made her very charming returned to her lips.

Luís took advantage of the first opportunity to speak of his love. His overwhelming passion—contained for an unbearably long time, because for someone who truly loves, twenty days seem like centuries—made him extremely eloquent. Filled with excitement, he told Rosa: "I saw the dream fleeing from my eyes but your bewitching image never left me for a moment, and I feared then that I would lose my sanity. I just know that I love you with all my heart."

Rosa, who had pinned all her dreams on Luís, accepted happily and graciously the love he professed. She told him that she too loved him, that her heart belonged only to him, and that she thought of him every moment since she had laid her eyes on him.

Luís stayed in Vigan for a month, visiting Rosa every night and never failing to reiterate his pledge of love. It was a month of happiness when hours seemed like minutes.

He returned to Abra but often went back to Vigan to see his beloved. They wrote love letters to each other every day, making plans for the future and believing that their love would never end.

VIII

Vigan, in our judgment, is the best provincial capital because of her beautiful buildings.

Wooden and nipa houses, so abundant in other places, are not very common in Vigan.

There are barrios, like those of the mestizos, where the houses are all made of stone.

There are two spacious plazas. In one of them can be found the city hall, the residence of the head of the province called Casa Real, the Bishop's Palace, the Cathedral, the Finance Building, the Local Court, the seminary of the Order of St. Paul, the Army Headquarters, and the house of a Spaniard, an old resident of Vigan whom the Ilocanos appreciate for his philanthropic acts. The Casa Real, the Palace, and the Administration are very good buildings. In the center of the plaza is a beautiful promenade with a simple monument of the illustrious Juan Salcedo.

Worthy of honor, too, is the memory of a mestizo born in Vigan, Don Miguel Vicos. He is honored for having killed the leader of a mutiny who attempted to incite a rebellion in Ilocos Sur in support of the English when they invaded the capital of the Islands.

In 1578, Vigan was granted the status of a city. Its residents are very sociable and quite illustrious.

The feast of La Naval, dedicated annually to the Virgin of the Rosary, is very famous, and many people from all over the Ilocos come to attend it. There used to be a lot of dancing, a diversion the mestizas of Vigan are very fond of.

Ilocos Sur used to harvest the most indigo, a product that made the province rich. Today, it is in a state of decadence.

The farmers have been planting other crops without completely abandoning the production of indigo, which was a lucrative trade. They now deplore the decline of this industry.

Unfortunately, the tobacco the province produces is of poor quality.

Its climate is healthful and pleasant, except during a season when a strong hot wind, called *dugudo,* becomes very annoying.

It has excellent bodies of water, rich minerals, fertile fields, abundant timber, cattle, fish, game, and woven fabrics. It maintains important maritime contact with Manila, Cagayan, Pangasinan, and

Zambales by means of boats, mostly coastal boats and schooners built in the province itself.

The main points of anchorage are Salomague, in the town of Cabugao; Pongol, a league, about 5.6 kms. away from Vigan; Pandan and Butao, in Caoayan, a beautiful town near the capital; one in Santiago and another in Bibingilan, in Candon. The last one is a big town with abundant coconut trees and a pleasant village.

The province has a population of about 180 thousand. There are numerous settlements of tribal folk in the hinterlands. Those closest to the towns pay contributions called *reconocimiento de vasallaje*. They plant tobacco, which they sell to the Ministry of Finance and trade with the Christians.

Vigan is 71 leagues, about 398 kms. from Manila.

Having given this brief information about Ilocos Sur and its capital, the birthplace of the heroine of our story, we will now continue to relate her love affair with Luís Domínguez.

IX

The first cloud that darkened the golden sky of the lovers was the arrival of Rosa's betrothed. Lovers when they are happy think only of their love.

The parents of the young lady welcomed Ramón with as much warmth as they would have welcomed a son. But Rosa could hardly hide her dismay at his arrival. Her dejection could only have been due to the prospect of not seeing Luís again.

Rosa's parents apologized for their daughter's indifference toward her fiancé. Thinking that it was just her shyness, they did not make much of it.

Ramón, who had fallen in love with Rosa at first sight, suspected something more or at least sensed what it could be.

Coincidentally, Luís also arrived in Vigan. He felt an immense heaviness when he learned about Ramón; he had been unaware of the betrothal arranged by Rosa's parents.

He thought she was quite insincere, but she convinced him how wrong he was, swearing it was only him she loved and not the other.

Ramón noticed Rosa's special preference for Luís and he was driven to tell her parents of his suspicions.

Capitán Mariano and his wife did not believe him. They called Rosa, and the young girl, who did not know how to lie, revealed to them her love for Luís. She explained that she had tried to fight her feelings but all in vain, and that she would be very grateful if they did not oppose her love.

Not only did they disapprove, they were very disgusted. They appreciated Luís's good qualities but they resented not having been informed of the relationship earlier. Besides, it was impossible to consent to such a relationship, not only because of the promise they had made to the father of Ramón Álvarez, but also because of the great advantages that the marriage could offer.

Luís was poor, Ramón was rich. Luís was a resident of Abra and could not leave the property entrusted to him. Ramón was from Vigan and he could be useful to the parents of Rosa as caretaker of their farm. Luís was of low origin while Ramón belonged to a family of principales.

Ramon had all the advantages; above all there was the wedding covenant to consider.

Capitán Mariano said so to Luís and begged him not to come to his house anymore.

X

Thus, Rosa and Luís faced a very big problem. She had just enough time to send him a ring, which she treasured very much, repeating her undying pledge of love for him.

Brokenhearted, Luís left for Abra so as not to make it harder for Rosa whose parents had forbidden her from seeing her beloved.

When a woman truly loves, trying to oppose her is like stopping an avalanche with a hoe or spade.

Rosa had an angelic nature, but now she became disobedient. She could not sleep; she lost her jolly disposition, forgot the piano, and instead of singing she would cry.

Her friends' behavior used to amuse her before but distressed her now. So they left her alone. Absorbed in her anguish, she did not feel like seeing anybody or having anyone see her. Only the memories of Luís kept her company. Her health started to fail and her friends feared she would soon get sick.

The unrelenting Capitán Mariano and his wife were determined to fulfill their agreement with Ramón's father. Nothing in this world could make them retract their word.

A relative who took pity on the suffering Rosa begged Juan Álvarez to free the capitán from the pact. Álvarez refused, saying that his son had also suffered much from Rosa's disdain.

The sorrow of the beautiful mestiza grew heavier day by day. The house, which used to be so full of happiness, was now filled with sad and discontented faces.

Rosa's parents thought that absence could make her forget her beloved, so they sent her to the house of relatives in Manila.

Rosa's illness was incurable. In Manila, as in Vigan, she cried over objects that belonged to Luís. The memory of him deepened her love for him; she cherished only the hope of seeing him, hearing him, and talking to him again.

Her relatives tried their best to amuse her, but strolling no longer attracted Rosa, the theaters only disgusted her, and the dances became unbearable.

Thus six months of agony for Rosa passed. She wrote to Luís

but she never got any answer. Their letters to each other were intercepted and they never received them.

Perhaps the pain might have ended her sad life had not Luís, whose only desire was to be by her side and face the issue, come to Manila, leaving his family and business in the care of a friend. He was tormented by the thought of not knowing what had happened to his beloved, since after leaving Vigan, he had not received any news from her.

Rosa's relatives tried everything to prevent them from seeing each other but to no avail. The lovers found ways to talk or even just to see each other. They tried to contain the intense passion that enveloped their hearts, but all in vain.

Seeing the futility of warning Rosa, the relatives wrote her father about what was happening. Capitán Mariano came to Manila as soon as he could. Since he realized that bringing Rosa back to Vigan was not without its drawbacks, he made her stay at the Colegio de Sta. Rosa under the special care of the Sisters of Charity. Only Rosa's relatives were allowed to talk to her.

Thus Luís and Rosa could no longer meet and talk, but they managed to see each other once in a while, when the students went as a group to attend a religious ceremony outside the Colegio.

XI

Luís was not rich, and to sustain his stay in Manila where he knew nobody, he had to work at difficult jobs to support himself. When he finished work he went to the Plaza of Santo Tomás, where he spent long hours hoping to see his beloved at the Colegio de Santa Rosa.

His situation became critical. He had left his business in Abra to a friend without enough resources. It was only his great love that made him continue to stay in Manila.

When news came that his friend had left on a sudden trip, leaving his business with no one to oversee it, and that his mother was seriously ill, he decided to leave immediately for Abra. He lingered in Manila for two days, hoping to see Rosa to say goodbye, but failed to see her. He returned to Abra with a heavy heart.

Many months passed without Rosa seeing or hearing from him. Her grieving heart was filled with sadness once again. Although at first the comfort of religion and the love of the kind nuns reduced her pain somewhat, this time the pain was too much for her to bear and she fell ill.

All the lavish care the nuns showered on her was useless. The doctor became desperate as Rosa's condition got worse every day.

Five months passed. By then her illness had become so serious that the nuns had to inform her father and begged him to come to Manila without delay.

Capitán Mariano came despite the difficult trip because it was the rainy season. He found Rosa almost dying.

The presence of her father and his solemn promise to take her back to Vigan revived her spirits. She hoped she would see Luís again.

From her father, she learned that her beloved's old mother had died and that the stress of caring for her had made him sick.

Two months passed but still poor Rosa continued fighting her ailment, an extreme weakness that kept her in bed. When she recovered she asked her father to take her to Vigan.

Capitán Mariano did as he promised, and soon Rosa was seen in town again. Although she had recovered from her ailment, her soul's sickness was harder to treat. Her deep sadness made her feel worse because every place she saw brought memories of the happy hours she had spent with her beloved.

She informed Luís of her return. Though recuperating from his own illness, he rushed to her side. They were able to talk. Their happiness was so great that they thought they would die from overexcitement.

"I thought you had forgotten me, Rosa. I was delirious due to high fever, it seemed I saw you beside me, but when I came to and realized it was a mistake, the pain nearly suffocated me. Why didn't you send me news about yourself?"

"What about you? I wrote to you several times but never got an answer. Do you think I can forget you? Just telling you about it hurts me."

"Forgive me, Rosa. I love you so much and my fear that you do not feel the same way, no matter how baseless, is unfair to you."

"Luís, I was on the point of dying. It was only the hope of seeing you again that kept me alive because it would have been more painful to die far from you and without being able to say goodbye to you."

"I also felt the same sorrow when I was sick but thank God we are able to see each other again. Do your parents still insist that you do not marry me?"

"I don't know. I am afraid to ask them because their negative answer will be more painful than death. They think that it is dishonorable to break their ridiculous pact, without understanding the absurdity of the custom, which makes couples infinitely unhappy. There is nothing we can do except to suffer."

"Our future is sad, Rosa. What grieves me most is that loving you has brought you so much unhappiness."

XII

Capitán Mariano felt his daughter's pain. He was afraid, however, that breaking an old covenant would earn him a reputation of weakness among his town mates, who never cared whether their children agreed or not to the marriages their parents arranged. And so he stood firm in his decision and became more resolved to hasten the date of the proposed union with Ramón. He set it for 22 September.

Towards the end of August, the preparations for the wedding proceeded hurriedly.

Rosa begged them on her knees not to marry her off to someone whom she did not love, for it would only make her unhappy forever.

Her pleas fell on deaf ears, and hurting so much, she informed Luís of the cruel decision.

As soon as Luís learned of it, he went to Vigan to tell Rosa about what they ought to do.

After a few days, he succeeded in seeing her. In an outburst, he cursed the overly harsh and cruel attempts of Rosa's parents to separate two hearts meant only for each other.

Her sufferings and her great love for him made them resolve never to consent to the marriage, which for them would be suicide. They were willing to sacrifice their lives rather than suffer the severe pain of being separated forever. They could not endure the thought of her belonging to a man she did not love.

Luís said to her, "In the most hidden part of the mountains of Abra is a settlement. Although still primitive because civilization has not yet penetrated it, it is powerful because of its rich agriculture, numerous residents, and abundant products, which command high prices among the Christians. I was born there. When a daring member of an expedition that penetrated the thick forest snatched me away from my parents, I was still a little boy. I only remember the people who were humbled in front of my father. My old mother never revealed to me the identity of my father. As she told me later, she feared that I might change my religion and lose my peaceful life in Abra because of the fierce disputes in the village where I was born, whose envious neighbors fight wildly without winning gold or glory."

"Before Mother died, she revealed that my father was the village chieftain. His power was absolute and discretionary; his will was law and everybody obeyed him. When my father died, his brother, who took care of me when I was small, took over the command. He loved me deeply, and upon learning where I lived from one of the rebels who came to buy supplies in Bangued, he sent a relative proposing that I reclaim in his name my paternal inheritance without prejudice to my new beliefs. For one who has known a better world, it is terribly sad to live in an uncivilized place where society hardly exists. But for two people so madly in love with each other, it is paradise wherever they meet, no matter how bad the situation is. I thought of going away to enjoy our love, far from the places where we have suffered so much, away from the bitter life that awaits us. There we will live happily. You will be respected by all. No one will equal you in power and you will be the queen of my heart. Moreover, we will be blessed. If you love me, don't turn down my plea. Follow me and my intense love will build you a new country. It will give you affection sweeter than what you lose by leaving your parents who want you to suffer and your relatives who were indifferent to your pain when it would have been so easy to make you happy. Before we go to my village, a priest will marry us in Bangued because I only desire your happiness and not your dishonor."

"I accept," Rosa said, deeply touched. "You are right. Where I feel the pleasure of your love, there my country will be, my most tender affection, my happiness. Without you, I don't want to live. And before I take my life, an act that would offend God, let's go to where we can adore Him even if the men in Vigan offend him. God will know the need that pushes me to make a very difficult decision. I leave my parents whose love, in spite of what they might do to me, I will never forget."

"I will hurry back to Abra to arrange everything so that our plans will succeed. As soon as I've done that, I will come back for you. Don't forget me. Goodbye, Rosa."

"Goodbye, and remember that 22 September is the date of my wedding. If you don't come, it will be the day that I stop living."

"I will not forget it."

They were, however, not aware that the parish in Bangued could not marry them without parental consent and a license from Vigan.

XIII

Luís went to Abra. Rosa, now more calm, awaited his return, believing it would end all her misfortunes.

She suffered from the thought of having to leave her parents. With so little time left with them, she tried to be her good self again, showing them all her affection. She was always nice and loving, and she never left their side.

They thought that this unexpected change proved them to be right in pressing for the union with Ramón Álvarez, and they congratulated themselves for this idea.

The twentieth of September dawned and Luís had not returned.

It was raining hard and Rosa began to be restless. The river could swell and delay his coming back. It would be distressing for her not to know what to do on the day of the wedding.

On the twenty-first her impatience turned to agony. Each hour that passed was tormenting. The weather worsened. The fear that misfortune had befallen her beloved filled her heart with anguish.

Night came. It continued to rain. There was no other sound but the monotonous rhythm of falling rain interrupting the solemn silence that enveloped the street where Rosa lived.

The young woman, now disconsolate, lost all hope. She started to pray since it was impossible for her to sleep. She had been listening closely for the signal agreed by them.

Moments before the stroke of twelve, her suffering heart was suddenly filled with joy. She heard the signal she had been awaiting so impatiently. Her beloved had finally come and with him, her freedom. Her happiness was overflowing. She was petrified for a while and would have remained so had not Luís's second call restored her composure. Then she brought a light to the window as a signal that she had heard him and was ready to follow him.

She unfurled a rope ladder she had kept hidden and fastened it to the window ledge. She took up a small bundle of clothes and left a note on a writing table for her parents, bidding a sad farewell to them and to all things around that were dear to her. She knelt before the image of the Virgin, earnestly asking for forgiveness for what she was going to do. She descended the ladder. Luís caught her in his arms while she fainted as a result of her intense emotions.

Rosa's parents, who were sleeping in the next room, did not hear anything.

She regained consciousness soon enough. Luís covered her with a rubber raincoat and led her to where he had left the horses. He helped her mount, and together they escaped towards the mouth of the river.

The strong rain muffled the noise made by the horses so that nobody heard the sounds of the escape.

The native women generally ride horses well, and Rosa who from childhood was no stranger to horses, rode ahead of Luís without fear, arriving shortly at the place where he had prepared a *vilog* with twelve good rowers, all trusted Igorots.

They rowed laboriously and after struggling against the strong current, the troublesome wind and rain, they succeeded in sailing up the river and arriving in Talamey. It was almost dawn, and they were exhausted. They gasped for breath, were dead tired and drenched.

They rested a little. After another journey on horseback, they walked a short distance. The torrential rain and the fearful fury of the wind were making it impossible for them to go on. The rising water of the river prevented them from crossing it. The horses could hardly go against the fury of the elements, and they did not have any recourse but to seek refuge in a house nearby.

The simple folks living there willingly received them, apologizing for not having enough food to offer them. They served the guests their ordinary fare.

The food Luís had brought was wet, so they were resigned to whatever food was on the table.

The wind calmed a bit but since it had rained very hard and the rivers were impassable, they decided to wait.

They worried about being followed but were calmed by the thought that was causing their worry—the bad weather.

XIV

The next day, the weather became worse. It rained harder and the wind blew stronger. For twenty-four hours no one in the house felt like eating. In the grip of anxiety they could only lament their grievous state. Never before had it rained with such fury.

The rainstorm had virtually converted the fields into a vast sea. They could not eat even a little food as they were burning with fever.

Rosa's anguish was immeasurable and her beloved suffered even more when he saw what she was enduring. He began to blame himself for having caused her misfortune, and the thought grieved him even more. Seeing him so distressed, Rosa felt like dying.

In the evening, the wind became erratic and the rain doubled its force. The water reached up to the floor of the house, and water poured from the ceiling. Then part of the roof was blown away.

"This is terrible," Luís said, very upset. "We are dying of hunger and we will all die from drowning. How unfortunate you are, Rosa, for having met me."

"Have faith in God," she replied. "Everything passes."

But it was not so. Water surrounded them everywhere and a gust of wind made the house lean to one side while it blew down some walls.

"The house is going to be carried away!" shouted the owner. "We are surrounded by water. There is no way to save ourselves except to climb those trees." He set an example by laboriously climbing up one tree close to his dwelling.

The rest of his family followed. Rosa and Luís, in turn, climbed another tree and set themselves on one of the thick branches.

It was one o'clock in the morning of 25 September 1867, a tragic date still remembered with horror by the residents of Abra.

"What a very unfortunate love ours is!" Luís told Rosa. "The thought that I have caused you much suffering is killing me. That I, who would give anything for just one moment of happiness for you if I had a thousand lives, should be the one to cause you a horrible death, alas! Curse me!"

"Are you mad, Luís? If God does not take pity on us and has willed our death, then I die happy together with you. What drives me to despair is to see you exposed to the same danger. It is the fear that you, too, may die."

"Why should I live without you? We will die together, loving each other with all our hearts. Then we will consider ourselves happy. What is life? Compare the pleasant times of your life with the unpleasant times and you will realize that a moment of pleasure is paid for with months of sorrow. Death will be good for our souls, perhaps, but no, we will live. You will live because I do not want you to die. I will save you."

The fever made him delirious. He embraced Rosa with a feverish strength, his whole body trembling. He felt as though he was going to faint.

Rosa, for her part, exclaimed:

"I am cold. I am hungry. I am going to die!"

"Come!" Luís shouted. "Come closer." He pressed her hard to his body to give her warmth.

XV

The wind, which had been blowing fiercely for hours, suddenly turned into a violent hurricane. The tree, where the poor lovers had sought refuge, was shaking and swaying like a reed.

It must have been two o'clock in the morning. Water was falling as if the sea, suspended in space, had fallen over the land.

A sharp cry was heard, a cry of anguish followed by sorrowful sighs. The branch of the tree to which the house owners had been clinging was struck by a powerful gust. The branch broke off, causing the unfortunate five to fall quickly and disappear as the torrent swept them away.

As if all these were not enough, a horrible flood suddenly engulfed the scene. The scary rumble of thunder and the furious roar of the sea proved no match for the deafening sound of the huge, devastating, monstrous, and uncontrollable surge of the floodwater.

Trees fell while houses were pulled out from their foundations and dragged away in the flood. The angry currents carried away thousands of animals, waste of all kind, and, most lamentable of all, a multitude of corpses, men and women, young and old. Taken by surprise, the victims had been unable to escape the destructive flood.

Luís and Rosa were becoming weak owing to the prolonged suffering. The tree where they sought refuge was about to give way, too, weakened from the buffeting of the storm and the flood.

"God is punishing me for disobeying my parents and for fleeing the home where they gave me life," Rosa said, about to breathe her last.

"Don't say that," replied her beloved. "The will of your parents went against your heart."

"I can't hang on anymore. The flood will sweep us away. The tree is going to fall. I am going to faint. Goodbye, Luís. I die loving you."

Luís held Rosa tightly. Her last words were muffled by the sound of the falling tree that held them. They quickly disappeared in the rushing flood.

There was a scream of terror. It came from the old owner of the house where the unfortunate lovers had stayed. The crown of a tree nearby had miraculously sustained them.

The flood razed everything. Places where houses and trees had stood were now covered with water. The mountains had disappeared. Only an immense waterfall was visible, as if heading for that big tomb known as the sea.

Countless cadavers and dead animals were submerged in the watery fields of death.

Such a somber scenario was reminiscent of the scourge of God against His ungrateful people during the Great Flood.

Public wealth and private treasure, the fruits of assiduous and patient work in the rich provinces of Ilocos and Abra, were destroyed and remained in ruins for a long time.

Some time later, the authorities initiated a gathering of signatures by which all the classes of society known for their charity and generosity agreed to share their produce for the reparation of the immense loss suffered by the inhabitants of those provinces.

Unfortunate were those beyond help. For them only bitter tears could be shed.

May God have mercy on their souls.

XVI

Many years passed.
It was All Souls' Day in the year 1873.

Following the custom of praying for the departed whom our hearts will never forget, we walked that afternoon to the Vigan Cemetery.

A multitude of the faithful filled the sacred space. Our attention was drawn to a group of beautiful young girls at the end of a narrow passage placing wreaths on a tomb with this inscription:

D. O. M.

Here lie the remains of Luís Domínguez and Rosa Yacson
who died in the flood of 1867.
Pray for the repose of their souls.

A short distance from the group was a very old man praying on his knees, his head covered.

Tears flowed down his cheeks. His grief and that of the young people who placed flowers on the tomb aroused our curiosity.

We respected their mourning and when they were about to leave, we asked the old man to tell us about the two whose deaths had caused them so much pain.

The old man stood by our side and over the tomb of Luís and Rosa told us the sad story of the doomed young lovers. He had narrated the same story of their last moments to Rosa's parents, whom he came to know after the tragedy.

The old man was the owner of the house on the outskirts of Talamey where Luís and Rosa had sought refuge. He was saved miraculously from what seemed to be inevitable death.

The unfortunate man fought the whole night against the wild and uncontrollable floodwaters.

Clinging to a fragile branch ripped off during the storm, he was pulled away helplessly like an inert mass and was struck by the remains of houses and trees carried away by the flood. He had to fend off logs and branches drifting with him in that terrible struggle.

He lost consciousness and became one of the many objects swept away by the raging waters.

The unfortunate man vividly described how he suffered bitterly before he lost consciousness. It was difficult for us to follow his touching story. One cannot really comprehend a horror one has not experienced.

When the rains stopped and when the water covering the land slowly subsided, the hilltops, the crowns of trees, and the fragile roofs of nipa houses that had survived the rush of the current began to appear one by one. The old man was found on a hill still desperately clinging to a small bush he had come upon during his agony.

There he fainted. A charitable family took care of him. It took two weeks for him to regain consciousness.

The young mestizas standing by the tomb of the tragic lovers were Rosa's good friends. After learning of her tragic fate and grief, they would gather every year to lay wreaths on her tomb in homage to their friendship.

The bodies of Luís and Rosa, according to the old man, were found together on an islet in the barrio of San Julián after the flood. They were identified by a relative and were buried in the place where they now rest.

XVII

Let us look back.

Rosa's parents suffered very much from the tragedy, but their pride and their obstinacy had already done their harm.

Their obsession and their ambition, perhaps, had caused the violent separation of two lives that were meant for each other.

Ramón's father also suffered deep remorse.

Regret filled the man's heart, and he was compelled to confess that he had caused the early demise of Luís and Rosa.

After the sad incident, he did not live long.

His son, the suitor of the beautiful but unfortunate mestiza Ilocana, also became very unhappy.

Did remorse pierce his heart? Was it perhaps filled with pain? We do not know.

Ramón never became interested in any of the young girls in town, nor did he ever attempt to get married. He remains a bachelor to this day.

The story of the sorrowful love we have just narrated is known in Vigan. It will take a long time for many people to forget the tragic end of the good Luís and the beautiful Rosa.

We ask God to grant their souls the peace and happiness in heaven that they found impossible to attain on Earth.

THE PIRATE LI-MA-HONG

I

Li-Ma-Hong, until he turned twenty-five, had been a peace-loving citizen of the Celestial Empire.

Not very fond of working, he spent his time wandering in the streets of his native city, flattering the beautiful women he encountered. Even the Chinese are maddened by the charms of the beautiful sex. And if they are naughty, as Li-Ma-Hong was, they never fail to flatter the women whenever they have the chance.

One afternoon, Li-Ma-Hong met his fate when he saw a lady of dignified ancestry entering a textile bazaar. The lady was of noble birth, judging from her luxurious *palanquin*, or sedan chair, in which she came, and the servants accompanying her.

She was young and beautiful—qualities that Li-Ma-Hong appreciated most in women; trivial traits that the Chinese have most admired in the fair sex from the time of Laon King to the last renowned Chinese philosopher. This attitude will demonstrate what one with such ideas is capable of doing.

Li-Ma-Hong approached the lady and said, "Beautiful lady, worthy representative of Tchangno[1] on Earth whose disdain has caused me to suffer the most horrible of sorrows, have pity on your adorer and make me the happiest of men by bestowing your affection on me."

The lady, who had seen Li-Ma-Hong before, thought he was crazy for speaking in such a manner. She sensed that he relished flattering her and she showed her displeasure.

Since the Don Juan persisted in being brash, she left the store, ordering her companions to take her home. Li-Ma-Hong was undaunted and he followed her, intent on finding out where she lived. They walked for quite a distance and he was astonished to see the palanquin enter the governor's palace. The governor was a mandarin known for his intransigence.

Li-Ma-Hong turned back and made his way down the road leading to the village beyond the city.

The lady, a favorite of the mandarin, complained about Li-Ma-Hong's impudence, and even before she finished talking, the governor had ordered some officials to look for that miserable wretch.

And so they took him to the governor, who ordered that he be paraded around the city, and at every corner he was to receive beatings that caused serious injury to his back. After the beatings, Li-Ma-Hong was ordered to leave the province in an hour

---

[1] Goddess of the moon.

and never to return. He was also tasked to beseech Confucius to keep the mandarin in good health because he was benevolent enough not to have him beheaded.

Li-Ma-Hong left the city with a body that had received 200 lashes, an excellent reason for him not to sleep on the hay although he could barely stand up. He stayed in a nearby town with a friend who bathed his wounds with water and vinegar. He recovered and left the town, but the memory of his wanderings in the city of his birth emboldened him.

Anxious to take revenge, he joined a band of thieves who admired his mischievous villainy and acclaimed him as their chief.

It seems that things did not turn out well for the chief thief. So Li-Ma-Hong changed his way of life and became a pirate. He finally found his vocation. In short, he came to command a powerful fleet of *champanes*. His vandalism, his rampages sowed panic all over China. The emperor, tired of hearing about the exploits of the notorious pirate, assembled all the warships of the empire and sent them in pursuit of Li-Ma-Hong.

Recalling the way he was treated by the mandarin of his city for the minor crime of merely uttering a few compliments to that official's favorite, Li-Ma-Hong pondered on what would happen if he were caught and the emperor ordered his punishment; so that he thought it would be prudent for him to go where he would cause less trouble.

He left for Tacootican Island and became a sultan at about the time this true story began.

II

It was around two o'clock in the afternoon.

Li-Ma-Hong, after a sumptuous meal, lay down for his siesta, smoking opium so that instead of dreaming of being disemboweled on orders of the emperor, he would envision beautiful Chinese girls offering him all sorts of delicacies. Such blissful prospects were banished by the arrival of Sioco, his aide-de-camp.

"My lord and my friend, I have come to relieve myself of the sorrows in my soul by confiding in you," said Sioco.

"What is the matter?"

"I have been the victim of the darkest perfidy in history caused by the fickleness and moodiness of women."

"Did you get beaten?"

"I would have preferred that."

"I can see you have never been beaten."

"Judge for yourself if I have reason to grieve."

"I'm listening, my friend."

"The most beautiful maiden you can imagine promised to marry me."

"She must indeed be beautiful."

"She was exceptionally lovely. She swore that she loved me and her parents promised that she would belong to no other man. I left her in all confidence in order to come and tell you the details of our last exploit, hoping to return to her soon. But my return was delayed and she listened to the false promises of her seducer who took her away to an island where I was told many of our compatriots have migrated and are doing well in business. I learned all of these from the chief of the squadron who has just arrived."

"So, what do you want to do now?"

"I wish that you grant me permission to go with some ships to that island so that I could take revenge for the fickleness of that woman and her hateful lover."

"What island is that?"

"It is called Luzon. The Spaniards have occupied it but they are a small force and cannot possibly defend their possession. The island is big and fertile and its inhabitants can be subdued easily. It is a very appropriate place for you to establish the foundations of your empire. It would not be difficult to conquer that region. Consider the fact that there are many seductive women as well as resources for you to create an empire which will rival that of the Son of the Sun."

"Great! Wonderful idea! Sioco, prepare all that is necessary and go ahead to the island of Luzon. Bring with you the greater part of the fleet. I shall follow later. Before the new moon appears, we will be the lords of that privileged country. No barracks. Surprise them at night and knife them! Do not leave anyone alive in the garrison. The natives who surrender will be our slaves. The life of the woman who has not kept her promise will be yours, and also the life of her seducer who knew very well that she was engaged to you."

"My revenge will be terrible."

"And I will gain a kingdom."

"And so I go to fulfill your orders."

"Let good fortune guide you, Sioco."

The fleet was ready—sixty-two champanes—well equipped with cannons and ammunition. When the troops had embarked, they sailed for Manila.

III

So the readers can have a good idea of the dangers confronting the growing colony called the Philippines in 1574, we shall give a brief summary of the situation then in that part of Spain's dominion.

The Adelantado Miguel López de Legaspi had set up his residence in Cebu, from where he made a reconnaissance of the other islands. He had heard of an island bigger than those that had been discovered, and he set out to search for it.

He took possession of Panay, composed of the provinces of Iloilo, Antique, and Capiz, where he stayed for a while and was welcomed by the people. After a difficult voyage, he discovered the island of Luzon.

He made his nephew, Juan de Salcedo, in charge of reconnoitering the area. Leading an expedition of 120 Spaniards and some natives, Salcedo came to the Pasig. The sight of that wide and navigable river flowing into a bay inspired Salcedo to establish a city on its banks. Forts at the narrow *bocanas*, or entrances, for ships would ensure protection and defense against any foe.

The territory, consisting of Manila and its main suburbs, was ruled by two rajahs, Soliman and Lacandola, who received Salcedo amicably. The leader of the expedition had no cause for alarm as he believed in the expressed peaceful objectives of the two chieftains.

But the indios under Soliman, rajah of Manila, suddenly attacked Salcedo's boats. The assault was repulsed and the aggressors fled. To punish them, Salcedo ordered eighty Spaniards to pursue the militant indios to their wooden fort, surrounded and besieged them, and captured the fort after a brief but ferocious battle.

The retreating indios set fire to the fort. Twelve cannons and some Portuguese jewel merchants fell into the hands of Salcedo. The defense of the expedition was led by a Portuguese who was killed.

Lacandola, the rajah of Tondo, did not take part in the aggression. During the battle, a white flag was seen flying above his house as a sign of neutrality.

Bad weather forced Salcedo to take refuge in Cavite. From there he sailed for Capiz to replenish food stocks and supplies. This active captain visited the island and continued to organize his small army.

Legaspi, on the other hand, went to Cebu to create a city. He distributed lands to the fifty inhabitants who had submitted to a census. He organized the city government and appointed a governor.

He then proceeded to Capiz on 15 April 1570, and from there sailed north with a squadron, intending to conquer Luzon. In Leyte, he reviewed his troops, now increased to 280. In Mindoro, he decreed the imposition of a tax, *tributo,* later extended to the whole country. He anchored at Cavite where the natives paid him homage.

The Tagalogs, who were supposed to be hardened men, did not show any sign of hostility. So Legaspi invited them to become vassals of the king of Spain, offering them his protection and aid. Lacandola was the first Tagalog to accept the invitation, followed by Soliman, thus ensuring the peaceful possession of the country.

Legaspi founded the city that he called Manila. He ordered the reconstruction of the burned fort, the building of a palace for himself, a convent for the Augustinian priests, a church and houses for the inhabitants, all made of wood. He declared the city the capital of the archipelago.

On 19 May 1571, the feast of Santa Potenciana, Legaspi solemnly took possession of Manila, and declared it as the city's patron saint. The *Ayuntamiento* swore to comply faithfully with its duties and this was followed by a reception.

After this primitive city was destroyed by fire, better houses were constructed. Legaspi pointed out the magnificent layout of streets that have since been conserved.

He sent ambassadors to China and allowed the Chinese merchants to settle in Manila.

The Tagalogs at that time were like savages with hardly any clothes on, living in overcrowded, badly constructed *nipa* houses without any furniture or utensils. They adored countless idols.

The elders applied the laws. Polygamy and slavery were practiced. Generally, the wrongdoers were punished with *la pena del Talión*.

They loved to sing, play musical instruments, and dance. Their songs were, however, monotonous. Their musical instruments were made of bamboo, and their dances were pantomimes.

Legaspi, with great tact, knew how to organize everything. He established the administration and dictated wise laws without neglecting even for a moment the evangelization of the islands. It was because of his heroism, his civic virtues, his superior genius, his great patriotism, and his noble lack of self-interest that the early, peaceful, and total incorporation of the Philippine Islands into Spain was realized.

Legaspi was a hero whose memory has not been honored as it should be. There is not even a single monument in Manila to remind the people, who were born there or the visitors to that capital, of the glorious accomplishments of the illustrious Miguel López de Legaspi, first governor-general of the islands. Only a town in Albay province and a modest street in Manila bear his name. He died on 20 August 1572, bearing with him the universal and sincere sentiments of the Peninsulares and the natives. His remains lie in San Agustín Church.

Upon Legaspi's death, Guido de Labezares, his *Maitre de camp,* came to be the highest in command.

Juan de Salcedo was in the Ilocos, busy conquering that part of Luzon.

With the small force thus distributed, Manila had only sixty Peninsulares to defend the city when the pirates arrived.

IV

Sioco, accompanied by 400 men, disembarked in the morning of 30 November 1574. He was not able to do so at night as Li-Ma-Hong had wanted him to, because of the winds.

The governor-general was prepared and he fought bravely, inflicting some casualties on the enemy.

Sioco had not expected to encounter any resistance. Fearful of suffering a disaster, he withdrew, telling his chief that he wanted Li-Ma-Hong himself to take the city so that the glory would be his alone.

Li-Ma-Hong was in Cavite, where he had anchored to launch his attack from there.

Sioco's withdrawal worked perfectly to the advantage of the city's defenders, who took advantage of the time to build up their strength and mount four cannons on the walls. The inhabitants of Manila barricaded themselves inside the fort. The city having been abandoned, enabled Li-Ma-Hong to penetrate it easily, committing the barbaric act of setting it on fire.

The attack started. The besieged people put up a heroic defense. They organized everything and spread out, gathering where the danger was greatest.

Li-Ma-Hong was also admired for his heroism, and now, greatly excited by the fight, was like a tiger. He could not believe that it was so difficult to conquer a fort defended only by some Spaniards while his forces were ten times stronger.

Agitated by the fight, the pirate redoubled his attacks. Maybe valor could have given way to numbers had Salcedo not arrived to lead his men.

This courageous leader was in the Ilocos, as we mentioned earlier. From an elevated watchtower in Vigan called *La Mira*, he saw a numerous fleet of Chinese champanes sailing towards Manila. Realizing that the purpose of the Chinese was to descend upon the capital, he left immediately for Manila.

Salcedo's foresight saved the country from the claws of the ferocious pirate Li-Ma-Hong, who had to withdraw hastily, losing 200 men in the process. This great achievement earned for Salcedo the position of maitre de camp.

Furious, the daring pirate disembarked in Pangasinan and demanded tributes from the natives, ordering them to build a fort reinforced with strong stakes.

As soon as Labezares was informed of the impending invasion, he ordered Salcedo to go and fight Li-Ma-Hong.

The indefatigable nephew of Legaspi, leading 200 Europeans and two thousand indios, left for Pangasinan. His arrival was fatal to the Chinese because he reduced all their ships to ashes.

The pirates wanted to try their luck but they were instead forced to flee, suffering many casualties. Some of them were able to take refuge in their fort while others did not stop until they reached the mountains.

In order to avoid further bloodshed, Salcedo surrounded the fort, confident that hunger would make them surrender.

The Chinese were aware of this. So night and day they built small boats with the wood that they could get their hands on and thus were able to escape through the river, although only very few made it and with great danger to their lives because their vessels were not very safe.

Salcedo is one of those heroes deserving eternal renown who worked hard to conquer and organize the country. He was unselfish and noble and had no ambition except to secure Spain's dominion in those regions. He was tireless in his patriotic endeavor. He subdued the whole of Luzon by persuasion and other peaceful means rather than by force. When he had to fight, as he did against Soliman and Li-Ma-Hong, he was always victorious.

He was loved for his kindness, feared for his courage, and respected for his dignity and nobility. He died in Vigan, a city for whom he had a special liking. He built a villa for the city and called it Fernandina.

In the main plaza of Vigan is a small monument to the memory of Salcedo, erected in 1850 by a zealous government official of Ilocos Sur. A town in Samar province and a street in Santa Cruz, a suburb of Manila, were also named after him.

V

The pirate Li-Ma-Hong and a few of his followers were able to reach Tacootican but not without great risk to their lives. Many days did they spend there under the cruelest conditions.

When Li-Ma-Hong remembered the destruction of his big fleet, the death of his best soldiers, his shameful defeat, the dishonor to his once respected name, the hardships he suffered, cornered like a wolf in his fort in Pangasinan, he cursed his unfortunate decision to support the vengeful designs of Sioco, his deputy, who had committed him to engage in an endeavor that only brought about the opposite of what it was intended to accomplish.

Li-Ma-Hong was a Don Quixote who wanted to right a wrong, straighten the crooked, and conquer kingdoms. Because of this, he almost suffered a round of beatings like the ones applied by scoundrels on the thin ribs of the nobleman from La Mancha, or like the ones he himself received on his back on orders of the mandarin who governed the city where he was born.

He, who was for some time the terror of the seas, was absorbed in these thoughts when he decided to call for his deputy Sioco.

"But sir, Sioco cannot come," they answered him.

"Why?" he asked.

"For a simple reason. Sioco was a scrupulous boy and was in love. The plan to conquer the island of Luzon that you undertook through his advice failed disastrously and his sense of honor could not permit him to show his face to you anymore. Furthermore, when he failed to take revenge on the unfaithful woman who deceived him but with whom he was still passionately in love in spite of everything, he tormented himself with the thought that she must be happy with her new lover. Because Sioco was jealous, he decided to end his life just now by strangling himself with a rope. Now you understand why he can not come."

"He committed suicide! The wretch! He was a hero!"

Li-Ma-Hong drank six cups of tea because a lump had formed in his throat caused by the pain of losing his deputy. Fearful of creating a bad impression, he asked for his pipe and began to smoke opium, hoping that it would give him images quite different from those that were in his mind, thinking of the fatal destiny of the unfortunate Sioco.

The very reliable documents, written in Chinese, from which we have taken the true accounts of Li-Ma-Hong's life, the authenticity of which we cannot doubt because we saw them in the archives of one of the famous pirate's descendants when we traveled to China last March, conclude at the moment where we left him—preparing to smoke opium.

We do not know how he ended his days. It is possible that the images appearing in his sleep were so entertaining that he died, drunk with the pleasure of contemplating them.

Manila still remembers 30 November of each year, when that ill-advised pirate endangered the island of Luzon with his foolhardy attempt to subjugate it. A religious ceremony is held, with corporate officials in attendance as a sign of thanksgiving for such a special favor from Divine Providence.

Since the event just described occurred on the feast day of San Andrés, this saint was chosen as the patron of Manila.

The glorious defense put up by those brave Spaniards is commemorated by having the *Alférez Real* carry the banner of Castilla through the main streets of the city. He is accompanied by public officials and a small troop of soldiers.

The people of the capital decorate their houses with bunting and cover the streets with tents while the city comes alive with joy. After the religious and civic ceremonies, the Alférez Real hosts a succulent banquet for his friends and government officials, evoking the glories of our own ancestors, and always ending with a cordial toast to Spain.

THE STUDENT FROM LA LAGUNA

I

anila was struck by the strongest storm of the rainy season during the last days of October 1873. Torrential rain fell incessantly with constant intensity, from the morning of one day to the morning of the next, so that throughout the week the morning star could not shine in splendor as it was obscured by very thick clouds. Tondo, San Miguel, and other barrios in the lowest places were so flooded that in their streets only a small boat could pass.

Despite the frequency of the storms that batter the Philippines for months, what happened during the aforementioned rainy season shocked the inhabitants. It was feared that the southeastern provinces would be destroyed by terrible floods.

On the twenty-fifth, the wind blew incessantly. The doors and windows of the cement buildings creaked frightfully; the roofs of the nipa and bamboo houses flew in the air, some houses collapsed, big trees were uprooted, and street lamps lay broken on the streets.

The steamships anchored in the bay fired up their boilers, while the sailboats were dragged from their anchorage, some of them running aground on the beach of Santa Lucia, which was littered with the debris of vessels.

That particular *baguio*, the devastating storm that occurs during the frightening season of stormy seas, nearly drowned the city of Manila.

Darkness was dense, the sky was terrifyingly dark, the wind blew at 343,000 feet per hour, roaring with a horrifying sound. Big drops of water driven by the wind were crashing with a deafening sound on the shell windows of numerous houses.

A gust of wind blew away the upright nipa roof of a house in the suburb of Tondo. Suddenly, the *dindines*, or partitions made of *saji*, or woven bamboo, flew off, leaving only the framework of the house. The family living in the house was caught unawares. Rain and wind lashed at their faces. They were exposed to the fury of the wind. A twenty-four-year-old *indio* jumped out into the middle of the street, despair written on his face. Others squatted on the ground, waiting patiently for the storm to end. Others did the same with equal calmness.

Afterwards, each one managed to find a refuge in the houses of friends, and when the hurricane ended, they began to rebuild their houses with *bejuco* and bamboo, which are useful and practical materials.

II

Three days after the storm, a light banca[1] came sailing rapidly down the beautiful Pasig River.

Two shirtless Tagalog rowers wearing wide palm-leaf hats, their tanned skin glowing like varnish under the rays of the ardent Phoebus, were speedily stirring the water with a pole that served as a rudder so their canoe could glide rapidly on the big river.

The banca had a *cayan,* a tent made of woven bamboo that protects the center part from the sun and the rain. It was occupied by some indios whose European clothes showed that they were students. Indios generally prefer to wear European clothes even if they feel warm in them because they want to feel *chichiricos.*[2] This, in spite of the fact that their native attire is cool and loose and well-suited for that country.

Everyone urged the rowers to go fast. The current was favorable and, together with the natural lightness of the banca, made sailing easier than on a steamboat. The compact mass of grass, called *quiapos,* which the river constantly drags along in great quantities, was easily cleared away from the path of the banca.

We already know one of the passengers. He was the one who had thrown himself into the street from the slightly elevated floor of his bamboo house in Tondo when the baguio blew away its roof and walls. He was called Juancho Alcira. Speaking in Tagalog, he said to his companions on the boat: "I cannot wait to see my town. If it is true that the last baguio has destroyed my house and flooded my fields, making it impossible to plant for some years, I am ruined, because the loss of my resources will force me to discontinue my studies at Santo Tomás."

---

[1] A narrow and long canoe made of one piece of wood.
[2] Well-dressed.

"Well, you can be sure of it," someone answered. "My family was left in the most abject misery, that is why I went back to Sta. Cruz when my classes had barely started."

"I, as you know, come from Tayabas," added another, who was tall and had an expressive face. "I am returning to my province for the same reason. The storm on 25 October will never be forgotten by our people in Laguna and Tayabas, the provinces devastated by its accursed fury. It was simply horrible, my father said. The rivers overflowed, towns were flooded, crops were destroyed and many kinds of livestock were killed. Our people were devastated by the cruel hurricane and the heavy rainfall. Their houses could not shelter them against the inclement weather because they were demolished by the baguio."

"What a horrible calamity!"

"Fortunately," said the second person who had spoken earlier, "the government always tries to save the people from such calamities, and has initiated a drive all over the archipelago to remedy these evils as much as possible. Philanthropy being a distinctive characteristic of the inhabitants of the Philippines, Peninsulares and the natives as well, you can be sure that in a short time a large amount was collected."[3]

The banca continued on its way and the beautiful vegetation on both sides of the Pasig made the wide river look enchanting. Now and then a crowded barrio of nipa huts would appear, perched on bamboo poles stuck in the water and shaded artfully by the long leaves of banana plants.

Some native women in the primitive attire of Eve, with shiny black unbraided tresses, were bathing, continuously pouring water over their heads with their *tabo*.[4] They prefer this way of bathing to full immersion.

---

[3] The drive raised over 10,000 duros.
[4] The concave part of the second covering of the coconut.

Others, dressed in the same cool manner, were doing the laundry, beating the clothes with a club to clean them. It is the club and not their hands that whitens the clothes.

In the Philippines, the people know how to wash well and iron with a device they call a clothes press, similar to what is known in Europe as a steam press. They press the clothes thoroughly, using wet rice flour instead of starch to moisten the clothes.

In other places, carabaos were bathing. These animals come from a species of buffalo; they are quiet, do heavy work, and possess unusual strength. But the problem is that they have to refresh themselves continuously during the hot hours so that the heat will not exhaust them. When allowed to rest, they look for the muddy places where they happily soak themselves, enjoying a mudbath with only their long horns sticking out.

On the other side of the river opposite where our students were going, there were other boats full of *banga*, or pots with a special shape. They are used to carry water and for other purposes. The other boats were long and narrow and were loaded with *zacate*, grass for feeding the horses. Many more carried different kinds of fruits. Other passengers on the river came from the towns, bringing merchandise to sell or simply going to Manila for one reason or another.

The boats passed the town of Pasig after which the river was named because it bathes the town as it enters the big Laguna de Bay, the source of the river and the namesake of the province of Laguna. The students who were guiding the boat on which they sailed separated when they reached the province, each one going to his respective town.

III

Laguna is reputed to be one of the best provinces in the Philippine archipelago because of its proximity to the capital, its beautiful river frequently used for travel to Manila, its luxuriant vegetation, its magnificent lake, its thermal waters, the great Bototan Waterfall, the tall mountains of Banajao and Maquiling, and its rich natural resources.

Laguna is also famous for its coconut oil, which is sold all over the country and abroad in significant quantities. It also produces delicious *lanzones* and *chicos-mamey,* fruits which the Manileños value highly and pay well to savor.

On Mount Banajao, the highest mountain in the country, standing almost two thousand feet above sea level, there is a volcano that was once active. Its crater, one league in diameter, is full of trees, and at its bottom is a winding river.

Mount Maquiling is very rich in thermal waters with many invaluable health-giving properties. In the place called Maynit there are baths where the water varies in temperature, from boiling and lukewarm, to cold and freezing.

Bacon Spring is noticeably peculiar because its waters become rough and agitated with noise, rising or falling according to the intensity of the disturbance.

The waters of Bombongan in the town of Pagsanjan are located in a lovely place, where tall bamboos provide shade and coolness. They are very effective for treating skin diseases. Springs with medicinal waters can also be found in other provinces.

The student Juancho Alcira was from the town of Majaijai, in the province of Laguna. When he arrived in his hometown, he saw that the destruction to his properties, as described to him, paled in comparison with the reality.

Seeing himself homeless, he walked to the great Bototan Falls situated northwest of Majaijai. He resolved to end his life by throwing himself from where the water majestically flowed down from a height of 500 feet, offering the most astonishing view imaginable.

Yet the sight of the lovely waterfall, whose foamy waters assumed many different colors when struck by the rays of the sun, distracted Alcira from the terrifying thoughts that had led him there. When the first moment of depression had passed, he returned to his town, determined to earn his living as best he could.

Shortly after, he obtained a profitable occupation. Juancho was a *filósofo*. That is the term provincial people use to describe a native who, after studying for some years at the University of Santo Tomás, returns to his hometown, feeling important like a great scholar. Such characters dress in European style and cut their hair in the romantic fashion; they look at their boots when walking and speak in a pompous way although unable to rid themselves of the habit of pronouncing F as P and vice-versa. In this manner, they earn a reputation and attract attention in their hometowns.

The filósofo in the Philippines is similar to the pedant in Spain.

If they fail to finish their studies, which happens frequently, and if their finances prevent them from continuing to reside in Manila, they end up occupying the position of clerk of court or *directorcillo* of the tribunal in the town.

Juancho Alcira ended up as one.

The *Pedáneo* of a town in La Laguna, whose name we will not reveal because the events we will narrate are too recent, gave him that position. Juancho, satisfied with such an honor, decided to celebrate it with a *catapusan,* or a dance, in the tribunal. This is how everything, even death, is solemnized in the Philippines.

The people who attended the dance were pleased with the *gaudeamus*, or merrymaking, telling themselves that anybody who inaugurates his office so generously cannot be bad.

IV

The municipal government in the Philippines differs greatly from that of Spain. Some provinces, like the majority of those in Luzon, are governed by educated elderly *alcaldes* who administer the civil government and serve at the same time as judges of the Courts of First Instance, assistant directors of Finance in the local branches, collectors of tobacco in the provinces where these plants are harvested, administrators of the post offices, military commanders, and chairmen of the Boards of Auctions and Primary Education.

Other provinces like those of the Visayas and Mindanao are governed by *politico-militares*, or governors who belong to the Army and Navy. They also hold positions identical to those of the alcaldes, with the difference that in these provinces there are judges for the administration of justice while in those of Luzon the governors are also the judges, together with an educated adviser who is the judge in the nearest province. In places where there are no administrators of public finance, they are also the finance officers.

In the towns the *gobernadorcillos* govern and become similar to the alcaldes and municipal judges of Spain because they perform simultaneously the functions of the judges and clerks with specific responsibilities. In the collection of tobacco, they are also the heads of the branch offices.

But even when the gobernadorcillos receive a certain percentage of the collection, or are given a gratuity for the tobacco and some other privileges, the total amount they receive is so meager that their position is regarded as somewhat honorific.

The indios, nevertheless, seek this position with amazing determination. Their ambition is to be important and rich. Almost all attain a comfortable state after only two years as gobernadorcillo. One is elected to the office by a committee, under the chairmanship of the chief of the province and composed of twelve *principales* of the town. Six of these principales are former gobernadorcillos and *cabezas de barangay*, while the other six are selected from among the present cabezas. The gobernadorcillo also votes in the election.

The person who obtains the most votes is recommended to the governor-general, followed by the second. The present pedáneo, or municipal judge, is the third so recommended.

The governor-general then nominates one of three candidates, with due consideration to the report of the election chairman.

As assistants to the gobernadorcillo, several lieutenants and constables are elected in proportion to the size of the neighborhood.

The cabezas de barangay are heads of fifty families from whom each collects the taxes, which are turned over to the offices of the Hacienda and the Gobierno.

The barangay, instituted before the conquest, is very useful.

The present and former cabezas, together with the gobernadorcillo and the *capitanes pasados,* as the former capitanes are called, form part of the *principalía.* Their usual attire is a black jacket, European-style pants, a bowler hat, and colored slippers. Many use patent leather boots. The shirt is short and worn over the pants. The gobernadorcillo carries a cane with tassels; the lieutenants, a stick. For important ceremonies, they dress in formal attire, a dress coat and top hat, clothes passed on from father to son.

When the gobernadorcillo assumes office, there is a *fiestahan,* or a big feast in the town. Everybody eats, drinks, smokes, and enjoys at the expense of the municipality.

In the tribunal, he occupies a huge armchair made two centuries before, showing the coat of arms of Castilla covered with fanciful designs.

On holidays, the gobernadorcillo goes to church. The principalía and the *cuadrilleros* form two rows in front of him while a band precedes them. He occupies a seat in the church more important than those of the principales, who occupy only benches of honor.

After the Mass, musicians play a loud *paso doble* while the officials return to the tribunal where they hold a meeting under the gobernadorcillo's chairmanship to discuss with the cabezas the public works scheduled for the week.

In many towns, the taxpayers listen to the orders communicated to them by the cabezas themselves after the Mass. The people have come to recognize the sound of drumbeats that summon them to the tribunal.

When the gobernadorcillo is active or is in a bad mood, the people fear and respect him a lot. But if he is irresolute, they become irresponsible and abusive. When he leaves his office, a constable precedes him, carrying the staff of authority.

Since the majority of the pedáneos do not speak Spanish, they are authorized to appoint *directorcillos*, who receive a very low salary.

The directorcillo prepares the draft of the judicial proceedings and the answers to the orders of the local authorities; he serves as interpreter of the pedáneo when the latter has to speak with Europeans, and exercises great influence in all matters. Consequently, it is quite a lucrative position. Sometimes he uses his influence to commit abuses. But the gobernadorcillo will tolerate him rather than be deprived of his services because there are towns where he will not find a substitute who speaks Spanish.

V

Advised on the manner in which the towns of those islands are governed, one will understand the importance and meaning of the position given to Juancho Alcira.

Vanity is one of the passions that dominate the indios in positions of authority. And, if we consider what we have said about the student filósofos and remember that Juancho was a student, one has an idea of how greatly presumptuous the new directorcillo would be to his province mates.

The old *manguinones*, or caciques of the town, were whispering about Juancho's conceit simply because he did not have the courtesy to ask their advice about the difficult problems that began to surface. Juancho's unexpected rise and his rapid prosperity awakened the envy and antagonism of many people.

Before Juancho came, some *abogadillos* were exploiting the indios' propensity to indulge in litigations, extracting money, livestock, and even land from them in exchange for the abogadillos' written work.

Juancho greatly reduced the clients of those pettifogging lawyers by introducing himself as an abogadillo. The quarreling persons would go to him, believing that his position was more important than the circumstances on which the written work should be based. Thus, the *pica-pleitos*, or pettifogging lawyers, declared war on him.

These abogadillos are a plague that causes more damage in the provinces than the locusts. Their greed is such that instead of advising their clients to desist from pursuing unreasonable legal cases, they encourage the complainant to proceed, thus leading the clients to their ruin.

Those so-called abogadillos, of course, have had no formal law studies but are filósofos like the ones we have known. They study a few years at Santo Tomás without learning anything useful. There are, of course, honorable ones, but they are more of an exception.

We should point out that while it is true that the native Filipinos have great facility in imitating everything, their higher intellectual capacity is limited. They are brilliant in music and have a propensity for the other branches of the arts. If they were more industrious and had instructors to guide their work, they could certainly produce valuable works of art. On the other hand, they do not accomplish much in the study of the sciences, which requires a conscientious exercise of the higher faculties of the soul. They are fonder of reading and writing. Rarely can one find an indio who is illiterate, even in the most backward provinces.

As for Juancho, we can honestly say that few directorcillos, and there are daring ones, can equal his cunning in enticing away the clients who have pending cases in the tribunal. He handled everything so well as abogadillo that soon he made enough money to buy a good house made of wood.

But he had annoyed so many that the *sementereros*, or farmers, and some industrialists finally realized that they were being abused, and they plotted to get him to leave the town.

One night, Juancho's enemies gathered together and the leader of the group, a naughty abogadillo, pointed out the advantage of getting rid of Juancho. The best way to do it, he said, would be for all of them to go to Juancho's house and force him to leave the province right away and never to return. If he resisted, they would kill him.

During the meeting, nipa wine, as intended, flowed profusely, overexciting the plotters who applauded the idea of the abogadillo.

Armed with bolos and spears, the native sementereros went in a mad rush to Juancho's house. Upon seeing them and guessing their intentions, he mounted a horse and escaped at full gallop. Some of the more hotheaded pursued him without catching him. Others, drunk as they were, set fire to his house, which burned immediately like a tinder box.

The winds were very strong and in a moment, the fire spread rapidly to the surrounding houses. Since the houses in provincial towns are mostly made of wood and bamboo, or bamboo and nipa or cogon, which are very inflammable, the fire quickly grew uncontrollable. Sparks and pieces of burning bamboo were jumping about like artificial rockets, carried farther by the wind as it spread the fire to as far as 100 meters away. In a short time, the whole town was on fire.

Alarmed by the sound of the drums calling all the townspeople while church bells were announcing the calamity, the inhabitants began to arrive at the scene in large numbers. They brought some *bombones*, or bamboo tubes, filled with water. Some brought metal hooks and threw them up on the houses to unroof them and bring down the *harigues*, or wooden posts, in order to isolate the fire.

The owners of the houses near those that had caught fire were covering the roofs of their houses with moistened blankets or were sprinkling them with the water from clay jars, placed outside their houses in case of fire. The sparks were immediately extinguished as they fell on the wet blankets.

The women were crying and pulling their hair as they rushed out to the street, bearing their clothes and furniture. There was terrible confusion. Everybody was shouting but no one could be understood.

Some houses fell and smothered the blaze. Eventually the fire was placed under control, but 500 families were now homeless. The voracious fire had reduced their homes to ashes in less than four hours.

This kind of calamity happens frequently in the Philippines, but the indios accept it with resignation. When their house has turned to ashes, they stoically exclaim, "That was my fate."

Then they go to the mountains to cut down trees for wood, and with bamboo, bejuco or rattan, and nipa, they build another house. But it does not take long for the new house to suffer the same fate. Wherever there is a *tinjoi*, a kind of bamboo lamp, the slightest gust of wind carries the flame to other houses constructed in the same way, causing a fire.

The mutiny against the directorcillo cost the people more than what the plotters had bargained for. This gave rise to a great deal of talk.

VI

While the town was burning, Juancho realized the danger he was exposed to, and he made his horse go faster. He had no desire to return to the province of La Laguna. He did not consider himself safe until he entered the jurisdiction of the neighboring province of Tayabas.

The pedáneo of an interior town was his relative and Juancho went to ask him for help. The pedáneo promised to help him and asked him to stay in his house while awaiting the results of what had happened in La Laguna.

Having achieved their purpose, which was to drive him away from the town at all costs, the mutineers did not think of him anymore.

His relative wanted Juancho to stay in the town and fill the vacant post of lieutenant of the cuadrilleros. The pedáneo proposed to the principales that they nominate Juancho for the job and he was thus appointed by the chief of the province.

Each town in the Philippines has a number of cuadrilleros in proportion to the community. They serve for three years and their only benefit is an exemption from paying the *tributos* and the *polos*. The tributo is the contribution of the indios and mestizos to help with the government's maintenance. The polo is the duty to work for forty days in local projects.

The cuadrilleros are armed with old rifles and lances. They serve as policemen, guards of the tribunal, the jail, and the *Casa real,* or government. They also go after criminals.

Juancho had never handled a rifle in all his life, but he tried to train himself and every afternoon he went out to drill with his troops, proud of his martial stance.

Tayabas is a mountainous province with thick, rich forests, ideal for the construction of ships. The natives prepare excellent wood for this purpose. The forests also have abundant animals for hunting.

Many *tulisanes,* as they call the bandits there, live in the forests of Tayabas. From their inaccessible hideouts, they go down to the towns and the roads to kill and steal.

It is almost impossible and extremely dangerous to catch these bandits. Since they know the land like the palms of their hands, they kill without fear those who try to harass them. People are afraid of them and there have been cases of sacking and burning of entire towns by bands of tulisanes.

When Juancho was designated lieutenant of cuadrilleros, one of these bands was roaming in the nearby towns. The gobernadorcillo ordered Juancho and his men to pursue them.

He assembled his cuadrilleros, and the former student-turned-general of that brave army took the road to the forest where the bandits had their camp.

His spies told him where the bandits were. Brave and determined, he led his men into the depths of the forest.

Near a spring winding around the massive trees of the thick forest, they saw a cogon hut and several saddled horses. Although it was noon, the forest was dark because the interlocking leaves of the trees formed a thick cover that sunlight could never penetrate.

Juancho ordered his men to surround the house.

The tulisanes were alerted by the neighing of a horse. Instantly, the bandits grabbed their guns and fired, wounding two of Juancho's men and killing another.

Juancho, ignoring the bullets, approached the hut and set it on fire; the flames shot up, illuminating the forest, while two bandits tried to escape being burned to a crisp. Taking advantage of the confusion, the cuadrilleros assaulted the bandits and victory was almost theirs when they were suddenly attacked from the rear. A bigger band of tulisanes came to the aid of the bandits Juancho was fighting. The cuadrilleros realized the odds were against them. Asked to surrender, the cuadrilleros answered that they preferred to die in battle. The fight resumed with renewed fury on both sides.

Almost all the cuadrilleros were wounded. Their opponents, greater in number, surrounded them and those who resisted were quickly captured. Five tulisanes died while eight were wounded. The cuadrilleros suffered six casualties.

Juancho had fought bravely. The indios, once they decide to fight, ignore death.

Some tulisanes felt that the cuadrilleros should be executed, but their leader ordered that they be taken to their chief, who was busy elsewhere and did not come to fight.

They went deeper into the forest and after half an hour they stopped.

The houses and the cultivated land revealed that it was the hideout of the criminals. Shortly after, their chief arrived with his followers.

When Juancho and the chief saw each other, they each let out a loud cry of surprise. Then they hugged each other, leaving the tulisanes and the cuadrilleros stupefied.

The chief bandit was none other than the student who had traveled with Juancho on the boat from Manila to La Laguna after the horrible storm of 25 October. Among his men he was known as Radjak.

Juancho narrated to his old comrade the incidents that led to his position as lieutenant of cuadrilleros in a town of his province. Radjak, after listening to him, said,

"My life has been even more agitated. I arrived in my native land and the condition of my house horrified me. Members of my family were dying one by one. I was a directorcillo like you. Nevertheless, since I was a good adviser to the pedáneo, I provoked the hatred of everyone so they decided to do away with me. They falsified documents in the tribunal, took out some and substituted others. You are, of course, aware of the corruption prevailing in this kind of office. My enemies accused me of those offenses and the gobernadorcillo, who had been won over by them, confirmed their accusations.

"I was imprisoned by the court while the charges were being substantiated. There was lack of evidence but I was helpless against the slanderers. So, I decided to avenge myself but the love I had for the most beautiful lady in my town distracted me. She reciprocated my love but her parents were opposed. I took her away but then my enemies connived and she disappeared from the house where she was staying. Up to now, I have not found out where they have taken her.

"I was blinded by fury and could not calm down in order to file a case against those who were abusing their position. I decided instead to go after those who were mostly to blame.

"My dagger left two of them dead. From then on it was impossible for me to remain in my province. I escaped to these forests, where I have been staying for three months as the leader of fifty men. I have declared war unto death on all my province mates. And the different encounters where I showed my savage fury endeared me to our chief. He died from a wound in one encounter with the troops and at his suggestion I was elected to take his place.

"These are the important events that happened since we last met. Now, even if you are my prisoner, we will eat together. My boys will take care of your subordinates."

The tulisanes led the cuadrilleros to their huts to feed them after attending to their wounds. Radjak invited his friend Juancho to his quarters.

VII

Radjak's servants placed a mat on the *saji*, or floor. Aside from the indispensable rice, they served different dishes of *gulay*, or vegetables, fish, salt, and green mangoes with vinegar, which the indios eat as appetizer.

Radjak and Juancho sat down and started to eat heartily.

"I admire you," said Juancho to Radjak in Tagalog, "for having been able to accustom yourself to this kind of life, after the life we led in Manila."

"Don't be surprised. My life is delightful. If the woman I loved so much were at my side, I would spend the rest of my days enjoying the charms of these virgin forests."

Radjak continued: "There are still places here where no man has ever set foot; streams of clear and healthy water where only I can drink, and mountains where one can breathe fresh air perfumed by the smell of the *caviqui, champaca*, and *romero* plants. From these high mountains, one can discover beautiful views never before seen by anyone else.

"Many trees and different kinds of root crops provide me with delicious dishes. If I want to eat fowl, I hunt them. Here, wood pigeons and sandpipers abound, and for good meats, I have wild boar and deer. I am the king of these forests and my soldiers adore me. When I want to entertain myself, I walk out into the roads and the small pathways. If I wish to rest, I lie under the pleasant shade of a tree where the gentle and delightful breeze constantly tempers the heat. Believe me, life in the woods is preferable to that in the towns."

"You say that so solemnly that it almost makes me want to go back to the mountains," Juancho said.

"Well, in order to convince you, stay with me for some time. Then, you decide."

"You are right. These places are beautiful, no doubt, but I find life in the populated areas less boring."

"For those who only look for material things, you are perfectly right, but not for those who wish for spiritual upliftment."

"Or dreamers, like you."

"As you wish. But since I have a high regard for you, I want to offer you a way of making your present life of suffering and work one of comfort and joy. Instead of being a lieutenant of cuadrilleros, which will not make you rich, why not be my lieutenant?"

"What, become a tulisan? That's not such a bad idea," answered Juancho, laughing at his friend's proposal.

"It is the fastest way to make a fortune."

"And also to die."

"Bah! That kind of death is like any other."

"What will they say of me?"

"That you are not the first cuadrillero who has done so."

"Now you are tempting me. But you can't make me bite."

"Well, it's your loss."

"We better take a siesta. I am exhausted."

"There is your pillow and mat."

"I will consult my pillow about the advantages of your job offer."

"Stop worrying and accept. It won't be hard for you."

In the afternoon, they went out together to wander around the forest. Radjak insisted on showing Juancho the advantages of staying with him.

Juancho still had his doubts, but the chief of the tulisanes was so insistent that he achieved his objective. When Juancho accepted, Radjak hugged him effusively.

The cuadrilleros had been fraternizing with the tulisanes during the meal. Due to the apathy or indifference that is characteristic of the indio, they offered no objections to Juancho's decision.

Radjak ordered some jars of wine to celebrate the company of the new comrades. They all drank wine from the tabo, sang, danced and enjoyed themselves until they were exhausted and woke up late the next day.

"Now, friends," said Radjak as he gathered his men to give each of them their duties, "you already know my plan. He who carries it out well will be compensated. For those who distinguish themselves and are wounded, I will double the reward. He who shows cowardice will be executed."

Radjak formed two bands. He ordered them to go to certain places that he pointed out. With his men, he left for Tayabas. When night fell, they were near the town where Radjak was born.

They waited until everything was silent before entering the town. Radjak ordered them to set fire to a house. When it started to burn, the neighbors began to shout. The church bells rang and all the guards of the tribunal and the gobernadorcillo ran towards the burning house. Moments later, the gobernadorcillo was informed that the bandits had invaded the town from the opposite side. The drum sounded the alarm and they fled from the fire started by the tulisanes, who were feared more than the fire itself.

The townsfolk came, armed with bolos, spears, and shotguns. A bloody fight ensued. The bandits resisted for a time, but since their enemies outnumbered them, they retreated, taking with them the guns that were in the tribunal. They sowed terror and death wherever they passed.

The men from the town tried to pursue them but when the tulisanes entered the forest, no one dared to follow them there.

The fire was finally put out.

Radjak was happy over the alarm they had caused as he had no other motive but to disturb his province mates.

When they arrived at their hideout in the forest, they slaughtered animals and drank much wine to celebrate their luck in the fight. Only a few of the bandits were wounded.

"Day after tomorrow," said Rajak to his men, "we will hunt deer. You will see how we will enjoy ourselves, Juancho."

"I would like that," Juancho answered.

The indios used to hunt deer at night. The tulisanes, following this custom, went deep into the mountains at night on the day agreed upon. They made bonfires in several places and positioned themselves, armed with lassoes and enormous arrows of wild palms. They howled ferociously in order to make the deer come out. Whenever a deer appeared, which they could tell from the sound it made when moving through the grass or between the high cogon fields, the tulisanes would skillfully shoot the arrow into the air. Hit by the arrow falling perpendicularly, the deer would then give out a strident howl. The hunters would approach the deer from behind and catch it. Many of these animals would die instantly. Others were caught alive. Their wounds were treated and later on the deer would be sold. The tulisanes caught six that provided them with a delicious meal. To preserve the meat, the indios usually cut them into thin slices and dry them under the sun. Meat prepared this way is called *tapa*, or dried venison, and is very much in demand. The Chinese buy the tendons of the animal when they are dry, and make glue out of them.

The natives are great enthusiasts of hunting. It is one of their main sources of livelihood and provides them with food. They also hunt for commercial purposes. They are very competent hunters.

Although they also use firearms, they usually hunt with bow and arrow. They use arrows that are bigger than the ordinary arrow.

Radjak told Juancho that he frequently went hunting in that area.

VIII

The tulisanes' attack on Radjak's town and the delay of the cuadrilleros' return to their quarters made their pedáneo think they had been killed by the bandits. This thought grieved him.

When the facts were communicated to the head of the Guardia Civil of that district, a division went in search of the wrongdoers, backed by cuadrilleros and some men of the town who were eager to avenge the killing of their relatives.

Radjak knew this through his spies. But far from fleeing, he waited until he felt confident of defeating them.

The band he headed consisted of hardened men. They were numerous and well-armed, and had the advantage of knowing the terrain well.

The chief of the Guardia Civil divided his force into three sections consisting of cuadrilleros and civilian province mates. He explained how they would attack, designating the place where they should meet according to the evidence he had and where the tulisanes were staying. The plan was well conceived because it took into account the different places occupied by the tulisanes.

Shortly after sighting each other, both sides immediately opened fire with their rifles. The civilians, armed with arrows, seldom missed their mark. The guards fought bravely. One of the sections that reached the right side started its attack, protected by the tree trunks, while the civilians who had climbed trees wounded the bandits with impunity, shooting arrows at them.

Radjak became desperate. He did not expect the opposing force to be so numerous. His confidence had made him neglect to prepare better means of defense.

Protected in their barricades, however, the tulisanes defended themselves well. Juancho and his men fought with their faces painted so that they would not be recognized.

The fight went on for a long time. The guards were not making much progress and their chief was hampered by the delay of the third column, which should have been the first to arrive. It was still nowhere in sight.

Radjak, upon seeing that the guards up front were yielding their ground, moved forward, followed by his best riflemen, most of them escaped convicts and army deserters who fought like wild animals. They attacked so fiercely that those who were helping the guards fled. The guards, however, were determined to die at their posts.

The guards would have had a hard time if the third column did not arrive, having lost its way in the forest the whole morning. Finally the shots were heard. Guided by the sounds, the column arrived without being noticed. The reinforcing guards fired a volley of shots, hitting the tulisanes almost in their very faces. Rajak and five of his men were killed instantly.

The guards, reinforced and recovering their spirits, threw themselves on the bandits, who did not know in which direction to flee, seeing themselves attacked on three sides simultaneously.

Juancho assembled as many of his men as he could gather and made a supreme effort to turn the tide in his favor, or to avenge, at least, the death of his friend, but his efforts were in vain. The tulisanes were discouraged by the death of their chief. The signal to withdraw was given and was followed in an orderly fashion. They kept their pursuers at bay by firing while entering the forest, hidden by the cogon plants and the bushes.

The guards were not familiar with the topography of the forest and to avoid more casualties, they withdrew, contented with the victory they had attained.

The exchange of fire was very important because it resulted in the death of the feared bandit who was terrorizing that area.

The people of Tayabas greeted the guards on their return as conquerors. Their bravery was rewarded later.

Meanwhile, Juancho and the bandits who followed him stopped at a secure place.

Some of the wounded were cured with oil of the *tagulaguay*, which heals wounds marvelously, while the others were treated with very effective herbs known only to them.

Afterwards, they sadly dedicated a memorial to their dead chief and moved to elect his successor. They instantly acclaimed

Juancho as their captain in consideration of his proven bravery and his friendship with Radjak.

The tulisanes admired Juancho. They believed that he had an *anting-anting,* because he had never been wounded in any battle. The indios have a superstition that there are persons who cannot be wounded by bullets or endangered in any way if they wear on their bodies a kind of amulet called anting-anting. The person believed to possess this talisman inspires greatest respect. Juancho, according to them, was saved from many dangers without being wounded because he had an anting-anting. This belief influenced them to elect Juancho unanimously as their chief.

After thanking them, Juancho said, "Our presence in these places is dangerous because the guards know where we are. If they attack us again, we will be defeated. Let us leave and return at a more opportune time to avenge the unfortunate Radjak."

"We are ready to go wherever you send us," they all answered.

"Well, then, let us go to the mountains of Batangas."

"To Batangas!" they shouted boisterously.

They started the trek to Batangas, passing through isolated paths known only to them, gathering edible root crops along the way, especially a plant with red leaves called *baino* and another called *alibamban.*

They walked a long distance; then they stopped to eat their frugal meal. They needed to light a fire and so they cut the branches from a resinous tree to build a fire. Rubbing two sticks together, they produced the flame. They burned tree trunks, which blazed like torches.

Lacking utensils, they cooked their food in a thick bamboo cane half a meter in diameter and cut down to 6 inches in height from one of its nodes. They obtained water, which was scarce, by extracting it from some hard leaves shaped like small cups that close when filled with any liquid. This rare plant, which the indios call *nepentes,* always keeps the water inside it pure and fresh, giving much-need relief to thirsty travelers.

The bandits' appetites were satisfied and as the heat was suffocating, they lay under a tree and soon fell asleep.

IX

Light white clouds started covering the skies and soon the brilliance of the lightning and the exploding thunder announced the approach of a storm in the dry season. These storms are dangerous and frequent in tropical climates. Lightning soon lit up the place, followed by the deafening sound of thunder.

The tulisanes were startled by the noise as the ground continued to tremble. The dark and overpowering sky frightened them. There was another flash of lightning and three sparks fell on the trees around them, setting them on fire immediately. The strong smell of sulphur was beginning to suffocate them.

Two more sparks sank into a mountain nearby, producing a terrible sound. Three of the tulisanes fainted and fell to the ground.

Juancho encouraged his frightened companions not to be afraid. Reminding them of the danger they were in, he ordered them to use their rifles to carry their unconscious companions and to leave hurriedly. At that very moment, another electric spark split into two the massive tree under which they had sheltered themselves. The thick branches started to burn.

Many more sparks fell on different places. The forest fire, fanned by a strong wind, was rapidly spreading wildly from tree to tree like a huge bonfire.

The tulisanes found themselves trapped, surrounded on all sides by the flames. The heat singed their skin. Their throats started to dry up and the lack of water tormented them. Some wild carabaos ran past them, howling horrendously as they ran.

Flocks of deer fled in all directions, utterly terrified. The crackling sound of the dry tree trunks as they burned, mixed with the continuous roar of the thunder, hurt their ears. But the sparks were falling incessantly. It was a virtual rain of fire. The electricity charging the atmosphere made breathing difficult while the constant lightning flashes blinded them. The tulisanes thought it was the end for them.

Juancho ordered them to leave the unconscious men behind because it was too tiring to carry them. He told his men, "We must break through the fire barrier surrounding us before we are trapped. Move on, let each one save himself."

Some were greatly discouraged and did not try to flee.

The others, led by Juancho, made a mad dash for the place where the flames were less intense, jumping over the cliffs and injuring their feet. Still, the sparks hit them and tree trunks uprooted by the lightning hampered their escape.

Some tulisanes succumbed to lack of air before reaching safety. Others, worn out with fatigue, consumed with thirst and breathing hot air, stopped running and waited with indifference for death.

Only Juancho, gripped by a frenzied zeal, ran frantically, jumping over ravines until he reached the last row of trees. As he crossed the fire barrier, his clothes caught fire. He spotted a lake in a gully, jumped in and drank the water avidly, experiencing a moment of joy as he felt its fresh touch after being almost burned to death.

His jump, however, produced a slight concussion. When he got out of the lake, he could hardly support himself. He felt bruises all over his body, as well as burns which, even if slight, made him suffer horribly.

The lake was separated from the forest by a wide fissure, and after walking a short distance he felt he was out of danger.

He searched for root crops that have the power to cure burns and after pounding them, he applied them to his whole body. He lay on the grass. The next day, he woke up cured.

He explored the terrain and he knew that he was in Batangas. He stayed there for two days but none of his companions appeared.

Some had perished, asphyxiated by the forest fire, while others had been devoured by the flames. A long row of trees had been razed to the ground. The fire extinguished itself only after a few days. Storms like the ones we have described occur very often in the thick Philippine forests, which are covered with astonishing vegetation.

At times these storms would lash the coasts. On 29 May 1873, Manila experienced one storm that lasted for 70 minutes. One continuous lightning flash and roll of thunder during the storm was enough to release forty sparks that fell on the city. In the bay, innumerable electric sparks broke out, some of which struck the ships anchored there. It was the most significant and impressive phenomenon that we had ever witnessed. Manila agonized painfully for an hour. Some buildings were considerably damaged, but fortunately, there were no personal tragedies.

X

The province of Batangas is a good example of how industry can make the people rich.

The Batangueños are, perhaps, the most industrious farmers in the Philippines. Their industry is often rewarded by abundant harvests and huge profits.

Annually, they harvest 100,000 *picos* [5] of coffee and 150,000 picos of sugar. Both products are of the best quality and are ex-

---

[5] The pico is 63.261 kilograms.

ported for huge profits. The 146,580 heads of cattle there are valued at P1,692,000. Textiles manufactured in increasing quantities sell at a good price in Manila and the neighboring provinces. They are very much in demand because of their durability. Furthermore, cacao, rice, wheat, corn, and cotton are harvested. The province also produces lumber of good quality.

Each year in Batangas there is a fair or an exhibit of agricultural and industrial products and cattle. The number of participants in these fairs is increasing. Prizes are awarded to those who display the best products or animals.

The population is more than 325 thousand.

Batangas has very healthy mineral water, especially from the Punta Azufre Spring, as well as excellent ports.

Such is the province in whose mountains the sorrowful Juancho found himself wandering. He had reason to be sad because the death of Radjak had deprived him of a loving friend. Only days before, he was surrounded by happy companions and was the chief of a band of brave men. Now, he could not find even one person to console him. He recalled the tragic deaths of his friends and the dangers he had barely escaped from. Surprised to find himself alive, he felt that he had been saved by something supernatural.

As Juancho walked towards a mountain not knowing what to do, he came across a deep cave that had been formed by a big earthquake. He entered it and found on a *lancape*, or bamboo bed, clothes, arrows, tabo, and bamboo containers with some leftover food. He inspected the spacious cave but saw no one. It must be a shelter of the tulisanes, he thought. The sight of the clothes made him remember that he had to change his own which were totally torn and scorched.

He put on a shirt, a pair of pants, and a *salacot*,[6] and strapped a bolo around his waist. Looking like a peasant in this attire, he

---

[6] A hat with a wide brim and cone-shaped on top.

left the cave and continued to walk along Macolot Mountain. A receding column of white smoke made him recognize the place as the outskirts of Taal town. He then decided to visit the big volcano in the lake of Bongbong. Perhaps he was moving towards it for the same reason that had brought him to Bototan Falls. Soon he reached the famous Taal Volcano.

The lake is 25 leagues in perimeter and connects to the sea through the navigable river of Pansipit. In the center of the lake is a cone 400 meters high. In this cone can be found the crater of the volcano, which is 100 meters in circumference and 500 meters deep.

On 24 September 1716, there was a big explosion from the cone. It was a great spectacle! The ground trembled with a horrifying sound, producing a tall column of fire that reached a distance of 15 miles towards Macolot Mountain. Lava and ashes were spewed out simultaneously in big quantities. The lagoon turned black and its waters began to boil, emitting a very strong odor of sulphur.

The frightened people abandoned the towns and did not recover their peace of mind for a long time. The sight of that mountain spitting out lava, fire, and smoke from its enormous crater was their constant nightmare. The eruption lasted for three days. Another terrible eruption that the people of Taal still remember with fear left Batangas in mourning. It went on for eight days, destroying the towns of Taal, Lipa, Tanauan, and Salas. The lagoon overflowed and its scorching waters burned wide fields. The volcano's ashes, carried by the wind, covered the towns situated more than twenty-five leagues from Taal, and even reached the provinces of Manila, Pampanga, Bulacan, and Cavite. The noise of the eruption was heard in distant places and caused great fear among the people. Since then, the volcano has continued to spew out lava and smoke. No other volcano has been known to equal its terrifying eruptions.

The view of the volcano is impressive. On dark nights, especially, it is a fantastic sight of unequalled beauty.

In the Philippines, there are many volcanoes: The Mayon in Albay can be seen from afar and serves as a beacon to ships crossing the San Bernardino Strait. In the eruption of 24 October 1767, Mayon destroyed the towns of Camalig, Palangui, Guinubatan, Ligao, and Malinao. In 1814, its ashes fell on Manila, which is 78 leagues away, and it threw out so much water that several rivers were formed. Mayon Volcano has a big crater and a very high cone.

On the big island of Mindanao, there are many volcanoes, the most important of which is in Buheyan. In 1640, there was an eruption that made whole mountains jump.

On the little island of Camiguin, a part of Misamis, there was a volcanic eruption recently that spewed out rivers of lava. The volcanoes of other provinces are not so important.

XI

Juancho climbed Taal Volcano. He leaned over the crater and devoured the sight of the black hole that was letting out a hoarse and powerful sound. At that very moment, only a small column of smoke was coming out from the opposite side.

He stayed there, absorbed for about half an hour, when he heard a sound behind him. He straightened himself and with a swift movement that almost made him fall into the crater, he was able to save a young *india* from throwing herself into the wide crater in search of inevitable death. She had not seen Juancho, who was bending over the abyss when she came running to jump into the volcano. Although Juancho saved her from certain death, she said angrily, "Why are you holding me?"

"Because it is my duty. Suicide is a crime," Juancho answered philosophically.

"What is it to you since it is not you who is committing it?"

"It is very important not to deprive humanity of such a beautiful young girl like you," he answered gallantly while looking at the beautiful india.

"*Aba!*" she exclaimed, at a loss for words.

"Yes, you are pretty and should not die so young."

"The man whom I adored has died so I must die. Life bores me," said the india loftily.

"And who was that fortunate mortal?"

"He was a hero."

"Some soldier killed in the plain?"

"No, a tulisan."

"A tulisan! And his name?"

"Radjak."

"Radjak!" exclaimed Juancho, astonished.

"And why are you surprised?" asked the india, startled by his surprise.

"Radjak, poor Radjak," repeated Juancho, disturbed. "He died at my side. He was my best friend."

"Were you with him? Are you a tulisan? Oh, tell me everything!"

Juancho told her in detail what she wanted to know. When he finished, he asked the india, "And why did you want to commit suicide?"

"Because my life, as I already told you, is unbearable. My name is Lelay (short for Manuela). My parents, in order to stop me from marrying Radjak, dragged me away from the house where I was staying. They took me to Batangas and put me under the care of some relatives living in Taal, who were ordered to keep me a prisoner. A few days ago, when I learned that Radjak was in the vicinity, I escaped. I roamed the nearby mountains, suffering horribly. I found no one to guide me until I learned from some hunters about the unfortunate death of my lover. The hunters tried to take me to Taal but I fled while they were sleeping. Desperate, not knowing what to do nor where to go because I did not want to go home, and tired of such a painful existence, I thought of putting an end to my life when I saw the volcano. And I would have done it if you did not stop me."

"Well, that makes me doubly glad. Now you know that Radjak was like a brother to me. In the other world, he will be grateful that I will devote myself to looking after you. I was also thinking of throwing myself into the volcano, not knowing what to do in this life. But now, I have a sacred mission to fulfill and I will live happily."

"Oh, thank you," Lelay replied gratefully.

"We must not remain in this place where we could be found. Let us go back to the forest and there we shall decide what to do."

"Let us go! I trust you."

"You have nothing to fear."

Juancho and Lelay entered the forest together, traveling slowly, eating root crops, the fruits of the *alinsanay*[7] and the birds that Juancho hunted with a snare. They drank fresh water from the springs or the water from the nepenthes along the way. A few days later, they arrived at the same place in the Tayabas Mountain where Juancho found Radjak for the first time. During those days that they spent constantly in each other's pleasant company, love blossomed in the hearts of Juancho and Lelay.

The life of a tulisan, which he had accepted just to please Radjak, was beginning to weigh on him. To live all their lives in the mountains was not very pleasing to Lelay so they thought of going back to town.

---

[7] Wild banana.

One day, Juancho said, "Lelay, I feel such great affection for you that I believe it is love. If you have some feeling for me, I think we can get married so that I can look after you better. If Radjak were to know, he would approve of this decision."

"I accept your proposal, Juancho, because, like you, I believe that given the great friendship you had with him, it will not be an offense against his memory."

"That is true. Today, I will carry out an idea I had so we can return to your town. Stay here and I will go to see my relative, the gobernadorcillo. I will return right away."

"I'll be waiting impatiently. Come back soon."

Juancho left, arriving in the town at night. He went to the house of the pedáneo and he saw that the latter was alone.

When the judge saw him, he screamed in terror, thinking he was the ghost of the dead lieutenant. Then he made the sign of the cross.

"What is the meaning of this? Did you think I was dead, by any chance?" asked Juancho.

"The tulisanes did not kill you?"

"What a funny question! Don't you see that I am alive?"

"Oh, I am very glad," said the pedáneo, embracing Juancho.

"Tell me what happened because I mourned thinking you had died."

"I will tell you briefly. The tulisanes defeated us. Some of my cuadrilleros died fighting and the others were made prisoners. When we were taken to the mountains of Batangas, we remained in the custody of some tulisanes. Maybe they intended to keep us for ransom while the rest of the band stayed in the jurisdiction of the province. The guardia civil defeated the tulisanes while those who were saved returned to prison where we were being held. That same day there was a storm and I was able to escape. I was very fortunate because, as I learned later, everyone there perished in the forest fire caused by innumerable sparks. Now, for me to be able to return here, you must ask the parents of Lelay Rivas to give me their daughter in marriage."

"What a pity! But you are late. Lelay has not been seen in this town for perhaps a year already. I think they do not even know what has become of her."

"I know. Do as I tell you and she will appear."

"That means you have her?"

"I found her in the mountains."

"What a happy encounter! I will do what you ask. Wait for me here."

The gobernadorcillo left. An hour later, he returned, happy with the outcome of his errand.

"You got your wish," he said when he saw Juancho. "Her parents' only condition is that you bring her here as soon as possible. They want to embrace the daughter they have been mourning for."

"I will then go and tell her. I will see you when I return!"

"God be with you," said Juancho's relative.

"I will wait impatiently for you. Come back soon!"

After two days Juancho returned with Lelay. Some time later they were married in a sumptuous ceremony with the gobernadorcillo as the godfather.

For weeks there was only one topic of conversation in the whole community—the adventure of Juancho's imprisonment and how he met Lelay. This was so until new events made them forget the teniente de cuadrilleros who, with his wife and under the efficient protection of the pedáneo and his parents-in-law, lives happily in that town of Tayabas.

Juancho, finding himself happy, peaceful, and respected, blessed the baguio that had ruined him and made him give up his studies. He also blessed the mutiny against him that had obliged him to leave La Laguna and take refuge in Tayabas; his encounter with the tulisanes; and, above all, Taal Volcano, on the summit of which he had met the adorable young girl who became his wife. He also blessed the anting-anting that had saved him from so many dangers during that agitated period of his life.

There is indeed sense in the adage that something good comes out of a bad situation.

CHANG-CHUY'S UMBRELLA

I

The Chinese in the Philippine Islands have established some kind of colony. They do not rule the country but they exploit it.

They have been trading with the natives from ancient times. A large number of them settled in the archipelago shortly after the Spanish conquest.

Currently, there are around thirty thousand Chinese in the Islands, besides the illegal ones. There they practice all kinds of crafts and professions.

The government's main objective in allowing them to settle in the country at that time was for them to engage in agriculture. They are very smart and skillful workers, and were granted many exemptions to encourage them to become farmers. But very few cared to devote themselves to farming. Because of their indifference to such an important field of agriculture, the immigration of the *Sangleyes*[1] brought no benefits to the country. On the contrary, it caused lamentable harm.

Agriculture in the Philippines is a great source of wealth which the *indios*, because of their natural indolence, do not develop as they should. If only they were interested in working the fields, this country could be the richest in the world.

The Chinese almost exclusively engage in commerce, and being competent traders, they monopolize it to such an extent that all the natives of different races cannot compete with them. They can only watch sadly how the Chinese, veritable leeches of the archipelago, extract wealth from Philippine soil to give to their own country without giving any benefit to this country.

No one can go anywhere in Manila and its most remote towns without encountering a Sangley store. There are suburbs like Binondo, where there is hardly anyone who is not a Chinese. There are also streets like Rosario, San Fernando, San Jacinto, Santo Cristo, Nueva, and others giving one the impression of being in a city of the Celestial Empire. On Escolta Street, except for some European bazaars, the stores belong to the rich Chinese.

Not content with the capital, the Chinese have invaded the provinces where they all engage in illegal trading activities.

The Chinese arrive in Manila poor. But after a few years of industry, talent, and frugality, they acquire a fortune that they later enjoy in China. Many of them marry indias or mestizas and settle in the archipelago.

The mestizos in the Philippines are descended mostly from the Chinese. They are numerous, hardworking, and rich. They in-

---

[1] The name given to the Chinese in Manila. It means "travelling merchants."

herited from their Chinese forebears their strong interest in commerce and owe what they have attained to these forebears. Their relatives and ancestors are Chinese but this does not prevent them from clashing with those foreigners and even hating them, although not as much as the indios, who harbor a mortal hatred for the Sangleyes.

The Chinese in Manila have preserved their costumes, language, customs, and religion. Even if the Sangleyes are ordered to use the Spanish way of accounting, not all do so. They prefer to use a special counting device called *suampan*. They are excellent in arithmetic.

Those Chinese who married and settled in the country are generally well-off. They reside in beautiful houses and own carriages. They are decent and generous to persons they trust.

The poor Chinese huddle together as best as they can in miserable shacks that look like chicken coops.

In general, the Sangleyes dress neatly. Some of them wear extremely loose clothes.

They speak average Spanish and Tagalog, while those in the provinces speak the dialect of the place. There are well-known schools that introduce recent arrivals to both languages. Some serious Chinese teach the newcomers the most frequently used words they pronounce in such a strange manner that one cannot refrain from laughing. They pronounce the "r" as "l" and at the end of verbs they add the letter "o" or "e." Thus, the word *comprar*, they pronounce as *complalo; jugar, jugalo; quiere* is *quiele*.

They have a guild exclusively for themselves. The *gobernadorcillo* of the Chinese exercises authority over his countrymen and carries a cane with tassels.

The Chinese are also the clerks of the town hall.

They pay a basic tax called *patente personal*. Merchants pay four classes of industrial tax according to the trade, or business, they are engaged in.[2] The fees they pay are meager and are increased in proportion to the benefits they receive.

The shopkeepers have limitless patience, always with a smile on their lips and a noticeable complaisance.

The Chinese are reserved and distrustful, humble and flattering to those who can serve them, haughty and proud to those from whom they expect nothing.

To the host country—I repeat—they do not remit any benefits. The profits from their trade are sent to China, where they retire after making a fortune. Every year, new Chinese replace those who leave.

On Christmas Day, they are generous. They give gifts to their best *suquis*.[3] To important persons, they give lacquered objects, ham, chestnuts, pears, apples, sweets, and other items imported from their country.

Laws passed by the Philippine government regarding the Chinese need to be reformed while others should be implemented.

The Chinese are organized, and increasing in number. With the excessive liberties they are enjoying, the importance they are given, and the influence they obtain in certain ways, there is no stopping them. If they are, as everyone knows, a state within a state, only God knows what they will become tomorrow.

This state of affairs goes against the political system. Considering the way they have constituted themselves, their stay in the country poses a constant danger. The history of the archipelago proves this contention.

Observe if this is not so. Witness the uprisings in 1590 and 1639, the assassination of Governor-General Dasmariñas when he

---

[2] In the 1868-1869 budget, more or less $234,400 was collected from both personal and industrial taxes.
[3] Regular customers.

went to fight in the Moluccas, their conduct during the English invasion, and other similar incidents.

This is a question deserving the attention of the government. We can only treat it lightly here because of the special nature of this book.

After this digression, which is too long for a prologue, let us now begin our narration.

II

Tieng-Chuy was known as one of the richest traders in the flourishing Sangley colony of Manila in 1870. He owned several bazaars and was an active and intelligent businessman.

When he arrived in the country in 1848, his only capital was a relative's recommendation to a merchant who was a countryman. Tieng-Chuy went to see him and was well received. The merchant assigned him to his *chuchelias*, or hardware store, to learn the business and some Spanish as well as Tagalog.

Tieng was smart and soon learned what he needed to know. With ingenuity, thrift, and steadfastness, he was able to make money after a few years and establish his own business.

He decided to become a Christian in order to have an influential patron to protect him and to have the legal right to marry, the only reason for speculators to change their religion. He was then baptized Ramón de Molina, the Christian name and surname of his patron, but he maintained his own name as well as his costume and his customs.

Fortune smiled on all his business ventures so that he soon became powerful.

Tieng became fond of the land that brought him his fortune. He built a beautiful house on Calle Rosario, in the suburb of Binondo, and married an india with whom he had several children. He dedicated himself to his business while his wife was busy caring for his needs and those of his children who were in school. Tieng-Chuy was enviably happy, respected by his relatives and esteemed by others.

When Tieng-Chuy saw that his eldest daughter, a dark-haired, attractive girl called Paning (short for Estefanía), had reached puberty, he thought of marrying her off to his nephew in Ningpo. This marriage, which was meant to unite her to his countryman, would suit his business ventures since the prospective groom's parents were of good standing in China.

Tieng, therefore, wrote to them and they accepted his proposal, aware of Tieng-Chuy's prosperity. They then dispatched their son aboard the English ship *Esmeralda*.

III

Ramón de Molina Tieng-Chuy, who was known for his generosity, wanted to celebrate the arrival of his nephew Chang-Chuy with a dance. He decorated the rooms of his well-furnished house and sent for an orchestra composed of native musicians. At nine in the evening, many visitors arrived.

The living room was full of elegant, luxuriously dressed mestizas. Their charms, their refined and inimitable grace, their ability to dance, we can safely say, had no equal.

There were groups of happy people, children of the Celestial Empire savoring the delicious nectar, the *cha,* or tea, in small cups slightly bigger than thimbles, as they fanned themselves with wide *paipais.* The others in more secluded places were dozing, rendered sleepy by opium. Some guests were in a hidden room, playing *llampó* and *monte,* which they, like the indios, were fond of. Many others, lazily reclining in armchairs with their feet up on the seats, were enjoying themselves watching the dance.

In the bedrooms, the respectable mothers were gathered around the lampshades, passing the time playing *panguingui* and *tapa-diablo*, enveloped in the thick smoke from oversized cigars, which they savored as contentedly as the *buyo*. Cigars and buyo were constantly passed around on big trays. The *caída* was full of musicians, onlookers, and servants bearing lacquered trays filled with sweetmeats and ice cream for the ladies.

The whole house was resplendent, profusely illuminated inside as well as outside, offering a lively and enchanting sight. In the front part of the living room could be seen a gigantic painting of Confucius at whose feet were set sixteen big red candles.[4] Some believers were burning small pieces of yellow paper printed with Chinese characters of different colors.

At 10:30, the dancing stopped so that the Chinese visitors could enjoy a theatrical presentation prepared by Tieng-Chuy.

Chinese music is considered by the children of the Celestial Empire as the most harmonious music in the world. Its composer, however, was undoubtedly deaf or had perhaps lost his reason, since in no other way could anything so lacking in harmony have been conceived. It was deafening and out of tune as it cast to the wind its hair-raising sounds; but it caused the passionate art lovers among the Sangleyes to jump with joy from their seats.

The harsh sound of the two-string *bandolín* started to fill the air. It shrieked, its noise more irritating than the sound of 100 cicadas, while beside it someone played the discordant *ty*, a bamboo flute with six holes, emitting a more deafening sound than the detonation of a battery of ten cannons fired simultaneously. The sound of the *batintín*, a bell of two metals in the form of a boiler, when joined to the incessant sound of the other instruments just mentioned, was

---

[4] The Chinese in Manila, although they have become Christians, revere this philosopher and build altars for him.

more than enough to deafen anyone not born in the wide expanse of the Chinese Empire.

The curtain rose and mandarins appeared on the improvised stage dressed in very luxurious woven silk costumes of lively colors. They were singing, with one hand placed over the other, their arms extended up to their faces, while several henchmen held the banners of the empire. Later, there was a very heated argument with the other characters who had arrived on the scene. The show ended with fancy dances while the music went on mercilessly, hurting the ears of the non-Chinese.

The Chinese actors and musicians left to rest from their exhausting activities, and guests could dance once again in the European style.

IV

Tieng-Chuy and his family, as hosts, did their best to make everyone enjoy the affair.

When the buffet was ready to be served, they moved to a gallery prepared for the occasion. The table was covered with exquisite dishes. Tieng-Chuy was truly being a wonderful host to his party guests.

The palate of the most delicate and demanding Chinese could not have asked for more. There was abundance and variety. Among the huge plates of rice, white as snow, the best brand from the Ilocos called *mimis*, there were platters of dried fish, *pansit*,[5] and *cutchay*.[6] There were dishes overflowing with shark's fins and *hog-shum*, or *balate*, plates of cured veal and deer ribs, capons and chicken side by

---

[5] A sort of paella with thick noodles of rice flour and small pieces of ham, chicken, veal and different spices.

[6] Herb imported from China.

side with plates of shrimps, lobsters, and small *babuis*, or suckling pigs. Attracting the eyes of everyone was an exquisite silver platter, prominently placed, full of *nidos de salangunes*,[7] a highly expensive Chinese gourmet delicacy.

In the middle of the table were elegant fruit bowls surrounded by flowers, bearing the most delicious fruits of the country like *manga*, *piña*, *ate*, *chicos*, *plátanos*, *lanzones*, and *guayabas*. There were also abundant desserts from China and Manila.

At the sight of that banquet, which the Son of the Sun himself could not have scorned, the eyes of his subjects shone like glowworms. They were also overjoyed at the sight of some bottles of Spanish wine. Many people, especially Filipinos, have started to develop a taste for it.

The Chinese armed themselves with their *sipit*, luxurious cylindrical ivory sticks which they manage so admirably, placing one stick between the thumb and the index finger and the other between the latter and the middle finger. With these implements they bring the food to the mouth. The indios, meanwhile, prepared the five fingers of their right hand, the only cutlery they use. Soon everyone started gobbling up the food like turkeys. Some frequently repeated the libations, unaware that the terrible *Mane Thecel Phares of Balthazar's Last Supper* had just placed himself above their heads.

Suddenly a bright light illuminated the whole house and the bells in Binondo Church began to ring to warn the people of a fire. A loud and horrible shout broke out from the lips of everyone—Tieng-Chuy and his family, because their house with all its riches was about to become fodder for the flames; the many guests, perhaps because they had to sacrifice such a delicious dinner to the urgent need of saving their lives.

---

[7] Glutinous substance used by the swallow Salangane to build its nest. A pile of the nest is worth 4,000 pesos in China.

The house beside that of Molina the Chinese was burning fiercely, as if oil were fueling the blaze. Soon, the sparks carried by the wind set Tieng-Chuy's house on fire.

Instantly, the party broke up like magic. The guests started pushing one another, the parents neglecting their children and the young men their sweethearts, all rushing into the streets like the soul of Judas rushing from hell. There was intense confusion, fear, and profound grief.

Tieng-Chuy and his family abandoned their house to the flames, more concerned with saving themselves than with trying to salvage their riches. Their lamentations and tears accompanied the burning of their house.

During that unfortunate night (29 March 1870), the flames devoured a great number of houses and warehouses of Chinese merchants. Some of them nearly died, when they refused to open the doors of their stores that the troops had to open by force. The losses caused by the voracious fire reached several millions. The cause of the fire remains a mystery up to now, although not for the man who had been hiding from the law for some time. His cadaver appeared on the beach of Santa Lucía early on the morning after the tragedy. They found on him proofs of his suicide.

V

The fire in that part of Calle Rosario where Tieng-Chuy's house was located lasted thirty-six hours. It was actually very fortunate that they were able to isolate his house. Otherwise the richest barrio of Manila would have been razed to the ground.

Tieng transferred temporarily to a friend's house. Chang-Chuy lodged in the house of another friend because the house of his uncle's friend was not spacious enough for such a big family. This pleased Chang-Chuy because it gave him more independence.

When he saw the cousin who was meant to be his wife, Chang believed himself to be happy. But he thought differently when, on the night of the ball, he saw the radiantly beautiful but most arrogant mestiza on Calle Jaboneros.

Titay (short for María) was also the daughter of a Chinese who was known to be a haughty woman.

Chang-Chuy showed Titay that he found her very attractive and that he liked her. She responded to his gallantry with the friendliest of smiles.

Chang was enraptured by her graceful ways. From then on, he would often walk up and down her street, hardly thinking about his fiancée.

One day, when for the fifth time, his uncle scolded him for this behavior, Chang got very annoyed and said that he did not want to marry Paning because he was in love up to the ends of his pigtail with the mestiza Titay.

On hearing this daring statement, his uncle, in a frenzy, threw his cap at him.

Chang rushed out shouting that his uncle could never expect to see him again. Tieng-Chuy replied that he was glad Chang was leaving and that it would have been better for all if he had not thought of him. Since Chang's arrival had coincided with the first misfortune he had ever experienced in the country, Tieng attributed this bad luck to his nephew and, consequently, held a grudge against him.

Paning cried upon learning of this affront. Her impending marriage to her cousin was known to everyone. Were it not for an admirer who, unknown to her family, had been writing her passionate love letters, it was possible that Chang's affront could have caused the sudden death of this beauty.

Because Chang-Chuy had some money, he was not worried when his uncle withdrew his protection. He moved to another place in order not to depend on his uncle, and spent the days walking in front of his idol's house.

Chang decided to end his uncertainty and demanded from María the affirmation that would make him the happiest of all the Chinese. The haughty Chinese lady almost exploded with rage, indignant at his insolence. At the height of her fury, she ordered her driver to tell Chang that she was not in this world to marry a *babuy*.[8]

Chang was so humiliated that he felt as if the sky had fallen on his head.

María was an impressionable girl, fond of reading romantic novels, somewhat vain, and rich enough to aspire to marry a rich man of another nationality. Although her father was Chinese, she did not quite relish the idea of marrying a Sangley. Even the mestizos and the indios were not good enough for her. She wanted no less than a Spaniard of noble birth, rich, young, handsome, intelligent, occupying a high government position.

Looking for such exceptional qualities, María wasted her youth waiting in vain for her ideal man who would be a far cry from the Chinese Chang-Chuy. She thought that her father had placed imaginary impediments to separate her from her lover. She dreamt that at the cost of everything, even honor, she ran away with him to a forest where they could enjoy their love freely, living the errant life of nomads or the delightful and peaceful life of shepherds of Arcadia as sung by the poets.

Her illusions were confirmed when she read in the novels that love does not bother with race or rank. So María would go to bed every night, dreaming that upon waking up, a prince, dying for love of her, would be standing by her door to ask her to be his wife.

---

[8] Pig. The *indios* call the Chinese pigs to show their contempt.

VI

When Chang-Chuy was spurned in such a disdainful manner after hoping to be loved by the elegant mestiza of Binondo who looked just like his countrywomen, he felt so cruelly deceived that he got sick.

His landlord called for the famous Si-coco, a Chinese doctor who had an enviable reputation among his countrymen. The doctor came, took his pulse, as doctors usually do, and after thinking a little, spoke with an air of assurance that would have been the envy of any practicing charlatan: "This man's sickness is due to too much heat. It is necessary to restore his well being with something cold. To do that, take this prescription to the pharmacy of Khai-Fung-Sing and he will give you some powder to be mixed with bath water. When cured, he must try to divert himself."

Sorrows are fleeting for people of Chang-Chuy's age so that, after two days, he accepted the wisdom of Si-coco's advice and left his bed and his home. From Santo Cristo de Longos, where he lived, Chang went to San Fernando, and entering the arcade on the left, he headed towards the river where he found many small stores of *sinamayeras*.

The sinamayeras got this name from the cloth they sell. Aside from *sinamay*, a cloth made of abaca and silk fibers, they sell silk and cotton skirts, handkerchiefs and shirts made of pineapple fiber, *tapis, guinaras, cambayas,* and other kinds of cloth. Most of these cloth merchants are Chinese mestizas who love to dress well and who by nature delight in festivities, pleasantries, and lively occasions.

Chang-Chuy was looking at a sinayamera who was very pretty. Her companions called her Charing (short for Rosario).

An indio known to Chang who was passing by approached him and asked: "What is the matter, sir?"

"Look at that *chabó-suy-suy*," [9] said Chang.

---

[9] In Chinese, beautiful girl.

"Oh, be careful, sir. That one has a Spanish boyfriend and he will not like you for that," warned the indio in the usual pidgin Spanish.

Since the mestiza's boyfriend was approaching, the indio left after advising the Chinese to do likewise.

The Chinese are more known to be loud-mouthed than brave. Chang, however, refused to follow the advice given him.

The sinamayera must have said something to her lover because when he observed the insolent attitude of the Chinese, he let Chang feel the force of a *palasan*, or a fifteen-knot whip on his shoulder. The whip's force made Chang jump to the bridge nearby, shouting like mad.

To console himself, he went to a *pansiteria* and ate big helpings of pansit, *tajo,* and some *jopia.* He left the restaurant satisfied.

Not knowing what to do next, he went to an opium parlor. Opium, or *anfion,* is an important source of income for the government.[10] The hacienda bids out the contract in all the provinces. The contractors, who are usually Chinese, establish public opium parlors in different places after getting an authorization.

Opium smuggling, however, is heavily fined. The opium parlors are filthy pigsties, dirty, dark, and infested, where only a Chinese is capable of entering.

Chang-Chuy reclined on a couch and was given a pipe. He spent the siesta hour smoking opium, gratified by his lascivious drowsiness while imagining Titay and Charing swearing eternal love for him.

When Chang left the parlor, it was already six in the afternoon. He went to see a shopkeeper who was sent by his parents to see him and who had just come from China. This man was the manager of the first store on the Escolta situated in the Plaza San Gabriel. They sat by the door of the establishment, talking amicably. After a few moments, Chang's eyes feasted on a very lively scene.

---

[10] In 1873, the government earned 221,686 pesos from this.

A procession that seemed interminable, composed of eight thousand women, was crossing the Barcas Bridge going towards Binondo. They were the cigarette girls of La Fábrica de Tabacos del Fortin on their way home.

Chang-Chuy enjoyed watching them. He admired their easy manner, the peculiar sound of so many slippers and the constant swinging of their arms.

Chang saw one with a coquettish expression who smiled at him affectionately as she passed by. This pleased Chang so that after saying good-bye to his fellow Chinese, he followed the girl.

When the *cigarrera* noticed that Chang was following her, she turned to face him and said in a special language that many indios speak:

"*¿Cosa quiere suya conmigo* [What do you want with me]?

"*Mia quiele platicalo*" [I wish to speak to you], answered Chang, speaking in broken Spanish as they usually do there.

"*¿Y para cosa*" [What for]?

"Because you are *magandan dalaga*."[11]

"*Aba!*" she exclaimed. "This Chinaman is falling in love with me!"

"Yes, *icao mariquit*" [Yes, you are pretty].

"*Kansia* [Thanks]," she answered him in Chinese.

"*Mia quiele mucho con suya y tiene cualtas para puede compla saya y candonga*" [I like you very much and I have money to buy you a skirt and a carriage], Chang insisted.

When she heard the word cualtas [money], the girl's eyes opened wide like windows.

"Very well," she said. "*Sigue suya conmigo para habla bueno-bueno con aquel mi tia*" [Follow me so you can have a good talk with my aunt].

Chang-Chuy, noting her willingness, was pleased to accompany her. She lived in Sibacon. The careless Sangley talked to the aunt of that Venus called Quicay (nickname for Francisca). The aunt,

---

[11] In Tagalog, kind young lady, beautiful.

who was very shrewd, allowed him to have an affair with her niece after he made a formal marriage proposal.

Chang agreed to whatever the two women wanted, and returned home happily because he had at last found an india who loved him.

VII

Chang-Chuy's money, given to him to marry Tieng's daughter, lasted two months. Quicay's love also lasted two months.

Aunt and niece were so skillful in spending Chang's money that not a centavo was left of it. And worst of all, they threw him out into the street on the day they had spent the last of his money.

Chang was replaced in Quicay's affections by an assistant in the factory whom she treated nicely. This person had promised to make her a supervisor, a position coveted by all the cigarreras.

Chang protested to Confucius against such an outrage, but Quicay ridiculed him shamelessly, threatening to tell the *ayudante* if he continued to annoy her.

Chang had to resign himself to losing her, wracking his brains to find a way to live without money. He realized that it was harder than he thought, but he had a plan.

The lottery in Manila, held monthly, favors the Chinese so often that they almost always obtain the grand prize. After selling some of the things he did not need, Chang bought a lottery ticket.

Fearful of losing his ticket, he thought of putting it inside the bamboo handle of his parasol, called *payo* in Manila and made of Chinese paper. The paper used for the Philippine lottery ticket is very fine. Chang rolled it like a cigar. After making a small hole inside the handle of his payo, he placed the ticket inside, covering it with a small piece of bamboo that he pasted on the handle.

The Chinese are skilled in working bamboo. The bamboo chairs, sofas, fans, and thousands of other objects they make with bamboo materials are fashioned so well that there are no dents or ruptures on the surfaces. Nor could anyone have feared that the ticket would be lost because even if the cover fell off, the rolled paper would simply expand inside the handle of the payo and there was no way it could come out.

Because the heat is so suffocating and it often rains unexpectedly, the Sangleyes are never without their payo, which they import from China. The payo is also widely used among the natives because it is cheap.

Chang was living as a guest in the house of some of his countrymen with the understanding that he would pay his expenses when the mail he was expecting would arrive from China. He did not want to work because he had pinned all his hopes on the lottery.

On the day of the lottery, while Chang was taking his siesta, he dreamt that his number won the big prize. When he woke up, he heard people talking about the official results. He rushed down to the street and bought a listing. He immediately looked to see if his number had won. His dream had come true. Chang's ticket had won the P15 thousand-peso prize!

The lucky descendant of Hoang-Ti expressed his joy by jumping up and down, making people think that he had gone mad.

Impatient to see his ticket, Chang rushed to the room that he shared with other boarders. He took hold of the end of the payo and broke the handle. But the ticket was not there. He split it in the middle, trembling at the thought that the ticket could have been stolen, but he found nothing.

His shock was understandably great. In the most guttural tone that the throat of a Chinese can make, the unhappy man started to lament his misfortune, tearing his hair with such violence that half of his pigtail came off between his fingers.

Chang raised his hands to the high heavens and in his despair he banged his head against a post. Since it was made of molave, a wood as hard as metal, his head must have ached from the blow. His outrage left him and he scratched his head.

Scratching one's head is certainly inconvenient, even rude. But in certain cases, it can give rise to new ideas.

It occurred to Chang-Chuy that maybe it was not his payo. There were other Chinese who slept in the same room with him. They each had their own payo.

He looked carefully and realized that it really was not his payo. He searched every corner of the room, but his payo was nowhere to be found. He went to the store in search of his companions in order to ask them if they had seen his umbrella.

One of them said, "Isn't it beside your trunk?"

"But the one there is not mine."

"Well, it's the same. During the siesta hour I had to go out but I could not find my payo so I took yours. I went to different places. I don't know how or where I lost it. The fact is, when I returned, I did not have it. So I bought you the one you found upstairs. I thought that you would not mind losing yours because now you have a new one instead of the broken payo you had before."

When Chang heard this, he thought he would faint. He controlled himself, however, and said, "Thank you, but it was not necessary to spend. You can find my payo by looking for it in the places where you went."

"That's impossible. I already searched carefully so that I would not have to buy another one for you, but my search was in vain. Do you think you could have better luck?"

Desperate, Chang left and went to his room. He was afraid his grief could make him reveal his secret. This would not be a wise thing to do because if no one knew, maybe he would be lucky enough and still recover his payo. With this hope, he continued to think of ways to recover his umbrella. He could not sleep or calm himself, thinking that were it not for his outlandish idea of putting the ticket in the handle of his payo, he would be a rich man by now.

At last, he had a great idea, but he needed money to carry it out.

The problem was difficult. As he was trying to think of a solution, the door of his room opened and one of his companions appeared with a bunch of letters.

"Are you asleep, Chang?" he asked.

Chang could have answered him like the Galician in the story, "aunque parece que dormo, nun dormo" [although I seem to be asleep, I am not asleep], but he was not in the mood. He answered, "What do you want?"

"The ship from Formosa arrived tonight with the mail from China. I have two letters here for you."

Chang stood up right away and started to read his mail. One letter was from a young girl from his country, with whom Chang had romantic relations. She was scolding him for his fickleness. She threatened to take revenge if he did not fulfill his promises.

In another letter, Chang's father reproached him for his strange behavior toward Tieng's daughter. Chang disregarded his father's advice. His father also wrote him a strong recommendation to his friend, Ho-Chau-Chau, a rich merchant living in Manila, who could look after Chang in case he needed protection.

This letter was like manna from heaven to Chang-Chuy, who finally slept happy after finding the means to carry out his plan using his payo.

VIII

The following morning, Chang-Chuy called for the barber, Lim-Juaco, who was famous for his skill as a barber of his compatriots.

Lim-Juaco shaved Chang's head, removing all his hair except that on the upper-right side of his head, which Chang usually wore in a long braid.

The barber then cleaned Chang's nose, his ears and his eyes, a very difficult task which the Chinese barbers do with admirable skill, making use of certain special instruments. Often, this cleaning process is the cause of eye disease if those who practice it are incompetent.

After submitting to this cleaning process, Chang put on a clean and well-ironed *visia*, a white cloth from Canton, and a pair of extremely wide white pants, closed in front with a cord. He put on a *bueca*, a belt with a money bag worn by everybody. He put on his black cloth shoes rounded at the end with thick soles, and proceeded with his father's letter to the house of Ho-Chau-Chau.

Ho-Chau-Chau lived on the Escolta. Chang gave him the letter after the former told him how much he respected Chang's father and that he would do everything to help him. Then Chang said, "I have a project on which my whole destiny depends. But it cannot wait for my father to send me the funds I need. I would like an advance of P6 thousand. I will vouch for it with my honor and I will pay it back as soon as my father knows that I have received it."

Chang explained the reason for his rift with Tieng-Chuy. He added that he knew the country well enough to be able to manage alone.

Ho-Chau-Chau gave Chang the money, firstly because he thought highly of Chang's father, and secondly because Ho had too much money. Most of his countrymen, like him, had a custom of protecting each other, a veritable free masonic practice of mutual assistance.

Chang-Chuy said goodbye to his protector, thanking him repeatedly for his generosity. That same day he rented a space at one end of Calle Jolo. Then he hired some clerks, his own countrymen, to buy all the Chinese paper umbrellas that they could find. When they had acquired a large quantity, Chang had the umbrellas brought to his rented space.

The following day, a strange announcement appeared in the Manila newspapers: "In store no. 4, Calle Jolo, new Chinese payos are exchanged for used ones of the same kind for free."

This same announcement written in Chinese characters, and in Tagalog and Spanish, was posted at the door of the store.

The people who read it entered to exchange their umbrellas. They were astonished to see that in exchange for a dirty and broken umbrella, they were given a brand new and attractive one.

The news spread among the indios, the mestizos, and the Chinese who were users of umbrellas. In three days, Chang had exchanged two thousand payo.

As soon as Chang received an umbrella, he would take it to his bedroom where, alone, he would break the cane handle to see if his lottery ticket was inside. This was his only reason for undertaking the ruinous business of exchanging a new object for a used one.

Since they all looked the same, Chang could not recognize his payo. He was forced to break the handle or bore a hole in each umbrella, but he did not always have the patience to do this.

Chang began to waste away but no parasol with a lottery ticket appeared.

The more charitable persons believed that he had become *chiflado*, a word which, in the Philippines, is used to explain what appears to be strange or extraordinary behavior. Others shouted that Chang had gone completely mad.

The Chinese umbrella vendors were furious over the extravagance of the famous Chang, but he consoled them a bit by buying their merchandise, although at a lower price.

No one, not even his own employees, could understand the reason for Chang's actions. Nevertheless, anyone with a broken payo would hurry to Chang's store.

Ho-Chau-Chau did not know what to do, while Tieng-Chuy could not sleep, thinking about his nephew. Even Lim-Juaco, the barber, took an extra hour in braiding Chang's pigtail, thinking that the head, which his razor blade had made so smooth, was hollow inside.

To the astonishment of the residents of Manila, Chang-Chuy worked four months in this business that was beneficial to those outside and harmful to himself. During that time, he broke twelve thousand umbrellas without finding his ticket in any of them.

His father, who learned what was happening from Tieng-Chuy, furiously wrote him a letter ordering him to stop his monomania and proceed immediately with the arranged wedding with his cousin.

Ho-Chau-Chau demanded from Chang the P6 thousand pesos he owed him, realizing that the latter was spending the money unwisely. Paning, deceived by the false promises of her lover, began to notice the interesting Chinese who, with his new style of making money, was getting to be a celebrity in Binondo.

Chang was thinking of how to get out of that difficulty. He was tired of breaking umbrellas and had lost all hope of recovering his ticket, when Tieng-Chuy came to confront his nephew.

Tieng-Chuy pulled him by the nose, took him to the most isolated corner of the store, and told him, "You are not worthy of my coming all the way here to look for you because of the way you have treated me. But considering the fact that in your veins runs the same blood as mine and that your father asked me to take his place, I have come to force you to carry out his order. Here are his letters. If you refuse, tomorrow you will immediately leave for China."

Chang threw himself in his uncle's arms and said, "Uncle, if I did not come to ask for your pardon before, it was because of shame. I am very thankful for your kindness. Of course, my most fervent desire is to be united with Paning."

"Well, in that case, come to the house. In less than a month you will be her husband. I will pay the debt you owe Ho-Chau-Chau."

Chang cried his heart out upon seeing the magnificent solution to the mess, and he went forth happily to declare his devotion and love to Paning. His cousin told him she had not eaten rice since the day she learned he did not love her anymore and that jealousy was depriving her of sleep. Chang was amazed at the news. He found Paning stouter now than when she was eating, and said, "I, crazy for your love and crazy with love, have been changing new umbrellas for old ones since I lost you without knowing what I was doing."

"Let us forget the past dear Chang. We are now happy together. I want to seal our reconciliation with a plate of pansit, to which I will add *bagon*, and *tinapa* that I have ordered them to serve. Come with me to the dining room."

Chang used his chopsticks proudly. Paning ate so naturally with the five fingers of her right hand as though she had never stopped doing that exercise. They ended the feast by drinking a *tabo* of water and feeling very satisfied.

IX

Two weeks had passed since Chang-Chuy had gone to live in his uncle's house. The preparations for his wedding with Paning began soon enough. The happy day was scheduled for the end of the month.

During that time, Chang-Chuy was absorbing the doctrines that would make him a Christian. As his uncle and future wife were Christians, it was easy for them to overcome their scruples.

One night, Chang-Chuy went to the immortal Teatro de Tondo accompanied by Tieng's family. They went to watch a drama in ten acts and 200 scenes depicting the historic period of a thousand years, featuring the most famous paladins of the principal nations of Europe.

The actors engaged in sword fights onstage. The music was very loud. The Tagalog verses seemed to be the most aggressive in the world, coming from the mouth of Charlemagne talking heatedly with the Gran Capitán Gonzalo of Córdoba and the last king of the Goths. The Sultan Saladino made his presence felt. Then the warriors of each faction started exchanging blows with the flat of the sword while dancing the *moro-moro*, when the ambassador of Persia arrived in a state of agitation. The battle that was about to start would transform the scene into another arena of *Agramante* but was held in abeyance in order to enable the ambassador to speak.[12]

Tieng's family was listening intently so as not to miss the relevance of the narration of the Persian character. Chang-Chuy was admiring the valor of those fierce warriors, when he felt someone pulling one of the wide sleeves of his visia.

A Chinese, seemingly impatient, handed him a piece of paper and left hurriedly. It was a note written in his native language, and he read the following:

> *He who solemnly promises to love a woman until the end of his days should be faithful to his promises.
>
> *He who has told a woman that he will never unite himself with another should not marry anyone else but her.
>
> *He who abandons her without any reason, should look for her and be sincere, if he still loves her.
>
> *He who deceives her and fails in his promises deserves to die.
>
> *Remember Ningpo and be afraid.

The letter was not signed and the characters used were unfamiliar to him.

When Chang-Chuy finished reading, cold perspiration bathed his body. He imagined that he was about to be killed, and he screamed in terror.

The Persian ambassador stopped his narration. The audience in the coliseum of Tondo all turned their eyes to the spot where the scream came from. Tieng's family, surprised at Chang's behavior and seeing him so pale and distraught, anxiously asked him what was the matter.

---

[12] Dramas with similar plots have been staged in the Teatro de Tondo.

"I feel sick," he answered.

"Let us go home."

"That is not necessary. This will pass," said Chang. He was afraid that something might happen to him if he left.

The performance resumed. Chang's cousins were again spellbound by the drama, but the unhappy, fearful Chinese hardly noticed what was transpiring on the stage. Without a doubt, his conscience was bothering him for some fault or wrong he had done.

During the performance, he was restless and worried. The stupendous tragedy ended and they went home. Chang kept looking in all directions. He was afraid that at any moment he would see the Chinese who handed him the letter in the theater. He had all the features of a killer.

Nothing, however, happened to Chang-Chuy. Upon settling himself safely in bed, he let go of the burden in his heart that was tormenting him, and his legs stopped trembling.

Eight days passed and Chang-Chuy was not molested by anyone. He could not figure out any reason why someone should plot against his life. He became calm, thinking that it was all a joke of one of his compatriots, and he forgot about it completely.

As the ceremony for his conversion to Catholicism was coming closer, his uncle Tieng began to distribute a notice requesting their friends to honor the occasion with their presence.

That same night, Chang's servant handed him a package, brought by a Chinese who had not waited for a reply. Chang opened the bulky package. It contained a precious copy of *Chu-King* by Confucius, the most respected among the five books written by Chinese philosophers. There was a piece of paper inserted in the book, and on it was written:

> If he who without any justifiable reason abandons the woman he loved and by whom he was loved, it is not surprising that he abandons the beliefs of his parents.

Read this book carefully, meditate slowly on what you are going to do, and may Kong-Fu-Tsen enlighten you.

The Geis[13] have taken power of your body and Ti-Kang[14] waits for you.

If repentance is far, revenge is near. Remember Ningpo and do not forget your responsibility.

This paper was not signed either, but Chang saw the point clearly. Far from being calm, he felt his fears increase. He feared a disaster should he marry. Preparations for the wedding were already in progress, and given the situation in which the umbrella business had placed him, it was now impossible to turn back.

Chang-Chuy could not find a way out of his troubles. He tortured himself with thoughts of his predicament. As he could not sleep, he read some pages of *Chu-King*. Reading thus made his spirit waver between indecision and despair. When dawn announced a new day, Chang-Chuy closed the book.

Tieng's nephew was exceedingly troubled indeed. A natural worrier, he worried more each day about what was happening to him. Relatives and friends feared madness would attack him again.

On the day of his scheduled baptism, he could not get out of bed. He had a fever. So the ceremony had to be moved to a later date.

Chang's illness was mild enough and on the second day he was well. He left his room for brief moments and when he returned he found a letter on his bed that said:

Kong-Fu-Tsen has inspired you. If your repentance is sincere, you will soon be pardoned.

Tomorrow, at five in the afternoon, I will wait for you in La Loma.

---

[13] Evil spirits.
[14] God of the underworld, Hades in Greco-Roman mythology.

The meeting should be kept secret, and for that reason I have chosen that place. It is the only assurance that will protect my identity.

Do not fear, and come at the indicated time. If you disregard my call, you will not be able to complain of the evil that will happen to you. Tomorrow, you will know who I am.

That appointment was less surprising to Chang-Chuy than the manner in which the letter was brought to him. Neither his servant nor anybody in the house could tell him who could have entered his room or brought the letter.

Although prudence dictated that he should not go to the place where the letter writer would meet him, the desire to know the mysterious person was stronger than his fear of possible danger. He was afraid, but he had an adventurous character and the letter said nothing really alarming, so he decided to go.

At exactly five that afternoon, Chang-Chuy was in La Loma.

X

La Loma is the cemetery for the Chinese who die in Manila. The converts to Christianity are buried in the Catholic cemeteries.

The Chinese who worship Fo, or Confucius, build slightly elevated graves on graded steps. The grave marker laid on top has Chinese characters inscribed in red, black, and gold, which could indicate luxury and wealth.

When Chang-Chuy arrived in La Loma, there were many carriages on the avenue leading to the cemetery, where there was a crowd of Chinese dressed in white with a black ribbon on the neck, as a sign of mourning.

In the center was the cadaver of a Chinese in a coffin made of molave filled with food. The coffin was overflowing with cutchay, cooked rice, and pansit. There were candles, pieces of red and white paper with Chinese verses in gold and black characters, a teapot, and two empty cups. The relatives of the dead person were crying as they talked to the people about how generous the person was when he was alive. Soon after, they buried him in the ground and covered the grave with soil and stones.

When the funeral was over, they left with a peaceful conscience for having fulfilled a sacred duty, knowing that the deceased had everything to satisfy his appetite on the journey he was going to make. That was why they had to put all the food that we just described in the coffin.

Necrophobia overcame Chang-Chuy, seeing a spectacle similar to what had been forming in his mind, so that he forgot why he had come to La Loma. For some moments, he did not realize what brought him there. When the people had all left the cemetery, he remembered, and was surprised to find himself alone.

He was about to leave when a noise from behind stopped him. Frightened, he turned his head and found himself facing the Chinese with a sinister face, from one of the plays presented in the Teatro de Tondo.

Chang-Chuy was shaken.

Politely, the sinister-looking Chinese invited him to follow as he walked among the graves. Chang followed him mechanically.

At the far northern end of the cemetery was a pyramidal mausoleum made of black marble crowned by a dragon, and here the mysterious figure stopped. He knocked loudly and twice on the high gravestone and it opened like a door revealing a small hall that was lit by the clerestory.

Chang-Chuy was pushed inside by another Chinese who closed the gravestone and stayed outside.

Believing that they were going to bury him alive, Chang-Chuy let out a cry of terror, but regained some composure when he saw the woman within the mausoleum. The woman was covered with a cape.

"At last, I see you, Chang-Chuy," she said in correct Chinese.

"Who are you?" he asked.

"Do you not know me?" The woman let the cape fall to the ground.

"Khukhu-noor!" exclaimed Chang, terrified.

"Yes, Chang, it is I. I who have come purposely to avenge myself if you are not willing to fulfill the solemn promises you made to me."

Chang-Chuy was aghast and frightened.

Khukhu-noor was a young woman from Ningpo to whom Chang had sworn his endless love. She loved him with all her soul. When she least expected it and when she thought she was very sure of Chang's love, he disappeared. She learned later that he had left China and was going to marry a cousin in Manila.

Chang had not informed her of his departure or even said goodbye. She was insulted, deceived, betrayed by the man she sincerely loved. Jealousy and the desire for revenge did not give her a single moment of peace.

Khukhu-noor was a person of forceful character. She was willful, excitable, prone to anger and revenge. Knowing what she was like, Chang began to worry about his future.

The Chinese lady was barely seventeen years old. Her eyebrows were arched too much, her eyes too slit, but her complexion was fine and delicate. These are the qualities that constitute supreme beauty in China. She dressed in typical Chinese fashion, but her extremely tiny feet indicated that she did not belong to the inferior class who had normal feet. The hobbled feet of Chinese women are a deformity that repels the onlooker. From birth, the feet are bound very tightly. The bonds are rarely removed and the feet are later encased in shoes of a strange shape. The caged foot is thus disfigured, acquires a repugnant form, and loses all its beauty.

Walking must be very difficult for Chinese women with such shackled feet. If they ever try to run, they lose their balance like a drunk.

In the Celestial Empire, it is a mark of nobility or at least affluence, for the women in the family to display disabled feet. Hobbling the feet of young maidens is intended to enhance their beauty. It is designed to prevent the ladies from wandering about or going out too much. They appreciate this constraint more than we do even if it is detrimental to the beautiful sex.

To continue with our story. . .

"Are you not going to answer me?" Khukhu-noor asked Chang, who seemed to have turned into a statue.

"Khukhu-noor in Manila!" the distraught Chang exclaimed.

"Yes. I have come to this country disguised as a man and accompanied by my faithful servant, who waits for my orders outside. I have come to prevent you from committing perjury. Your sentence is my love or your death. I will not accept anything other than that."

"But that is impossible," Chang said.

"Impossible! Nothing is impossible if there is a will."

"Listen, Khukhu-noor. I loved you very much and I still do. My father obliged me to leave hurriedly the beautiful city where we had been very happy to enter into a marriage that my heart rejects. In the beginning, I refused. But since I am indebted to my uncle and my condition is precarious, my father has arranged my marriage and if I do not obey I will suffer many misfortunes. For these and other reasons too long to tell you, I have to go against my desires and marry a cousin I do not love. Now you see how great is the sacrifice!"

"You lie, Chang. Is it possible that you leave me for her because of trivial reasons? That you have no passion for that mestiza? You say you loved me but why did you abandon me for her, and why did you renounce the religion of our parents that together we exalted in the temple and which is revealed in the sublime pages of *Chu-King*, which I sent you?"

As she gave vent to her feelings, Khukhu-noor seemed to be in the grip of a passionate rage, judging from the ire evident in her face and actions.

"Although you doubt it," answered Chang, "what I have told you is true. I do not have any choice but to do as I am told. It would be well for you to go back to Ningpo."

Khukhu-noor could not restrain herself. Swiftly, without thinking, she struck the shaved head of Chang with the handle of her umbrella. Chang's head sounded like a coconut when struck and the pole of the umbrella broke in two.

Chang-Chuy uttered a pitiful cry but the pain suddenly eased when he saw a piece of paper peering out of the broken handle of his beloved's umbrella. He reached for it like a hungry lion seizing its prey. He recognized it and he surprised the impassioned Chinese lady with exclamations of joy instead of the cry of pain she was expecting to hear from him. He seemed to have lost his mind as he jumped happily.

Khukhu-noor became speechless.

When Chang finally calmed down, he told his beloved the story of his lost ticket, which had suddenly appeared in a way he had never imagined. The paper that came out of the handle of the umbrella was none other than the missing ticket.

"But my servant Kuei-Cheu got this umbrella in China several months ago from someone who came from these islands!" she said, surprised.

"Confucius is protecting us," Chang answered her philosophically.

Chang and Khukhu-noor embraced ardently. They were both glad about the tremendous blow she had dealt him as it had brought back the treasure that he thought was lost forever.

Chang's head became doubly swollen from the caresses of the young lady, but he did not feel any pain. The pleasure of having found his ticket made him crazy with joy.

Chang-Chuy and his beloved left the La Loma cemetery followed by her servant, Kuei-Cheu. That night, his uncle Tieng-Chuy waited for him in vain. Chang never appeared again in the house of his uncle.

For two days, his uncle anxiously searched for him everywhere in Manila. Finally, the pitiful Tieng received a letter from his nephew. In the letter, Chang told him to forget his planned marriage to Paning because that same day he was leaving for China with the only woman he loved. With the letter were bank notes totaling the amount he owed Ho-Chau-Chau and an additional P1 thousand pesos for the expenses and heartaches he had caused since his arrival in the capital of the Philippines.

Chang claimed the prize for his lottery ticket the day after his reunion with Khukhu-noor and left for China, where they were married. They went on a pilgrimage to Kio-Len-Hien, a city in the province of Can-tung, the land of Confucius, to make amends for his intention to renounce his religion.

Then they went to Ningpo. As money solves everything, Jalung-Chuy, Chang's father, pardoned him for his disobedience, seeing that he was richer than when he left their country. Kia-Ling-Kiang, Khukhu-noor's father, could not contain his happiness, considering that his daughter's disappearance had resulted in an advantageous union.

Tieng-Chuy and his relative Jalung cut their relationship after a bitter exchange of letters.

Paning, the unlucky young lady who was about to marry Chang twice, and twice failed, could not accept her fate. To stay away from the eyes of people who pointed at her wherever she went, who talked about her misfortune to those who did not know, she finally entered the convent-college of La Concordia. She believed this was the right place for her because it was far from Manila and she could live there in peace.

La Concordia is a beautiful building in the happy vicinity of Sta. Ana where many girls and young ladies from the provinces are educated and learn useful chores. They are interns and are under the direction of the Sisters of Charity who render valuable services to the Philippines, especially in hospitals and in the field of public instruction. Games and the pleasant camaraderie of her classmates distracted Paning from her sorrows. She came to believe that another lover more faithful than her cousin Chang, would take her out of that quiet mansion and lead her to the altar someday. She did not lose hope of joining the society of married women. No woman loses this hope, although wrinkles line her face and lovers pass like the seasons of the year. It is so distressing to remain a spinster.

We do not know whether Paning finally fulfilled her illusions or not.

With regard to Chang-Chuy, letters from China have informed us that he is as fat as a mandarin and is doing good business with tea. The Chinese, after breathing the tea's delicate aroma and savoring it in slow sips, dry the leaves under the sun and export them to Europe at a very good price.

Now, how can anyone still think that the Chinese are stupid?

He who does not know this well and feels like verifying it need not go to China. It is enough that he goes to Manila.

THE VENGEFUL CALAO

I

Twenty years ago, in the town of Mabalacat, province of Pampanga, there lived a native sexagenarian named Don Hermenegildo Basco de los Reyes. He enjoyed great prestige due to a privilege granted to his father as a reward for the important services he rendered during the English invasion. At that time the governor-general of the Islands was Don Simón de Anda y Salazar.

Don Hermenegildo was also *gobernadorcillo* of the town twice, a position known in that era as *juez de ganados*, or local judge.

He was respected and loved by the people for his wealth, his services, his age, and the traditional nobility of his family. Even the most prominent persons heeded his pronouncements.

The deeds of Don Hermenegildo's father are so praiseworthy that we are going to point them out to serve as a lesson to the Pampangos, who should be proud that the good patriot, Don Luís Basco, was born in their province.

For this purpose, we will have to remember certain historical events.

England and Spain were at war in 1762. The governor of the Philippines at that time was Archbishop Manuel Antonio Rojo, who was unaware of the outbreak of hostilities between the two nations. He was greatly surprised when he saw on the bay an English fleet composed of thirteen vessels carrying 6,800 men ready to disembark.

The head of the fleet informed the archbishop of an order to surrender the plaza but his response was to defend the city.

On the night of 23 September, the Englishmen carried out their disembarkation plans and laid siege to the capital. On the 29th, three more ships arrived to reinforce the attackers.

When the nearby province of Pampanga learned of this event, Don Luís Basco convened a good number of *principales*, province mates, and their servants, and told them: "The country is in danger. Sixteen English ships have invaded the bay, and Manila is surrounded by numerous foreign troops. If the Peninsulares are conquered, we shall become slaves of the English, who will only make us their contemptible instruments in exploiting the wealth of the country, as they have done with their colonies. It is necessary that we support the cause of Spain, which is our own cause. The Spaniards saved our parents from an uncivilized life in order to give them a culture envied by all the neighboring countries. They are not tyrants who enslave us, but guardians who govern us with paternal care. The laws that

Spain has imposed on the Philippines are kinder than the ones that are in force in the peninsula. They respect our properties and our customs. They do not feel humiliated when they marry our children or our sisters. They have built schools for the education of our children. We owe them what we are and what we have because when they arrived on these shores, our ancestors were living like the Igorots now do. Had they not come with the noble mission of civilization, we would still be uncivilized. They have given us the knowledge we have in agriculture, industry, and commerce. They have taught us how to build ships. They have introduced us to all the arts, enabling us to equal European nations. We owe them immense gratitude and this is the opportunity to show them our appreciation for such benefits, so they will see that we realize the advantages we have obtained from their government. If we allow another nation, be it English or German, Portuguese or Chinese, Dutch or Russian, to take over this land, the most abject form of slavery awaits us and we shall have labored for our own eternal misfortune.

"The place where duty takes us is Manila. Let us hurry to defend the country or die faithfully beside our compatriots, the Spaniards. Is there anyone who disagrees?"

"No one! No one!" shouted everyone, inspired by great love of country. "Let us hurry to Manila where our brothers are in danger. You will lead us," they said, clamoring for Basco to lead them.

"Let us go, partners, and long live Spain!" shouted Basco.

"Long live Spain, and let us go!" answered everyone.

II

On 3 October, a considerable number of Pampangos, led by Don Luís Basco and armed with lances, arrows, bolos and *campilanes*, entered Manila by land. The besieged welcomed them with cheers and embraces.

The English intensified their attack on the city's strong points and entrenchments made by the natives. But these could not compete with the invaders, who were well-armed and better in strategy. Nevertheless, they were amazed at the courage of the natives.

The archbishop, although inclined by his profession to have peace rather than war, agreed to the surrender of the city, knowing the futility of defending her.

Don Simón de Anda y Salazar, *oidor* of the Audiencia, believed that the city had to be defended to the end. But when he saw the defenders being routed, he abandoned the capital and went to Bulacan in a light boat with no one but his faithful servant.

The head of the province called all the Spaniards, the religious, and the *principales* of the capital, and upon disclosing to them his plan on how to resist the enemy, they swore fidelity and obedience to him.

On 5 October, official news was heard about the surrender of Manila. As captain-general, the heroic patrician Don Simón de Anda y Salazar issued a proclamation to the inhabitants of the archipelago urging them to unite and defend the Islands against the invaders. He established his residence in Bacolor, capital of Pampanga.

Don Luís Basco was the first to volunteer under Anda's command, and together with a loyal army of natives committed himself on that day to wage war against the English aggressors.

The province of Pampanga and other provinces that sent volunteers were greatly honored on that occasion.

The loyalty of the native Pampango is worthy of lasting fame. The English chief had committed the perfidy of offering P5 thousand to anyone who could deliver Anda to him dead or alive. No one turned traitor; on the contrary, they faithfully obeyed the orders of the illustrious old man. Basco was the one who best supported Anda's projects.

When Spain and England made peace, the English government ordered the evacuation of the plaza. The English communicated this order to Anda but he refused to carry it out because they did not treat him as the captain-general of the Islands. His refusal showed strength of character, as well as the security he felt in Bacolor.

When the Spanish government announced that a peace pact had been made with England, Anda proposed to the English the suspension of hostilities, pointing out to them how the plaza of Manila was to be relinquished.

This was done but not without serious displeasure from the archbishop and the other oidores, who complained to the government despite the fact that they could not have imitated Anda's patriotism during the fight. Anda resigned after someone more competent was chosen to take his place.

Don Simón de Anda y Salazar gained prestige for his heroic and dignified conduct. The memory of his valor lives on as a glorious episode in history and a lesson for coming generations.

In front of Fort Santiago, at the entrance to the Malecón, between the Pasig River and the sea, there is an obelisk 14 meters high, made of Italian marble with a granite base. The people raised funds to erect it in Anda's honor. Bacolor also dedicated another monument to him. A town in the province of Zambales and a street in Manila were named after him. The remains of this illustrious magistrate were placed under a stone slab behind the main altar of the cathedral. When the earthquake of 1863 destroyed the cathedral and the debris had to be removed, Anda's remains were transferred to the Church of the Third Order, where they now repose.

He was generous with everyone who helped him in his noble undertaking during the campaign.

Don Luís Basco, as we have mentioned, received an honorary award in appreciation of his loyalty, his personal valor, and the human and material support that he had generously given.

He was held in the highest esteem and given lavish care and attention by the head of the province and his compatriots. Spaniards who went to Pampanga visited him. He bequeathed an illustrious name to his son, Hermenegildo, mentioned at the beginning of this story and about whom we will hear more.

III

One stormy night, the residents of Mabalacat prayed very hard, entrusting their souls to their favorite saints. Thunder rumbled in the sky, continuous lightning tore the clouds, and the heavy rains lashed the humble houses of the town.

It was about ten o'clock and no human being could be seen in the streets. The night was very dark because there was no public lighting then, nor is there any now in any of the provinces of the Philippines. Mabalacat was in total darkness so that it was difficult to see a shadow within two feet.

There was complete silence in the town and only the sound of thunder and the heavy rains disturbed the solemn tranquility. It seemed as if all the people had gone to sleep or had deserted the town. Inside the houses, however, the owners were offering praises and supplications to God before images lit by blessed candles.

With every clap of thunder and spark of lightning, the men turned pale and the women's hearts were filled with terror, fearing they could be struck. There was reason to be afraid because the storms in the Philippines, and these are frequent, often cause lamentable tragedy. Fortunately, on that night, no serious harm or damage was done, except to two tranquil carabaos whose enormous horns had a particular attraction to electricity.

The storm passed without causing any damage. The lightning became less frequent and less intense, and the thunder quieted down. The neighbors of Mabalacat said their final prayers, extinguished their miraculous candles, and went to bed to get the much-needed rest of which the storm had deprived them.

The town remained in deep silence; and the streets, like before, were completely deserted.

The church clock slowly struck twelve. After the echo of the last stroke died away, a galloping horse was heard approaching faintly at first, then growing louder. The horse hurriedly crossed some streets and stopped at the entrance of one of the best houses. The horseman got off and knocked loudly at the door. After a while, he knocked again with more force. As he waited, he wrapped himself carefully with a blanket that he untied from the saddle. When asked who he was, he answered with a vicious curse. Recognizing the voice, the people behind the door opened it at once.

"I was not waiting for you tonight, Juan," said a woman. A little girl beside her greeted him: "Good evening, Father."

Without answering, he proceeded inside and locked himself in his room. He ordered them to take the horse to the stable and to go to bed at once because he wanted to rest.

The one who opened the door was his wife. She attributed her husband's bad humor to his having been caught in the storm. She surmised that he had left Angeles that night, where he had gone on an errand the day before .

As she was going to bed, she saw that her husband's room was locked. Thinking that he was asleep, she went to another room with her daughter.

Everything was silent. The man whom we saw arrive on a horse earlier now went down to the basement of the house, lifted two tiles revealing a deep hole into which he placed some carefully wrapped objects.

He set the tiles back and cleared away the dirt that was dug out. After seeing to it that everything was just as it was before, he returned to his room.

That man was livid; fear was written all over his face. He remained meditative for some time with his head between his hands, his elbows resting on a table. Later, more serene now, he raised his head and a kind of sarcastic smile shone on his countenance. Having resolved not to doubt, he was beginning to calm down, and when he went to bed, he seemed completely calm.

IV

The following day, the gobernadorcillo of Mabalacat was in the tribunal talking to several people about the typhoon the night before and trying to find out what damage it had caused so he could report it to the *Alcaldía Mayor*.

He was beginning to get impatient waiting for the *capitán de cuadrilleros* to report to him, when he saw the capitán coming, followed by some police officers and laborers. The capitán got off his horse and ran to notify him that they had found the cadaver of a man horribly disfigured in the thickest forest leading to the town of Capas.

Immediately, the gobernadorcillo ordered someone to call the *directorcillo* and left for the scene of the crime accompanied by the witnesses, the cuadrilleros, and the police officers. When they arrived at the place, they followed all the legal procedures, put the cadaver in a handbarrow and headed for the tribunal.

They identified the body as that of the former captain, Don Hermenegildo Basco de los Reyes. He had been shot in the face, had two wounds caused by a sharp weapon on the heart, and many more wounds inflicted on the face to disfigure it.

The assassination of such a well-respected and loved person and the cruelty of the crime pained and angered the people present.

The gobernadorcillo immediately ordered the cuadrilleros to look for evidence everywhere while he started his own investigation to find the perpetrator of that horrible crime. The news spread among the people and filled the neighborhood with dismay. They made speculations and absurd comments while they talked about the dastardly crime.

The large family of captain Hermenegildo exerted every possible effort to find the murderer, promising a considerable reward to whoever could give any information. They were relentless in their investigation.

The *Juzgado de primera instancia* of Pampanga, which received the first investigative report in Mabalacat, was unable to accomplish anything in spite of its enthusiasm. Neither could the gobernadorcillo and his agents nor the captain's family. It was, therefore, necessary to stay the proceedings without the slightest evidence pointing to the assassin, and all concerned considered the crime impossible to solve.

There was a pervading sadness and desperation because of the terrible crime. Government authorities and the general public showed great interest in solving it. Everyone was anxious to know the name of the culprit and his motives.

Nothing, however, was discovered and the killing of such a well-liked person as Don Hermenegildo Basco de los Reyes remained shrouded in mystery.

V

Pampanga is a rich province near Manila. Its plains are well cultivated and it produces abundant sugarcane. Instead of the wooden sugar mills constructed by the workers themselves and used in other provinces, there are steam mills for extracting cane juice. With these machines, time is saved, the cane is well crushed, and the carabaos intended for the sugar mills are used for other tasks. Pampanga's sugar is well-liked in the foreign market because of its good quality.

A great part of the province is uncultivated. Thick growths of tall cogon grass serve as a hiding place for the most feared bandits of the country. Between Mabalacat and Capas is a dark forest with red soil, where countless large-scale robberies and murders have been committed. At present, with detachments of the Civil Guards stationed there, such crimes are less frequent.

The mountains of this province contain quarries for jasper stones and marble. It has many large rivers that are very useful for the fields and are wide enough for navigation, facilitating the importation and exportation of fruits and the development of industry due to the easy connection between the province and Manila, Bulacan, Pangasinan, and Nueva Écija. On a wide plain, named Candava, a big lake forms during the rainy season.

The streets or the highways are wide but badly paved, so much so that during the rainy season, they become impassable.

In the principal towns, there are families that rent out coaches, horses, and wagons with thin but strong horses.

There are many barrios, or *visitas*, each one with a small chapel and a *bantayan*, or group of guards, composed of natives under the command of a lieutenant.

Near these bantayan are houses inhabited by businessmen who discharge the duties of innkeepers like those in Spain, providing ample shelter and food to transients. On the other hand, the tribunales offer very poor service to travelers, serving food and handling baggage slowly, poorly, and so expensively that it is better not to patronize them. There is a plan to construct a railway from Manila to Pampanga, and a proposal to extend it to Northern Luzon. If the project is realized, there will be great benefits for this province.

The Pampangos are hardworking and good farmers. Bacolor is a beautiful town, San Fernando has good country houses, and in Guagua, where the Department of Finance is located, there is much business activity. It is bustling with life. The river through which the boats sail to Guagua presents a delightful view. The stretch of cultivated land is a beautiful sight to see. Some of its towns are very picturesque.

Mount Arayat, found in the center of Pampanga, rises over all the bordering provinces. It is a magnificent watchtower from which one can see the sea at a great distance.

The population is 200,700. Bacolor is 12 leagues, about 68 kms. away from Manila. Its natives are illustrious.

VI

We will now recount what we know about the murder that deeply disturbed the minds of the people of Pampanga, the murder of Don Hermenegildo Basco.

Juan Ibana, a native of San Isidro, capital of Nueva Écija, was a sugar harvester in Pampanga. He married Eugenia Basco, a niece of Don Hermenegildo. Because the parents of this young lady obliged him to live in Mabalacat, he moved there.

Juan was boastful, arrogant, domineering, and vengeful. Shortly after the marriage, he became at odds with the family of his wife due to some personal interests or disagreements that she managed to solve tactfully. Eugenia, a model of meekness, deplored her husband's bad character; but she knew how to live with him patiently, thus avoiding more quarrels.

Ibana was a hypocrite but so clever at hiding his true nature that in the town he was considered a model husband. He never showed his disgust at his wife's relatives who protected the interests of her family. He hated them and he was tired of their advice and suggestions.

Don Hermenegildo Basco de los Reyes, in particular, prohibited Ibana more than once from taking risks in certain types of business and speculations. He warned him that his parents-in-law were afraid to provide the money he was asking for. Ibana wanted more independence, less advice and, above all, money for his business deals.

Eugenia's uncle gave good advice, but he was an annoying meddler, and Ibana considered him an eternal nightmare.

After his wife's parents died, Ibana thought of taking exclusive control of her inheritance. Don Hermenegildo, however, wanted to retain some control, as agreed upon with Ibana's in-laws. Juan could not accept that and he went to court after exhausting all his resources for a settlement.

Reason was on the side of Don Hermenegildo and that was how the judge resolved it. Ibana appealed and the court confirmed the previous decision. Seeing that he was about to lose a good part of the lands that he felt belonged to his wife, he swore to take revenge. He pretended not to be angry and treated his potential victim in a cunning way in order to deceive him.

Ever since he nurtured that idea, he acted differently toward his uncle-in-law. Deceived by Ibana's feigned humility, Don Hermenegildo said with satisfaction that finally God had touched his heart; that arrogance did not blind him anymore, and that reason had overcome his pride. Happy with the transformation he attributed to his own skill and good advice, and owing to the typical assertiveness of elders whose authority is recognized by the natives, Don Hermenegildo visited Ibana more frequently to offer him counsel. Ibana had to adjust to all the acts and whims of his uncle. The natives have much respect for their elders, who believe that they are the only ones who can do everything well. Confident in this belief, the elders are accustomed to making all the decisions.

Ibana was exasperated with his uncle's desire to have things done according to his will and at his convenience. He considered this impertinent and offensive to his strong character. Determined to avenge himself for the litigation he had lost, and angered for having been denied the loan of a certain sum, he decided to destroy his uncle at any cost and lost no time in finding an opportunity to do so.

Knowing that Capitán Basco was going to his hacienda in Capas, Ibana feigned a trip to Angeles. When Basco was on his way home, Ibana hid himself in a thick forest between Mabalacat and Capas and stationed himself near the path where Basco usually passed.

Don Hermenegildo, as expected, came down the said path, and halfway he was caught in a storm. The elements unleashed seemed to be an omen of the horrible drama about to unfold in the dangerous forest, where he was about to seek shelter. Since he could not find shelter, he rode on, making his horse run faster.

In the middle of the forest, where sensible people would not dare pass because of the dark, someone shouted, "Who is there?"

"A man of peace," answered the capitán.

"Move on," a voice said.

He proceeded carefully, but suddenly, someone pushed him hard. He lost his balance and fell to the ground. His horse was terrified and ran away. Don Hermenegildo was held down by the neck and chest, and he heard his nephew say, "At last I'm freed of you, impertinent old man. Now, file lawsuits against me, rob me of my possessions, and meddle in my affairs." Uttering those words, Ibana shot his uncle in the face.

At the sound of the gunshot, a gigantic *calao*, perched on a branch of a tree above, let out a shrill and terrifying croak. It moved closer to another branch so that its wings lightly grazed Ibana's body. Frightened, he dropped the pistol and was about to flee. His uncle was not dead, only wounded, and gripping Ibana's arm, he said, "You are a scoundrel. Why are you trying to kill me treacherously without respect for my age and our relationship? God will not allow this crime to go unpunished." "Calao," he added, looking at the bird in the flashes of lightning that illuminated the forest, "you who are the only witness to my death, avenge me."

The bird seemed to understand. It flapped its wings noisily and began its dizzying flight, making sad and frightening sounds before it gradually disappeared.

Great was Ibana's terror, but he was emboldened when he saw that his uncle was getting up. With a knife he stabbed him, first in the heart and then in the face, leaving him horribly mutilated.

He quickly gathered his murder weapons, mounted his horse and rode home dripping wet and spattered with blood.

We have seen how, upon arriving at his house, he buried his shirt and the weapons he used in the crime under the tiles of his basement; how he smiled upon seeing the happy ending of his wicked assault. We witnessed, too, how his uncle entrusted his revenge to the calao.

VII

Ten years after the incidents we have just narrated, Juan Ibana was the most powerful and the happiest person in Mabalacat.

The much-talked-about death of his uncle, Don Hermenegildo, was forgotten. No one suspected that he was the perpetrator of the crime because he was a close relative of the victim. He was also one of those who showed much grief when the people learned of his uncle's death, and who appeared to be the most interested in finding the murderer.

One day his wife said to him, "Someone from the hacienda in Capas came to advise us that the palay is ripe. Since the land was only acquired last year, we should be there to witness the harvest personally. It is not right to leave the first harvest to the tenants. In this way, we will know the exact number of *huyones* it can produce."

"You are right," he answered his wife. "Tomorrow we will go."

They went to the hacienda and spent some time there. Night fell on their way home, and it began to get cloudy. A cold wind was blowing and there were signs of a heavy rain. Thunder could be heard and lightning flashed on the far horizon from time to time.

"It seems like we will be caught in the coming storm," said Ibana's wife, pointing to the dark clouds.

"Yes and we have to hurry to the next forest before it reaches us. If there is a storm, it will be dangerous to cross that dark place at this time."

The riders left hurriedly but just as they feared the storm overtook them. When they entered the forest, a very bright flash of lightning illuminated the entire forest. The thunderclap made the earth tremble and big drops of rain fell noisily on the leaves of the trees.

A few moments later, the forest seemed like hell. The violent beating of the rain on the branches, the frightening noise of thunder, the dazzling flashes of lightning that illuminate a forest, only to plunge it in complete darkness the next instant, can terrify even the bravest of men.

The natives are extremely superstitious. They believe that tall trees whose green leaves turn into different colors with the blue flash of lightning are *cafre,* or *asoan.* These are horrible ghosts and the mere mention of their names scares not only the ignorant class of the archipelago but the educated as well.

Ibana's wife, who was trembling with fear, told her husband that she could no longer retain her hold on the horse. Her husband, as well as the servants who accompanied them, were as terrified as she was.

"It is necessary," said Ibana, "that we leave the forest at all costs. Stopping and staying here so late is unwise and risky. Let us move."

His wife, who was overcome with terrifying thoughts and mistook each shadow for bandits who abound in the province, asked her husband:

"Isn't this the place where my uncle Hermenegildo was murdered?"

Right after that question, a long, bright flash of lightning lit up the entire forest. At the same time a calao of extraordinary size flew from a nearby tree, its wings grazing Ibana's forehead while repeatedly making a harsh squawk that was drowned out by the deafening thunder.

Ibana let out a terrible scream and fell from his horse, unconscious.

At first, neither his wife nor their servants could attend to him as they were also terrified. After recovering from the shock, they ran to help him.

Ibana's face was disfigured with fear; he was pale like a cadaver, and trembling like quicksilver.

"What is wrong? Are you sick?" his wife asked.

"No, the calao is lying. I did not murder your uncle," he muttered deliriously.

"What are you saying?"

"Do not believe the calao; somebody else murdered him," he murmured.

Ibana's wife was dumbfounded. His incoherent speech aroused her suspicions.

Ibana had stopped talking. Shortly after, he sighed and came back to his senses.

"Where am I? What happened?" he asked.

"Nothing," his wife lied. "The thunder might have frightened you."

"Oh yes, that last thunderbolt frightened me, and I do not know why it affected me so."

Ibana was lying. His wife's unexpected question, the sight of that enormous calao and its terrifying squawk reminded him of the murder of his uncle, whose revenge the dying victim had entrusted to the bird. The bright lightning made him recognize the scene of his crime. Coincidentally, it was exactly ten years ago, on this very same night, that he had committed the murder. These extraordinary coincidences, not what he said to his wife, made him utter a sharp cry and blubber like a madman.

When he recovered his senses, he decided at once to leave the place that awakened dire memories. They left hurriedly, despite the heavy downpour, not speaking a word on the way.

Eugenia was terribly frightened and was determined to clarify her doubts.

When they arrived home, Ibana had already calmed down. He was happy to have come out safe and sound from that storm and that dark forest. After changing clothes, he started to converse with his wife.

VIII

Juan Ibana was worried. From time to time, he interrupted the conversation with a sardonic laugh, the reason for which he did not want his wife to know.

She kept asking him why he laughed, but he evaded her question, laughing nervously from time to time.

The reason for Ibana's laughter, which he tried to control, was the thought of how his uncle had entrusted his revenge to the calao. It seemed that the calao was a gifted bird and was capable of fulfilling a mission entrusted to it.

He had more reason to laugh since ten years had passed without anyone suspecting that he was the perpetrator of the crime. It seemed the incident had been forgotten. Moreover, he was happy, independent, and rich, without having to account for his actions. Neither did he have to put up with the advice or the impertinence of others.

Under these circumstances, he began to laugh more frequently, making his wife more curious and suspicious. Finally, she fell sick because her husband refused to tell her the reason for his laughter.

She badgered him continuously until he gave in and revealed the real reason for his happiness. He narrated to her, without hiding any detail, how he had murdered the capitán, Don Hermenegildo.

She feigned her feelings but remembering Juan's revelation when he was delirious, her suspicions were confirmed. Nevertheless, she showed a calmness that she thought she was not capable of. To comply with his demand, she promised not to reveal his story to anybody.

They changed the topic of their conversation. When Ibana had finished his story, his wife pretended she had to buy food for dinner. She left the house, fearful because of what she had just learned.

Instead of going to the store, she ran to the house of an old relative who had always been a second mother to her. Unable to keep the secret that was consuming her, she revealed to the old woman what her husband had confided in her, adding that she was afraid to go back home.

The relative cried to the heavens and advised Eugenia not to return home. The kindly old woman left the house and went to the *pedáneo* to narrate what Ibana's wife had told her.

It was about ten o'clock in the evening but the gobernadorcillo was still working in the court. After listening to the woman's narrative, he issued a warrant of arrest. With a lawsuit in mind, he immediately went to Ibana's house to arrest him, accompanied by witnesses and cuadrilleros.

They lifted the tiles of the patio, and there they found the pistol and knife that Ibana had kept hidden for ten years. Although rusty, they still showed bloodstains. They also found the shirt, which was almost rotten.

When Ibana saw that his foul deed had been discovered, he lost his composure and confessed to the crime.

IX

One warm morning, when the rays of the tropical sun were falling like rains of fire, there was unusual excitement in the town of Mabalacat. As if it were a holiday, the fields were deserted by laborers, the stores were closed, and the workers rested.

People from different parts of town were rushing in the same direction, their faces filled with emotion, their hurried movements revealing great anxiety.

People of different classes, ages, and races crowded the spacious town plaza. They were stepping on each other to get a better place. The multitude had come from all over the province. In the center of the plaza was a platform with a terrible instrument of death, beside it the sinister figure of an executioner from Manila, clothed in red. A group of native infantry soldiers surrounded the scaffold.

At nine o'clock in the morning, the chapel in the plaza opened. Between lines of armed soldiers and cuadrilleros and amidst the beating of a drum, Ibana walked slowly, accompanied by two Augustinian friars. Repentance, sorrow, and shame were written on his troubled face. After ten years he was going to be punished for his premeditated and cruel murder of Don Hermenegildo Basco de los Reyes.

The prisoner mounted the scaffold together with the priests who were assisting him. He prayed and humbly asked God to pardon him for his crime. Then the executioner made him sit on a stool, tied his feet and hands to the pole, and placed a steel collar on his neck. While the priests continued with their prayers, the executioner turned the screw that ended his life.

At that moment, the frightening squawk of the calao was heard. When the immense crowd in the plaza looked up, they saw the gigantic bird flying and circling the scaffold. Then it disappeared, but not after letting out a terrifying cry. The bird had fulfilled its mission; Capitán Basco had been avenged.

The prayers of the priests kneeling down before the body of the condemned mingled with the cries of the people who marveled at what they considered a miracle.

No matter how one hides a crime, no matter how much time passes, and no matter how carefully the criminal tries to mock human justice, Providence provides the means for its discovery and inflicts the deserved punishment. Providence abhors crime and does not allow the culprit to get away with it. May this episode in the province of Pampanga serve as a valuable lesson to the natives throughout the Philippine archipelago.

May they not be carried away by their passion to the point of criminality, the worst form of human degradation.

THE ADVENTURES OF A CRACKPOT

I

n 1860, a frigate from Mexico anchored in the magnificent bay of Manila. Aboard were a large number of passengers. Lured by the fame of that new *Jauja*, they had come in search of fortune in the Pearl of the Orient. Among the passengers was an old man named Don Facundo Matasanos, a kind of herbalist in his native land. He was unique in a number of ways. He was in love and loquacious like a student who, after years of seclusion, eagerly ventures out to live fully as a man of the world. He was proud of his science and his profound knowledge of botany. Although he was ugly and poor, he could capture the sympathy of the women by virtue of his pharmaceutical remedies, which, according to him, would help them recover their lost beauty or their youth and enable them to keep their loved ones. He flattered them with the admirable rhetoric of a charlatan, a quality for which he was universally famous.

This extraordinary character, upon hearing that one of the boatmen who came to pick up the passengers complained of pain in his legs, offered to provide medical treatment. For his fee, he asked that he be brought ashore. The native would have wanted cash more than a doctor's prescription, but since Don Facundo didn't have fare money, the boatman agreed to ferry the latter, whose sole luggage was a box, which, according to its label, contained drugs.

The good fortune, which seemed to have been promised to the Mexican, was lost in no time. Upon entering the Pasig, the boat carrying this unfortunate person bumped the cable of a coastal vessel. The fragile boat rocked, Don Facundo panicked, stood up suddenly, lost his balance and fell into the river.

The unfortunate man struggled in the water to hold on to the same cable that had compelled him to take an untimely bath. The boatman, fearing Don Facundo's ire at getting so wet and losing the box of drugs, which went down to poison the inhabitants of the Thames of this archipelago, immediately left the place where the catastrophe had just taken place. He did not care anymore about the pain in his legs or the cure that was offered him. Wanting to escape, he left the furious Don Facundo in a most critical situation. Neither Don Facundo's voice nor his gestures, neither his pleas nor his threats could move any charitable soul to help him. He remained in that miserable state for some time until a compassionate ship captain, taking pity on him, came to his aid and delivered him to the Customs office.

In the Customs office, some curious people surrounded him, laughing at his appearance and his practice of taking a bath with his clothes on. He was bruised, hurt, and shivering. He began to make use of his rhetoric, lamenting his sad destiny, the inhuman behavior of the boatman and, above all, the irreparable loss of his baggage containing the drugs, with which he had expected to become a millionaire. Moreover, he believed that the powers of these drugs could make him a dispenser of health, a consoler of humankind, and an angel of well-being who would spread happiness wherever he would bring his lifesaving potions.

Meanwhile, a respectable pharmacist was looking at him curiously. He either felt pity for the old Mexican or saw in the unhappy man a very happy discovery. He invited Don Facundo to his house.

Don Facundo accepted the offer with a million thanks.

II

Installed in the well-stocked pharmacy of his generous guardian, Don Facundo marveled at his good fortune. He could not attribute this happy turn of events to blind chance of destiny. He walked proudly around the place, talking aloud to himself, when, upon looking up, he saw a charming brown lady staring at him from the window of the neighboring house. She was laughing, innocently, it seemed, at his gestures and his ridiculous clothes.

Don Facundo, overly affected and beginning to fall in love, let out a plaintive sigh upon seeing the beautiful lady. He made a gesture of respect and expressed his ardent love by looking at her tenderly, but he began to feel ashamed of his shabby appearance, his miserable clothes. He ran to the mirror to see if the attractiveness missing in his suit was in his face, which he considered charming.

Unfortunate illusion! The mirror revealed a starved and repulsive figure. In spite of his excessive self-love, Don Facundo was overwhelmed by disgust and could not help but scream horribly when he saw how ugly he was, and in his customary rhetorical style declared to himself, "Irreparable misfortune! I have probably lost the opportunity to feel the joy of love for which my heart is dying! I shall never see the fulfillment of my ardent desires! Judging by her appearance and her house, this very beautiful neighbor is a fortunate daughter of a wealthy family. What does she think of me in this miserable condition? Will this adverse situation cause my misfortunes if I am deprived of the opportunity to persuade this incomparable beauty to behold me in a different light?"

Plagued with such inconsolable thoughts and wanting to remove the cause of his lamentable condition, Don Facundo approached the pharmacist, his guardian, and assuming the funniest stance he was capable of, addressed him in a melodramatic tone:

"You know, my generous friend, I have experienced all the misfortunes since I arrived in the land of Magellan, Legáspi, Salcedo, Urdaneta, Labezares, and Anda. The naked truth, my misery, my penury is not hidden from you. Considering the immense profits you will obtain due to the efficacy of the pills, the ingredients of which only I can prepare, I beg you to advance me an amount that will enable me to be worthy of your respectable establishment and face people with confidence and dignity. Nothing honors the chief more than cleanliness that is evident in the washroom and the elegance of his employees. From experience, I know, my beloved master and friend, that physical looks and appearances capture, seduce, and inspire the vulgar and the ignorant. Consider how everyone admires an elegant coach with passengers dressed luxuriously and pulled by two fine chargers at the speed of light. Wherever it passes, coach and passenger are admired, respected, and given space on the road. No one, seduced by that pageantry, will fail to take off his hat to render humble homage to the owner of that luxurious coach. He may be just a braggart full of stupid pretensions but devoid of intelligence and most unworthy of the gifts that capricious destiny has given to magnify his vanity and insolence. Well then, if you surround your office with features that appeal to the public, and if your employees dress neatly and properly according to fashion, you will achieve the most important objective of an establishment—to attract attention and to please the eyes. Therefore, there will be an infinite number of patrons to whom the appearance of your salesclerks could be more gratifying than the medicines recognized by the science of Hippocrates. Remember that if . . ."

The pharmacist had to leave precisely at the moment that the loquacious Don Facundo began his discourse, and so, bored with lengthy conversations, and dreading the prospect of maintaining this crackpot for a long time, he interrupted, saying, "Well, Don Facundo, I already understand the purpose of your eloquence. Take this money, and get yourself whatever you think is necessary."

Don Facundo accepted the money and before he could deliver a thank-you speech, the pharmacist left, murmuring to himself, "If this charlatan, so fond of his eloquence, works as much as he talks, I will have found the most precious gem."

III

It was a Sunday. A group of idle people, resting from the week's tasks, was leisurely reading the fourth page of a Manila newspaper.

At a glance, an astonishing announcement in letters the size of almonds caught the group's attention, evoking admiration and questions. Its headline said:

YOUR HEALTH ASSURED!!!!
NO MORE DISEASES!!!!

The most awaited era has arrived. Humanity can now
be free of the interminable pains that oppress her so cruelly.
The world is to be congratulated. The sacrifices of
the martyrs of science, the true heroes who consecrated their
precious lives in search of the remedy necessary to universal

public health, have finally achieved the goal longed for through many centuries and after such praiseworthy abnegation and backbreaking research.

The pride of Asia, the valuable gem, the cultured, the Pearl of the Orient, in a word, Manila, is the capital of the world that enjoys the incomparable fame, the incredible fortune of being the first to know the advantages of the most recent noble discovery made by the famous genius, the sublime wise man, the gloriously eminent, the inestimable Don Facundo Matasanos.

This immortal man, this brilliant light of medical science is in Manila, oh unexpected happiness!

Yes, agonizing public—we have in our midst the most fortunate inventor of the Panacea that will bestow eternal health to humans. Those who want to meet the kind and illustrious Don Facundo will have a chance to admire him in the famous drugstore of. . . . At a small price for such a tremendously important cure, the most effective security against all diseases can be acquired.

Who would not hurry in search of the saving remedy for the assurance of enjoying complete health? Laziness, the goddess that absolutely dominates the tropical countries, was astonished at how young and old, men and women alike, rushed to the drugstore, not minding the heat of the sun that transformed the stones into meringue. They gladly emptied their pockets before the excellent and incomparable Don Facundo.

The shipwrecked traveler from Mexico was truly hard to describe. The money from his guardian transformed him completely. Hair dyed, well-applied pomade, a neat hair style; a ruffled collar and a big necktie, an English coat all buttoned up; brown pants that fitted tight on the legs, and white boots too small for his big feet— these were the trimmings of the now famous healer.

His eyes were not big enough to see his arrogant figure in the mirror that decorated the living room. With an effeminate bustle, he studied before the mirror the gestures that would capture the affections of the suffering ladies who would buy the remedy that would restore their health.

Ninay, his interesting neighbor, whose real name was Saturnina, had fun watching him. Vain and madly happy, he mistook her curious mockery, or perhaps lack of better entertainment, for ardent love for him and admiration for his elegance.

The drugstore was invaded that day by a great number of innocent people who gave up their gold in exchange for the silver-coated pills that contained their protection against diseases. Don Facundo was losing his grip on his mind. So much happiness threatened to rob him of his sanity.

The pharmacist could hardly eat or take a nap. Great was his admiration for Don Facundo. The continuous sound of gold being deposited in the wide boxes on the counter, in exchange for the boxes of pills—whose preparation cost him only an increase in the daily cost of bread and a jar of water as requested by Don Facundo—took away his appetite. The thought that he had in his care a truly cunning man, wise in the ways of the world, priceless during these unfortunate times, made him drunk with satisfaction.

The pills, by chance, produced marvelous results.

IV

The inhabitants of the capital of the Philippines came to recognize Don Facundo's power when they experienced the excellent effects of his discovery.

Musicales, dances, and parties were held in his honor. Wherever he passed, people praised him and the most beautiful young ladies threw flowers at him as a sign of gratitude and admiration for the sublime being who saved them from dying of boredom at home because of some wretched ailment. Now they were able to go for a *paseo*, attend dance parties and gatherings, or go to the theater.

There were praises for and protests against Don Facundo's popularity. The real physician, Dr. Garrido of Manila, was no longer consulted by patients in his clinic, for they now preferred to consult the famous healer of the hopeless in the famous pharmacy on Calle Luna.

The name Matasanos was on everybody's lips.

Everywhere, this conversation or something similar was heard:

"Good morning, neighbor."

"A very good morning, Doña Pánfila."

"How is your headache?"

"Oh, my friend, let us not talk about it anymore. It has disappeared completely."

"Really? Tell me how it happened."

"Well, do you not know that we have in Manila the greatest wise man of the world? He is the humanitarian Don Facundo Matasanos, inventor of the pill that enables one to recover his lost health and makes sure that he stays healthy for the rest of his life."

"I knew it could not be anything else. How would I not know the famous Mexican when my daughter, who had been suffering from chest pains for a long time, recovered completely the first time she took the lifesaving pills."

Another instance:

Two men were talking, the younger one aged sixty.

"Don Nicomedes, are you not going out for the usual morning walk?"

"I would like to, Don Judas."

"Well, what then? Are you feeling bad?"

"Very bad, my friend. Since yesterday, I have not been able to do anything. I feel so bad that I do not even dare look out of the window. I am thinking of taking a purgative."

"A purge? Are you crazy?"

"My friend, has it been discovered that purging is deadly?"

"What has been discovered, inhabitant of limbo, is a remedy, which neither you nor I could have figured out. It is an admirable amulet, a wonder belonging to the century of great advancements, the universal panacea!"

"Well, man, tell me about this wonder."

"Look at this, Don Nicomedes, read this announcement."

"Holy God, is this true?"

"Are there still sick people in Manila since these pills have proven their efficacy? Have you not heard about the amazing healings of Don Ruperto and Doña Gerundia? Or how old Don Homobono was saved from death even as his heirs were about to divide his possessions?"

"How would I know? No one ever came to my house to tell me. I will send for those pills right away. I cannot wait to take them."

Half an hour later, Don Nicomedes had swallowed a boxful of pills and told his friend, "How marvelous! Incredible! Do you know that they have brought back my appetite?"

"Well, you have to give the body what it needs. Tell them to bring out the ham, the bread and wine, together with dinner, and then you will know."

After the monstrous collation, Don Nicomedes said happily, "I am well! I have been saved! Thank you, my adored friend, my savior, Don Judas. Come with me—I am going to congratulate and shake the hand of the renowned genius, the wise man whose glory surpasses that of Hippocrates, the illustrious inventor of the Panacea."

Such were the conversations and the immense prestige earned by Don Facundo with his pills. But that was not all. In the next two or three days, the happy inventor received love letters, tender quatrains, and fragrant flowers from the daughters of Eve carried away by the ardor of their hearts.

Don Facundo spent the nights flattered by the sweetest illusions, dreaming not of glory and wealth but of love. He sensed the quick fulfillment of his heart's desires: innumerable seductions, some ladies silently longing for him, others more daring or less patient, revealing their love for him in perfumed and sentimental notes.

A certain grief, however, tortured his soul. The attractive neighbor, the graceful and smiling brown lady, whose sweet glances had made Don Facundo aware of his misery and shabbiness, hardly showed any interest in his transformed person and fortunes. She remained elusive even when his lips already hurt from smiling so much and his eyes grew tired from staring at her to express his passion.

The disheartening behavior of the pretty Ninay made him the most miserable of all mortals. "What is the use of all these," he said to himself, "the acquired glory and wealth, the respect and gratitude of my fellowmen, if at the end I am deprived of the luminous torch, the brilliant light that banishes the sorrows of my unfortunate being? What an unhappy fate! One may redeem oneself from the afflictions of slavery by immersing himself in the tedious task of cataloguing diseases of past centuries, but one is not freed from suffering cruel deceptions on Earth nor the bitter pains that persecute less illustrious men. Is it possible that I, idol of the most precious ladies of this city, have to lament the harshness of an ungrateful one whose heart can never appreciate the treasure of love in a heart like mine, a heart in love and ever faithful?"

Filled with sadness, Don Facundo devoted four days entirely to the making of his famous pills but could not produce anything on the fifth day.

His guardian shouted at him, "Beloved friend, distinguished physician, honor of pharmacology, more illustrious than all the wise men of Greece, what is wrong with you? What pain so afflicts you that your hands remain inactive and only pitiful complaints come out of your heart?"

Don Facundo did not answer. He was determined once and for all to put an end to the anguish that was consuming him. He went to the house of his charming Dulcinea and fortunately found her alone. Kneeling down, his face distraught, his voice trembling and his eyes glowing, he said to her:

"Ninay, my love! Purest angel of first love, most beloved of the girls that caught my eye, idolized with more fervor than the loving turtledove, more beautiful than the blooming flowers of the most beautiful garden at daybreak, which, when covered with dew, open their petals to the sun; like these flowers you are fragrant, tender, and seductive. You should know, oh, virgin lady, that the most fervent love, the inextinguishable flame consumes my soul. One sign of affection from you transforms my pain into the most grateful consolation that sweetens all the moments left in my existence. My dear Ninay, return my love with your most desired and invaluable love. Do not destroy forever with just one blow the joy of a heart that idolizes you. Be generous. If any woman has been made happy on Earth because of my pharmaceutical ability, I will make you even happier. I will put you on a pedestal so that anyone who looks up to you will have to turn away at once with astonishment because it will be like staring at the brilliant sun of the ardent sky of your happy country. . . Please listen, privileged daughter of the day, capricious sylph, haughty Nereida, gracious little wave, sweet mermaid, gentle fairy, tender perspicacious lady, celestial light, active tranquilizer, sweetest syrup, beneficent infusion, enchanting flower, divine star. . ."

"¡Abá! ¡inacú!" the surprised Ninay finally exclaimed. "cosa está vos jablando conmigo, seguro si aquel mi señor llega ha de enfadar con nosos; espera vos primero con aquel mi abuela que habrá de entender ese que vos platica.[1] [Oh, mother of mine! What are you saying? Surely,

---

[1] A type of pidgin Spanish understood by those who reside in or have stayed in the Philippines.

if that employer of mine arrives, she will get mad at us. Wait for my grandmother who will understand what you are telling me]."

Don Facundo, carried away by his passion, heard her complaints, and said, "What are you saying, divine lady? Is anyone capable of getting mad at you? She must be a fierce tiger and you the most soft-hearted pigeon. Are you afraid that your grandmother who undoubtedly exercises authority over you as a mother will disapprove of our love? Well, according to what I have gathered and based on the feelings that suppress you and torment me, you are responding to my desires, you reward my sleeplessness. Are you willing to cure my injured heart? Clear your young imagination of such childish fears. Your employer will see how noble is my conduct, how salutary the ideas that guide me, the purity of my motives. She..."

The door suddenly opened and the señora of the house was both surprised and angered by the last words of their neighbor. She threw in his face his doubtful ancestry, his impudence in going up to the house in the absence of the owners, in order to influence Ninay with his daring propositions. Sad and crestfallen, Don Facundo departed from the house while the sought-after Ninay suffered from a sermon that is better heard than narrated.

V

Ninay, a pure native, worked as a maidservant in the house of the woman who had bitterly reprimanded Don Facundo and stopped the flow of his loving speech at the height of his enthusiasm.

To the inventor of the valuable pills, she was the queen of beauty, a treasure of graces and the only woman on Earth worthy of his honor and love.

The señora who could not believe that her maidservant was innocent, placed the unfortunate beauty in a situation where she had to protect herself from the ire of her señora.

Ninay's excessive curiosity caused the drama to end much sooner than she thought. One afternoon, as the carriages went by rapidly, Ninay went to the window to watch the elegant ladies because their accessories and clothes delighted her. Her employer, who thought that she was at the window to look at Don Facundo, reprimanded her and finally dismissed her.

Don Facundo, on the other hand, was almost crazy with happiness, thinking that Ninay, softened by his tears and ardent propositions, would finally reciprocate his love. At the same time, he was very disgusted at the irascible woman who he thought was the grandmother of his adored and tormenting vision of love.

Instead of making more pills, he busily spied on the house across the street, hoping to see his beloved. He wondered why he could not see Ninay anywhere, although he used to see her often on the balcony. He asked one of the male servants about her, and this heartless servant answered, "Oh, sir! Ninay does not stay here anymore. Our employer sent her away because of you."

So surprised was the enamoured Don Facundo to hear the unexpected and shocking news. Speechless, he fell to the ground as if lightning had struck him. Were it not for the utmost care of his guardian, he would certainly have been consigned to the cemetery of Paco.

When he recovered his senses, he cried bitterly, "Curse me! I am the cause of her misfortune, I am the monster who destroyed the happiness of the most innocent of women. I swear that I will atone for her misfortune and with my love, I shall heal the deep wound inflicted on her by her grandmother."

One can understand the bitter pain of Don Facundo, overcome as he was by such sad thoughts. Incapable of being productive, he spent hours weeping and grieving over the fate of his idol, whose whereabouts were impossible to find out.

His generous guardian did not fail to notice the change in the behavior of the genius and offered to help. And so he said to Don

Facundo, "My respected friend, I am very worried about this secret pain that afflicts you. It has come to a point that you have forgotten your acquired glory and the immense income that your invention has brought to this house. I thank you in the name of the good friendship that I have offered you since the beginning. Unburden your heart in mine as a son would to his father and maybe I can relieve your pain. That way you can go back to making the pills of which there is a shortage that is damaging our business."

Don Facundo did not answer. His eyes filled with tears, his heart beat with unusual force, his hands trembled, and he sighed from the depths of his heart. He understood, however, the reasons of his comrade. He asked for bread, water, and the other health ingredients that constituted the marvelous pills, and withdrew to the most isolated corner of the drugstore to produce them.

He was so disturbed by unbearable misfortune that he did his work awkwardly and mechanically. A deadly carelessness made him use the wrong containers for the mixture. These containers had just been used for a medicinal solution with properties so different that it could not possibly produce the beneficial results claimed by Don Facundo. Shortly, we shall see the fatal consequences of his mistake.

VI

After a couple of hours and thanks to his skill, Don Facundo produced a large quantity of pills, most of them moistened by the tears that streamed from his eyes as he worked in misery and grief.

The pills were put on sale and the ingenuous believers of the city by the Pasig, after having been deprived for some time of the famous cure-all, caused the pills to pass rapidly from the *boticario's* hands to the buyers. Even those who were not sick hurriedly purchased them in order to avoid illness in the precarious future.

Alas, that night, more than four people feared they had been attacked by cholera.

Hardly was there a house where not one of its occupants was stricken by the evil disease. Fearful shouts, gasps, and groans could be heard everywhere.

The doctors doubled their efforts to stem the terrible tide of disease and death. Fifty people made urgent calls at the same time. When medical succor was delayed, panic and disorder increased in the houses stricken by cholera. Certainly, it was a very bad night for the unhappy inhabitants of Manila, victims of the wretched Don Facundo.

The pills were subjected to chemical analysis and when it was proven that a harmful ingredient in them had caused the cholera outbreak the night before, an angry crowd rushed to confront the frightened pharmacist, demanding that they be refunded the cost of the defective pills and indemnified for their expenses on doctors and medicines.

The pharmacist tried to protest, but to explain matters was to risk being taken to court, so he had no recourse but to pay a considerable sum. All his earnings from the pills and some of his savings disappeared like magic. If the people were quick to buy the pills days before, they were quicker to demand a refund.

This turn of events provoked an argument between him and Don Facundo that ended with the former throwing the latter out into the street. Nonetheless, this was for the better. The absence of malice and the fact that Don Facundo was indeed crazy were considerations that spared the disconsolate inventor the fate of having to sleep in a not-so-pleasant prison cell in Bilibid.

As he was already well-known, and because of his extravagant manner of dressing, boys followed him in the streets shouting and making horrible faces at him. But such mockery was not what grieved him most. His dearest Ninay was lost forever because he had made the mistake of not asking for permission from her so-called grand-mother. The memory of those happy moments he had spent contemplating the bewitching face of a homely dishwasher who appeared to him as resplendent and beautiful as the morning sun, made him restless, sorrowful, and disgusted with himself.

Overpowered by his sad thoughts, our hero went to the beach of Santa Lucía one afternoon, wrestling with the thought of drowning himself. There he saw a salesclerk of the drugstore where his tragic destiny had overtaken him. The salesclerk approached Don Facundo and greeted him affectionately, saying, "Dear friend, what are you doing here, why are you so pensive? I am not one of those who burn incense before the powerful only to abandon them in their misfortune. Confide in me, for if I cannot solve your problems, at least I can cry with you."

"Thank you, true friend, I will do that, for I know that I have always deserved a special affection from you. You must know that the reason for my sorrow is the disappearance of the divine woman whom I shall never forget."

"Ninay?"

"Ninay, yes, the unfortunate Ninay."

"Oh! What I am going to tell you is sad, but I trust that you will bear it bravely. Ninay, seeing herself abandoned, alone in the world, desperate due to the wickedness of people who took pleasure in her misfortune, swore to leave society and take to the forest."

"What are you saying? Is that true?"

"I know it for a fact. Ninay is in the country of the Ilongote."

"Where is that country?"

"That is the territory between the provinces of Nueva Écija and Nueva Vizcaya."

"And she is among uncivilized people!"

"Yes, my friend, but do not fear for her, because those infidels also know how to respect the beautiful sex."

"It is my duty to look for her and make amends for the misfortune that she is suffering because of me. I shall go to the land of the Ilongote.

"I think that makes sense. I am leaving tomorrow for Nueva Écija to run an errand for the family. If you want to accompany me, I shall take care of the expenses."

"You are providence, my friend. I accept and I will always be grateful to you."

The following day, they both left for Nueva Écija, arriving in the capital after a twelve-hour trip. The salesclerk stayed in San Isidro to attend to his errand. Don Facundo took refuge in the mountains where the tribes of infidels lived.

VII

Various uncivilized races inhabit the mountains of the Philippines. We are going to give you an idea of this.

The Aeta, or Ita, primitive inhabitants of the archipelago, wander in the highest mountains. They are short, agile, lighter skinned than the Africans, and have very curly hair. Probably due to instinctive modesty, more or less developed in all men, they cover a certain part of the body with the bark of a tree called arandong. They eat root crops and wild fruits, and take delight in tobacco and dogs. They have no regular sleeping hours. When they feel cold, they build bonfires and lie on the ashes even if these are still hot. They are never without their bamboo quivers that hold their poisoned arrows, terrible weapons that they handle with admirable skill. When the Malayos, ancestors of the *indios* took over the archipelago long before the coming of the Spaniards, they forced the Aeta to take refuge in the mountains. As a consequence, the Aeta hate them. This hatred has been perpetuated from generation to generation, so that the Aeta cannot live peacefully until they are able to kill an indio. To satisfy such a barbaric desire, they hide in the trees to spy on the indios as if they were hunting fierce animals. They kill the indios once their victims come within their reach. Their women always accompany these nomads everywhere. The most notable tribes are the Dumaya, Malanao, Manobo, and Tagabote.

The Igorrote, a race entirely different from the Aeta, are robust, big and well-shaped. Their skin color is somewhat darker than the quince. They have straight hair, thick, black, and shiny. They use underwear called baae, made from the bark of a tree. They paint their breasts and arms with the sap of a tree called saleng. Its color is indelible. The figure they normally copy is the sun. They live in settlement camps and build bamboo houses. Their most common weapon is the talibong, which has two blades and a roman tip. They also use the bow. They eat the root of the létaro, wild boar meat, and deer. Some are cannibals.

The Busao display flowerlike paintings on their bodies. They decorate their heads with a cap of quiao feathers; they wear earrings of different sizes. Their weapon is the alioa, similar to an axe with a protruding piece of metal from which they hang the heads of their victims. They themselves make this weapon with the metal from their mountains or by casting the *carajais*[2] which they get from the natives in exchange for tobacco.

The Burik have the same customs as the Igorrote. Their only difference is that they have a more vigorous build.

The Itetepane are short, and have flat noses. Although in general they have good features, they are very dark. They cover their heads with a red skullcap. The most important ones decorate their caps with feathers entwined with silk. They are armed with lances and arrows. They also use the alioa. When it rains, they put on a

---

[2] A special frying pan.

short cape called anao, made of anahao leaves. Many Ilocanos still use the anao, and they value it.

The Tinguiane, descendants of the Chinese, have a fair complexion. They are mostly in the province of Abra. Many have been subdued. They like doing business with the Christians. They wear only the jabaque and a turban on their heads. The women wear a kind of tapis that covers them from waist to knee; their arms, neck, and legs are adorned with beads. The converts dress like the natives. They are in constant war with the Guinaane, a warring tribe, cruel and revengeful.

The Ifugao, descendants of the Japanese, are the bloodiest race. Their constant occupation is to kill. They use the skulls of their victims to adorn their houses. For every person killed, they receive an earring. The one who wears the most earrings is the most respected. They like to steal and they are very good in using the rope. They never leave their alioa behind.

The Gaddane have the color of dark copper. They are small and have very flat noses. The majority are residents of the neighboring places of Isabela and are under the government. The Ifugao make war with them.

The Calaua are more civilized. They live in settlements within the jurisdiction of Cagayan, with whose inhabitants they deal frequently in harvesting tobacco of superior quality.

The Apayao have good houses made of cedar wood from the mountains they occupy. They harvest beeswax and cacao, which they sell to the Christians.

The Ibilao and Ilongote rob and kill. They poison their arrows, and always wound treacherously because they lack the valor to face their enemies. They are feeble and short.

There is also the race of Albino, the so-called Children of the Sun.

Most of these tribes believe in a Supreme Being and they adore many idols. The settlements of Ilamunt and Altasanes revere the so-called Cabiga and his wife Bujan. The Gaddane revere Amanobay and his wife Dalingay. The Ifugao and the majority of Igorrote worship Cabunian, the Supreme God, and his sons Lumabit and Cabigat respectively, and his daughters Banigan and Danugan, whom they believe to be the ancestors of the human race.

They adore Pati, the rain, as a divine benefactor. They often pray to it as they do to the goddesses Libongon, Tibagon, and Limoan, whose images are carved in wood and occupy a place of honor in their houses. The lesser but well-respected divinities are Balitoc, Linian, Piit, Sancan, Tatao, Banguiis, Oasiasoias, Batacayan, Ladibubu, and Dalig, each with its particular attributes. The images with heads between their hands and elbows on their knees are the most important because they represent beatitude and repose.

The cult of the gods is private. Sometimes, all the members of the tribe gather around an old woman, a Sibyl or fortuneteller, who offers up a sacrificial animal such as a carabao or wild boar. She dips the idol Anito in the ceremonial blood and pretends he transmits his revelations to her. For this, she performs an extraordinary ceremony, invoking the god Cabunian with grand gestures, contortions, and howls. All those present shout madly, and brandishing their weapons they swear to carry out the commands of their idol. The ceremonials climax with an orgy of merrymaking, dancing, and drinking until they are dead-tired or sometimes dead. Their common drink is the *basi* that they make from the unfermented juice of sugarcane. Their food consists of rice, root crops, fruits, birds, wild boar, and deer.

Several tribes adore the sun. Some invoke the honors of the divinity for the souls of their dead relatives, and others, like the Apayao, carefully keep their weapons. When a tempest threatens, they sacrifice a pig to Cabunian to pacify this deity. Later, when a rainbow appears in the sky, they humble themselves as a gesture of gratitude. Generally, the most valiant man governs the settlement while sharing authority with the Barnaas, or Bannanes, who have a certain number of slaves. The Barnaas are very much feared and their orders are obeyed promptly. When someone dies, they roast his intestines so they can foretell the future. They put the cadaver on a chair and they dance and sing praises to it until it reaches an advanced stage of decay. They drink and eat all the food there is, and if these are exhausted, there are tribes who will eat the flesh of their dead.

The Barnaas are buried in a place called Londent, which is equivalent to a cemetery. The lower ranks are buried elsewhere. Marriages are arranged by the families of both parties. The most essential requirement is the dowry. Once this is agreed upon, the couple is locked inside a house and not allowed to go out for eight days. Only their parents can see them when they bring food. Their relatives and guests sing and dance around the house to the beat of cone-shaped drums while the women sing. They dance in a circle, turning around with one foot raised. After eight days of seclusion, the wedding is solemnized. Both have the right to separate if they so agree and the dowry is lost. Adultery is punishable with death if they are caught in the act. Robbery is punishable only on the third offense. In all cases, if the accused makes a settlement with the offended party or family, the sentence is not carried out.

If they decide to go on a trip, they build a bonfire. If the smoke goes in the opposite direction of where they plan to go, they forego the journey, believing that it will be fatal to them. Finding a snake is also a very bad omen.

Medicine is practiced by old people who know the efficacy of many roots in healing all kinds of diseases. Every time the head of a family dies, the relatives around him observe how many of his fingers were open when he expired. When the opportunity arises, they kill several individuals, believing that this is necessary to pacify his spirit. This superstition is still believed in many Christian towns of the less civilized provinces and it has been the cause of lamentable crimes.

War is an irresistible attraction for all the mentioned races, some of whom can never live in peace. They celebrate a victory or conquest with festive banquets lasting an entire month. If they are defeated, they flee in order to reorganize and win over their conquerors, using the most incredible schemes. They do not forget revenge while they live and once this is carried out, losing their lives does not matter. Their frequent wars have notably decimated these uncivilized people. Nevertheless, there are approximately 200 thousand living in Luzon, and 800 thousand in Mindanao occupying an area of 450 leagues.[3] They speak the dialect, which is the name of their race and they differ a lot in beliefs and in customs.[4]

VIII

Having given this brief information about the different races that occupy the hinterlands of the Philippine archipelago, we will now follow the journey of the daring Don Facundo.

Penetrating the mountains of the province of Nueva Écija, and enduring all the sufferings that one who is less in love would find unbearable, he arrived in an Ibilao settlement. Fatigue and hunger on his painful journey had transformed him into a specter. The savages became speechless and stupefied upon seeing him. They brought him before the chief of the settlement, who was surrounded by many men, women and children, all naked, who were shouting and looking at him threateningly. He was asked, in a dialect unknown to him, what he was looking for in those hidden mountains.

---

[3] Padres Buceta and Bravo.
[4] In the Philippines, there are many dialects as there are provinces. The important ones are Tagalog, Visaya, Ilocano, Bicol, Pampango, Pangasinan, Ibanag, Cebuano, Panayano and Sambal.

Using sign language, Don Facundo said he did not understand and so one of the Ibilaos asked him the same question in Tagalog. Although he did not speak Tagalog, Don Facundo understood and said, "I have come in search of the most beautiful daughter of Manila, the one and only Ninay whom I passionately love. I unintentionally caused her to decide to take refuge in this land; and so, despite the dangers, which I face, I have come to ask you for her. I trust that you will be kind enough to inform her of my arrival, that is, if she is here with you."

The savages looked at each other without understanding what Don Facundo was talking about. The chief of the savages called a young girl who was at the end of the hall where they took the unfortunate Matasanos. She interpreted correctly what he was saying because all of them burst into laughter, exclaiming: "He is crazy! He is a liar! He is a half-wit!"

"What do we do with him?" the chief asked the people around him.

"He will be the target of our arrows and by the happy omen that has fallen in our power, we are going to have a banquet."

"Then, tie his feet and hands and put him in a secure place. Tomorrow he will die."

"Bravo!" everyone shouted.

Don Facundo was tied and imprisoned in a small cave. In response to his protests and speeches, he was whipped with a cane.

The Ibilaos built a bonfire and danced around it between frequent libations. Later on they went to bed happy, thinking of the feast that awaited them the next day.

Don Facundo, bitter and suffering, cursed their vileness and his fate.

At midnight, he heard a noise in the cave. He thought the hour of the sacrifice had come and he screamed in terror.

"Silence," a voice said.

"Who are you?" Don Facundo asked.

"A friend who comes to save you," the native, who served as interpreter of the chief of the settlement, said in faulty Spanish.

"Oh! You are an angel."

"I was born in Manila. It would take too long to talk about the misfortunes that obliged me to come to this place where I enjoy great power with the chief of the Ibilao. I know they have resolved to kill you but I am decided to stop it because I was moved by the passion you feel for a compatriot of mine. Go immediately and may God guide your way," the girl said while untying him.

"Thank you, beautiful and compassionate lady. All my life, I will be grateful to you for this service. But before I leave, I want to know if it is certain that Ninay is in this place or somewhere near here because I was told that she had taken to the forest."

"That is impossible, I should know. I do not believe she took the risk of taking refuge in these mountains. Go to Manila and you will find her there. You are a victim of deceit."

"That is probably true. I will go back to Manila as fast as I can. Goodbye. I long to see my beloved and I will punish the treacherous friend who deceived me."

He left hurriedly for the town at the foot of the mountain and for six hours, he did not rest. Once he reached the town, he ate little and shortly after, continued his journey without delay until he finally arrived in San Isidro. There, he learned that he was the victim of a joke. Desperate, he immediately left for Manila.

For half a month, he did nothing but go to the farthest reaches of the capital without achieving what he was longing for. Ninay could not be found anywhere nor could anyone say anything about her whereabouts. The unfortunate Don Facundo, like a disconsolate spirit, walked and walked through the streets. He ate very little as he had no appetite, and he slept irregularly. One afternoon, children mocked and laughed at him wherever he went. As he was going to the barrio of Tondo, he heard very loud and continuous shouting coming from the *gallera,* or cockpit. He entered to find out the cause of the uproar.

For the native Filipinos, the gallera is the temple of happiness, the *summum* of their joy, their unrivaled recreation. The roosters are their major enchantment, their most delightful entertainment.

Before sunrise, one can see natives squatting by the door of their houses caressing their roosters, talking to them, blowing cigarette smoke between their feathers, lavishing them with care. For them, this is a gratifying recreation and makes the hours pass like minutes.

On the days when cockfighting is allowed, countless people come to the amphitheater. The owners of the roosters and the players sometimes bet among themselves but usually with the *cazador.*[5] Together, they formally arrange the conditions of the fight and the amount of betting.

Once the game is set, they put the sharpest two-edged blade the Tagalo call *tari* on the roosters' legs. They make the roosters furious by alternately bringing them close to each other and separating them. The roosters are then let loose in the arena and the fight begins. The energetic birds attack each other and defend themselves valiantly and with masterful agility. The fighting cocks carefully observe each other. As they leap and slash to wound each other, the people are seized by indescribable emotions. They scream, shout, and cheer for the rooster by its color: "mapula [red], maputi [white], and maitim [black]." They follow closely all the drama of the fight, bending and leaning forward to see better, their faces showing various expressions.

As the fight goes on, the shouts and cheers increase and the zeal for betting on the favored rooster heightens. If a rooster is wounded

---

[5] A representative of the owner of the cockpit.

severely and begins to show fear, the shouts grow even wilder. When finally a cock is defeated and the other stands victorious over the cadaver of its enemy, the cheering, clapping, and shouting sound like thunder all over the place.

The owners of the winning rooster and the players who bet on it fill the victor with joyful frenzy. The losers pull the vanquished cock's feathers by the handful and hang them on the bamboo poles around the cockpit arena.

The players who are confident in their roosters fear the advantage should the opponent rooster have two blades and theirs only one. Thus, there is a considerable cross-betting in favor of one or the other.

Without the rooster, the natives do not understand the meaning of life. To prohibit cockfighting would be to condemn them to die of sorrow. To prevent a victorious rooster from dying of wounds suffered in a fight, no native would spurn the sacrifice of inoculating it with his own blood, although he knows this could cost him his life.

IX

Don Facundo wandered among the players admiring their enthusiasm, although feeling somewhat annoyed by the noise.

Around the cockpit arena, the natives and the Chinese put up a multitude of stalls that served coconut wine, *magcacarig, apulit, bibimca, lúmpia, chau-chau, pansit,* and *ampao*. The people in the cockpit arena enjoy these inexpensive drinks and delicacies.

Imagine how surprised the starving Matasanos was when, passing by a line of interesting betel-nut vendors, he heard a piercing shout. Its echo produced in his passionate heart the effect of ten machine guns fired from the mouth of a jar. Then he heard an unpleasant voice shout: "¡Inacú! ¡Ang diablong boticario D. Pacundo, por quien despidió conmigo aquel mi ama! [My mother! That devil of a pharmacist Don Facundo—because of him my employer fired me!]"

"My Ninay!" exclaimed the spurned inventor, barely able to express his emotions. "Is it possible that after thinking you were lost forever, I find you here and my presence is a happy surprise for you? Your disappearance was an irreparable misfortune that has made me the unluckiest of all men. Yes, now there is no power in this world strong enough to separate me from you. I will tell you my sorrows when we are calmer. Tell me how you were during the days that for me were centuries, when cruel destiny separated us. Have pity on me, answer me, my beloved, because I am so eager to know everything."

Ninay was amazed, truly surprised by the fervent words uttered by Don Facundo. Finally, not knowing what to say or do, she offered the loquacious individual a betel nut and he thanked her with a very long speech, so that the gathering of happy vendors, friends of his Sylph, thought he was crazy. He put the betel nut in his mouth and swallowed it, his facial movements emphasizing his ugliness.

His humble and adoring behavior must have pleased the sentimental Ninay. Fifteen days later, the people celebrated the marriage of Ninay, the betel-nut vendor of Tondo, to Don Facundo Matasanos, inventor of a remedy that gave health to all but whose merit the world did not recognize.

Fate had exalted him to the heavens and then dropped him into the depths of the earth, but Matasanos is now happy with his new status. The illustrious hero, the wise man second to none, who was about to mount a universal revolution with a panacea that would put an end to all medical prescriptions, believed himself lucky beyond all measure, selling betel nut beside his beloved spouse.

It may seem strange that his wife's status in life did not make Don Facundo realize his mistake and the absurdity of his past platonic love, the cause of so much unhappiness on his part. She owned nothing but her bag of clothes, a jar of lime, betel leaves, and the red betel nuts, and yet he believed her to be blessed by fortune. Now, the inventor of the celebrated pills found singular pleasure in selling his cheap merchandise in the open air, sleeping in a cool nipa hut beside the sea, dressing simply, singing the *Passion* in chorus with other families by the light of a *tinjoy*, with no sorrows to afflict him, no concerns to bother him, no work to do. And when alone, he had the enviable luck of having someone take care of him.

He rationalized to himself the change in his beloved's destiny. He believed that when her grandmother sent her away because she was not pleased with her love for Facundo, she also deprived her of her hacienda, and that was the reason for Ninay's humble state. Because she was good and honorable, she chose a kind of work that could be bothersome but was ennobling, rather than pleasant idleness or the life of a criminal.

One may wonder if Don Facundo remained a happy, contented creature, or if he lived in the grace of God with his wife as promised by the beginning of their joyful life together. One may wonder if they did not end up throwing pots at each another. We do not think so. The chronicles of the Philippines do not say if that kind of madness, which the distinguished Matasanos suffered from, was ever cured. In that country, a born crackpot will not recover from his disease until judgment day.

GLOSSARY

¡Aba! ¡Inacú! – A Tagalog expression for surprise, fear, dejection, or any other emotion.

Abacá – Inner fiber of the plant (*Masa textilis*) woven into hemp.

Abogadillo – A lawyer with few clients, or a lawyer of little importance.

Adelantado – Governor; considered the person with the highest, political, military, and judicial powers in America at the time of the Spanish conquest.

Administración Central de Rentas Estancadas – Central Administration of Monopolized Products.

Aduana – Customhouse.

Agramante – A character in Orlando Furioso; figuratively means a place of turmoil, confusion, chaos.

Alcalde – Mayor.

Alcaldía Mayor – Mayoralty.

Alcanfor – Camphor.

Alférez Real – Official designated as standard bearer.

Alitaptap – Firefly.

Aljaba – A bamboo container for arrows.

Almacenes generales de tabaco rana – Main warehouses of tobacco leaves.

Anting-anting – A talisman.

Arráez – Captain of a boat.

Ate – Atis, or custard apple.

Audiencia –Tribunal that performed the triple function of hearing important cases, advising the governor, and sometimes initiating legislation. The term also refers to the geographical area in which the tribunal has jurisdiction.

Ayuntamiento – Town hall or city hall.

Bagon, or *bagoong* – Salted small fish or shrimps.

Bahai – Hut, house.

Balete – A species of Ficus, strangler fig.

Bata – Houseboy or child.

Bejuco – Long piece of rattan used as a whip.

Bodegas – Warehouses.

Bolos – Native knives, hatchets.

Bonga, or *buyo* – Betel nut.

Butaca – Easy chair.

Cabecería – Head office.

GLOSSARY

Cabeza de barangay – Head of the community.

Caída – Wide and ventilated part of the house that serves as waiting room.

Cálao – Hornbill; a bird of the Old World Tropics.

Camisas de piña – Shirts made of pineapple fiber.

Campilan – A long and straight saber.

Capitán de cuadrilleros – Head of rural police in charge of hunting down criminals.

Capitanía del Puerto – Port captain.

Carreras de caballo – Horse racing.

Casa Real – Royal House.

Catapusan – Culmination.

Champanes – Sampans.

Collas – Southwest monsoon with strong winds and rain.

Comandancia General de Carabiñeros – General Police Headquarters.

Compoblanos –Town mates.

Consejo de Administración – Administration Building.

Cuadrilleros – Government armed guards.

Cutchay – Chinese herb grown locally; chives.

Dalag – Mudfish.

Datu – Patriarchal head of a barangay.

Directorcillo – Official who acted as adviser to the *gobernadorcillo*.

Duros – A Spanish coin worth 5 pesetas.

Ensamaidas, bizcochos – Pastries.

Enteomania – Obsession, or compulsion.

Frac – A frock.

Guingon – Woven fabric.

Gobernadorcillo – Judge with correctional and civic jurisdiction over minor and specific affairs.

Habanera – A type of Spanish dance that originated in Habana, Cuba.

Hacienda – Estate.

Hacienda Pública – Public finance.

Halobaybay – A small sardine.

Hito – Catfish.

Horchata – A refreshing drink from ground and squeezed almonds, other nuts and watermelon seeds mixed with water and sugar.

Houris – The beautiful maidens of the Muslim paradise.

Huyones – Bundles, parcels, or bales.

Igorrotes – Indigenous group of the Asiatic Mongoloid type, inhabitants of the island of Luzon.

Ilang-ilang – A tree with dark yellow and fragrant tubelike flowers.

Ilongotes – Ilonggots, natives of Nueva Vizcaya.

Intendencia – Executive Headquarters.

Intervención General de Aforo – Office in-charge of auditing weights.

Jauja – Larousse Gran Diccionario (1894) states that the Spanish noun Jauja is used in allusion to the Peruvian town and province of Jauja, noted for its wealth and the clemency of its climate. Tierra de Jauja refers to a land of milk and honey.

Jopia, or *hopia* – Flaky pastries filled with sweetened ground mung beans.

Juego de sortijas – Ring game.

Juramentados – Fanatics who swear to attack the enemy to the death.

Jusi – Chinese word for silk.

La Mira – The Watchtower.

La pena del Talión – Punishment that consists in making the guilty suffer the equivalent of the harm done.

Lancape – A suitcase made of palm leaves or any other leaves.

Lantacos or *lantacas* – Cannons used by the Moros; a piece of artillery that is long and of little caliber.

Llampó – A game of chance using Spanish playing cards.

Luisiadas – An epic on Vasco de Gama's voyage; the most celebrated work of Luis Camoens, renowned Portuguese poet (1524–1580).

Maestranza – Military school.

Maitre de Camp – Field master.

Mane Thecel Phares of Balthazar's Last Supper – These seem to be the Aramaic names for weights and monetary values. (Book of Daniel 5:25–28).

Mestizo – Half-breed person.

Monte – A game of chance using Spanish playing cards.

Moro-moro – Drama about the wars between the Christians and the Moors presented in the open air.

Narra – A species of red caoba; now the national tree of the Philippines.

Nido de salunganes – Bird's nest.

Nipa – Palm leaf thatch-roofing material.

Nito or Jipijapa – Plant whose fine strips are used to make the famous Panama hats.

Oidor – Judge of the Audiencia.

Paipai – Fan made of buri.

Palay – Unhusked rice grains.

Palenque – Market.

Panguingui – Card game popular among the inhabitants, using a Spanish deck of cards.

Pansit – A rice noodle dish of Chinese origin.

Pedáneo – Municipal judge who presides over affairs of little importance.

Pico – A unit of weight equivalent to 63 kilos and 261 grams.

Plaza – The plaza referred to in "The Pirate Li-ma-hong" is now the Plaza de Roma, located in front of the Manila Cathedral.

Polistas – A native or half-breed who did menial work.

Pontín – A light boat.

Practicante – Medical auxiliary, self-trained and able to do minor surgery.

Principales – The *ilustrados, cabezas de barangay*, civil and public officials, and people of means.

Principalía – A group consisting of *principales*.

Puspas and basa-basa – Chicken porridge and plain porridge, respectively.

Quingua – Now Plaridel, Bulacan.

Reales – Spanish silver coin equivalent to 25 *centimos* of the peseta.

Reconocimiento de vasallaje – Acknowledgement of vassalage.

Sampaguitas – Small white, fragrant flowers now the national flower of the Philippines.

Sangleyes – Denotes the Chinese in Manila. Traveling merchants

Sinamay – Woven fabric from abacá.

Solteros – Bachelors.

Sota – A houseboy assigned to take care of horses.

Sui generis – Unique; of its own kind.

Tabo – Receptacle made of one-half of a coconut shell.

Tagulaguay – Oil from herbs.

Tajo – A popular dessert made of curdled soya milk with light syrup.

Tapa Diablo – A game of chance using Spanish playing cards.

Tapis – A wide piece of cloth tied around the waist, worn by native women.

Tchangno – Goddess of the moon.

Telégrafo de banderas – A system of Marine communication using flags.

Tenorio – Allusion to the principal character of *El Burlador de Sevilla*.

Tercena – Warehouse where tobacco and other monopolized goods can be bought wholesale.

Tiangui – Flea market.

Tinapa – Smoked fish.

Tinjoy – A small open lamp using coconut oil.

Tinola – Chicken stew with unripe papayas and green leaves.

Tribunal – Court.

Vilog – A small boat.

Vintas, pancos, calisipans – types of boats.

LIST OF PHOTOS